"I JUST ⟨ ✓ ⟩ ... M LOSING YOUR VIRTUE, AND THIS IS HOW YOU THANK ME?

"What would you do if I had saved you from drowning," Alex growled, "toss me overboard?"

"Don't be ridiculous." Diana sent him a look of cold fury. "I would tie the anchor to your feet first."

"That mouth of yours will get you into trouble."

"Not as much trouble as you will have when I scream."

As she opened her mouth to carry out her threat, Alex pulled her close and stopped the cry with a kiss.

The taste of her exploded through him, as exhilarating as standing barefoot on a deck in a storm.

With such a woman a man could be tempted to forsake almost anything . . .

───── ∽ ∾ ∽ ─────

"A delightfully witty tale of romance
on the high seas,
with passion that sizzles!
Absolutely wonderful!"
May McGoldrick

Other **AVON ROMANCES**

THE BELOVED ONE by *Danelle Harmon*
THE DARKEST KNIGHT by *Gayle Callen*
ENCHANTED BY YOU by *Kathleen Harrington*
KISSING A STRANGER by *Margaret Evans Porter*
THE MACKENZIES: PETER by *Ana Leigh*
THE MEN OF PRIDE COUNTY: THE REBEL
by *Rosalyn West*
PROMISED TO A STRANGER by *Linda O'Brien*

Coming Soon

THE FORBIDDEN LORD by *Sabrina Jeffries*
UNTAMED HEART by *Maureen McKade*

And Don't Miss These
ROMANTIC TREASURES
from Avon Books

ON BENDED KNEE by *Tanya Anne Crosby*
SO WILD A KISS by *Nancy Richards-Akers*
UPON A WICKED TIME by *Karen Ranney*

DEBRA MULLINS

Once a Mistress

AVON BOOKS ◆ NEW YORK

This is a work of fiction. Names, characters, places, and incidents either are the product of the author's imagination or are used fictitiously. Any resemblance to actual events, locales, organizations, or persons, living or dead, is entirely coincidental and beyond the intent of either the author or the publisher.

AVON BOOKS, INC.
1350 Avenue of the Americas
New York, New York 10019

Copyright © 1999 by Debra Mullins Manning
Inside cover author photo by A Portrait Studio/Wayne, NJ
Published by arrangement with the author
Visit our website at http://www.AvonBooks.com
Library of Congress Catalog Card Number: 98-93306
ISBN: 0-380-80444-1

First Avon Books Printing: January 1999

AVON TRADEMARK REG. U.S. PAT. OFF. AND IN OTHER COUNTRIES, MARCA REGISTRADA, HECHO EN U.S.A.

Printed in the U.S.A.

WCD   10 9 8 7 6 5 4 3 2 1

This book is dedicated to my father,
Daniel J. Mullins,
who didn't live to see this book published,
and to
Kim Lewis,
critique partner and friend,
who showed me the way and always believed.

Chapter 1

Jamaica, 1680

At last he knew the name of his enemy.

From the shadows of the garden, Alex peered into the ballroom and studied the faces of the couples who danced past the open doors. His mouth watered for the taste of revenge.

A laugh rippled from the ballroom as two people stopped in the entryway. With a low curse he retreated behind a large hibiscus bush, standing motionless until they moved on. Then he slipped from his hiding place and lingered in the shadows, where he continued to watch.

Henry Morgan passed by the doorway. Dressed in fine scarlet silk, the lieutenant-governor of Jamaica had even deigned to wear his wig on this occasion, rather than the pirate bandanna he so preferred. Alex stepped forward, then halted. He glanced from his casual black shirt and the dagger in his boot to the dark-skinned servant guarding the door.

1

"Blast," he muttered. "Look this way, Morgan. *See me.*"

Morgan spoke to the lady on his arm, his booming voice merging with the music, which rendered his words indistinguishable. Then he moved away.

Alex stabbed a hand through his long hair and let loose a harsh breath. "Bloody hell, Morgan. At this rate, I'll be captured and you'll have to preside at my execution."

The sound of footsteps brought his head up like a wolf scenting prey. A tall woman with hair the color of a sunset swept out of the ballroom. With a quiet oath he pressed himself against the stone of the house and became one with the darkness.

Diana Covington stormed out into the garden. She snapped her silken skirts and kicked a nearby frangipani bush, scattering leaves everywhere. Papa's business partner or not, one more suggestive leer, one more secret fondle, and Lord Chilton would lose a body part.

She stared at the damage she had wrought on the shrubbery and released a shaky breath. Then another. Closing her eyes, she tilted her head back, inhaling the loamy scent of damp earth as a soft breeze teased her hair. Insects sang their mating songs, playing harmony to the music drifting from the ballroom. Her shoulders sagged.

"Diana!"

Her eyes popped open, and serenity shattered like glass. Slowly she turned as if to face the executioner.

From the doorway of the ballroom, Chilton's nasal tones trumpeted into the night. "Here you are, my dear. I knew you must have fled to escape the wretched heat of the ballroom."

She bared her teeth in a parody of a smile. "Quite so, my lord."

"You cannot wander the gardens alone in the dark." Chilton sauntered toward her, a tall, thin man who dressed the fop and wore a blond, curling wig that fell over his shoulders. "I insist on accompanying you. A gentleman would see to your safety."

"That will not be necessary, my lord. I was just returning to the dancing."

He stepped in front of her as she tried to slip past him. "Stay, my dear. Enjoy the night air."

"I have had enough." Once more she tried to pass.

"But it is so dreadfully hot inside." He held her arm with one hand and traced his fingers down her throat with the other. "Surely you, too, are feeling the . . . heat."

"Stop it!" She peeled his hand from her arm as a barber would a leech. "I will thank you to keep your attentions to yourself!"

"Cease your maidenly protests, my dear." He stepped close to her, his sharp features demonic in the eerie shadows of the garden. "There is no need to play the innocent. I know that you came out here so that we might be alone."

"You are mistaken."

"Am I?" He loomed over her, and she fell back a pace. "You are a woman of passion, Diana. You crave my attentions as a drunkard does his ale." He advanced on her, and she retreated until the harsh bark of a tree bit into her back. Here in the privacy of the garden he was bolder. Here in the darkness anything might befall her.

Chilton trapped her with his body, bracing his arms on either side of her head. He bent toward her, his overwhelming cologne contending with the odor of his seldom-washed flesh. "You want me, Diana. I can see it in your face."

Diana tensed at the lust that thickened his voice. She took a deep breath, her nose wrinkling. Grasping her skirts, she inched them up and moved her knee into position just as Chilton placed his hand on her breast.

"See how you tremble at my touch," he whispered.

"Don't touch me, you lecher!" Jerking her arm upwards, she landed a spectacular blow to his nose with her flattened palm.

With a howl he clapped both hands to his face. She dodged around him and had taken two paces before he grabbed her arm in a bruising grip and yanked her back against the tree. "You bitch," he panted. He held a lace handkerchief to his swelling nose while he boxed her in with his other hand. "Lecher, am

I? How dare you? You, the daughter of a common seaman!"

"I dare," she snapped back. "Now release me, or—"

"Or what? You will scream?" With the deadly grace of an adder he tossed aside the bloody handkerchief and closed his hand over her windpipe. He squeezed until her eyes widened in alarm. "So easily could I crush your throat."

"My lord, you misunderstand," she rasped. "I am to meet someone . . ." His fingers tightened once around her throat, and she gasped for breath.

"I see no one else. Perhaps your swain has deserted you. All the better for me."

"Nay, he comes. I swear he does." She added a touch of disdain to her voice. "He will kill you if he sees us thus."

Chilton's nasty laugh echoed through the garden. "Where is this lover of yours? This man who would take you from me? We are alone." Sliding his hand from her throat, he coiled his fingers into her hair. "I will have you here and now, my love. Then your father will certainly accept my suit."

Her jaw dropped. "Your suit? You wish to marry me?"

"Of course. But Frederick keeps putting me off." He touched his wet mouth to the bare skin at the base of her throat, then raised his triumphant gaze to hers. "After I have breached your maidenhead, he will have no choice but to see us wed."

Diana stared at the man she had dismissed as a foolish fop. Before her very eyes he had transformed into a creature she didn't recognize, someone dangerous and evil. Fear gripped her with icy talons. "My father will never agree to it."

"He will see us wed," Chilton assured her with cool menace, "or he will see his precious daughter's reputation torn to shreds when word gets out of her whoring ways."

"I think not." The deep voice rang out from behind Chilton. Hope swelled in Diana's breast as a man in black clothing stepped from the shadows. He stood half a head taller than Chilton, and his shoulders looked capable of supporting a cask of rum each. His white smile gleamed from the darkness shrouding him. "Should you harm this lady, I shall dispatch you to hell with all expediency."

"Who the devil are you?" Chilton demanded.

The stranger ignored him in favor of Diana. "Darling, are you all right?"

" 'Tis about time you arrived," she cried, in the voice of a woman who had waited too long.

"Do not be angry, my sweet." He stepped forward. Grabbing a handful of Chilton's coat, he thrust him aside like a discarded neckcloth. The nobleman stumbled and crashed to the ground. "I was unavoidably detained."

Diana stepped away from the tree. Moonlight filtered through the leaves to sparkle off the gold earbobs her savior wore. His dark eyes gleamed with mischief, and his black hair hung loose to his shoulders. His simple clothing marked him less than a gentleman, but he was all that stood between her and a future as Chilton's unwilling bride.

"Have you nothing to say, my sweet?" the stranger prompted. "I pray no angry words will pass your lips."

Chilton scrambled to his feet. Diana darted close to the stranger's side, and he settled his well-muscled arm about her waist. "I am not angry," she said.

"I am," snarled Chilton. He attempted to straighten his crooked wig. "I demand you unhand my future bride."

The stranger looked at Diana and arched an eyebrow. "You would marry this?"

"I would rather swim naked through sharks."

He swept his gaze over her body. "A fascinating image."

"Diana!" Chilton's voice cracked with outrage. "Such disgraceful language shames you."

"Are you still here?" The stranger regarded Chilton as if he were a mongrel pup that had followed him home. "I suggest you leave now."

"Do you know who I am?" Chilton sniffed and looked down his beaklike nose. "I am a peer of the realm, you baseborn cur. And who might you be? A stablehand?"

"No." With a smile, the stranger drew a pistol. The barrel of the weapon gleamed in the half-light as he pointed it at Chilton. "I am the man who will blow a hole through your empty head unless you take yourself off. Now."

Chilton's jaw worked as he stared at the pistol. The stranger cocked the weapon, and the click of the hammer made Chilton jump as if he had already been shot.

"I suggest you hurry, my lord." That white smile flashed again. "I think I feel my finger slipping."

Diana snickered as her thwarted suitor fled the garden as fast as his legs would carry him. Her rescuer chuckled as well and uncocked the weapon with an ease that displayed his experience in handling it.

"That went well." He shoved the pistol into the black sash around his waist and looked down at her. "Are you unharmed?"

"Yes." She pushed away from him. His arm fell from her waist, but the heat of his touch lingered. Bewildered by the unfamiliar sensations, she fell back on the manners drummed into her from birth. "Thank you, sir, for helping me. Lord Chilton was becoming most persistent."

"Chilton?" The way he spat the name made her fall back a step. "That was Chilton?"

"Yes."

His expression hardened as he followed the nobleman's path with his cold-eyed gaze. "Chilton," he whispered.

Diana shivered from the icy rage that cloaked the word. She realized that she knew nothing about this man. What if he was dangerous? Her heart pounding, she asked, "Who are you?"

He paused for a long moment. When he spoke again, his words were calm. "Does it matter?"

"I would know the name of the man who rescued me," she said softly.

"You may call me Alex."

"I am Diana." She took a shaky breath and continued, "While I thank you for your intervention, I would know its cause. You are, after all, a stranger trespassing on my property. Perhaps you mean me harm."

"Would you believe me if I said I do not?"

"I would."

He raised his eyebrows. "You are a most trusting young woman."

"Do not mistake trust for stupidity, sir."

"Never."

Stiffening her spine, she warned, "And do not mock me."

"Of course not." He took her hand and brushed his lips over the back of it, the gesture oddly aristocratic for one not of the gentry. "Do you need an escort back to the ballroom? I will be happy to offer my services."

A blush crept into her cheeks as the strange warmth once more stole through her at the stranger's touch. She tugged her hand from his grasp. "Lord Chilton is by nature an arrogant coward. He would not want anyone to know that I had refused his advances. Or that another man had sent him scurrying off like an insect exposed to light. I shall be quite safe."

"I understand." He glanced down at his plain, serviceable black clothing. "You do not wish to be seen with a man of my class."

She bit her lip in consternation. Her body tingled with awareness of this stranger, making it difficult to think. She forced herself to concentrate. Entering the ballroom with a dangerous-looking man like he would start tongues wagging for certain. "Thank you for your concern, but I believe 'tis best we part here. I can handle myself."

He cocked an eyebrow at her.

She correctly interpreted his skepticism and tilted her chin with pride. "If you are thinking of the incident with Lord Chilton, I was about to extricate myself when you appeared. You gave me no chance to do so."

"Oh? And what would you have done, wench, if the fool had done . . . this?" He took her by her shoulders and yanked her against his body.

For an instant she could do nothing, not speak or think, or even breathe. Never before had she been so aware of the differences between a man and a woman.

"Well, wench?" he taunted.

She shook off her distraction and curled her fingers into the muscles of his chest, giving him a sweet, innocent smile. "I would do this."

She stomped her foot. Hard. He moved his own just in time. She fell against him, and they both went down in a flurry of petticoats and curses.

Alex relished the jolt of pleasure as her feminine body sprawled on top of his. She struggled to sit up, muttering unladylike oaths under her breath as she regained control of her layers of skirts. Then she pushed her hair out of her face and gave him a look of triumph from her perch astride him.

He wanted her.

The thought struck him hard and without warning, like a shot to the broadside. Denial followed. He had no time for a woman, nothing to offer her. He could not afford to be distracted. Not when he sought a murderer.

"Are you all right?" She tilted her head, her lips curving in an impish smile. "I did not mean to injure you."

"You did not." The words came out more harshly than he intended. It was best to deny his desire now, in its infancy.

"I disagree." She raked his supine form with obvious pride. "You, sir, are bested."

He rolled, toppling her to the ground. Pinning her under him, he immobilized her flailing limbs with ease. "Am I?"

"Release me at once." She squirmed. "Sir, this is not the act of a gentleman."

"Who said I was a gentleman? You are certainly no lady." He grinned down at her. "Perhaps I acted precipitously in coming to your rescue."

She glared at him. "You are no better than Lord Chilton."

He stiffened, a chill entering his blood. "Had I been Chilton," he breathed, "you would have found your skirts tossed some time ago and your maidenhead a mere memory."

He released her and stood, holding out a hand. She took it, and he helped her to her feet. As he watched her slender hands straighten her clothing, he tamped down his unexpected sexual urges and focused on the matter at hand.

"Please accept my apologies," he said sincerely. "I did not intend for things to go so far."

"Oh?" She brushed clinging soil from the back of her skirt with a vicious swipe of her hand. "And just what did you intend?"

"I need your help."

"Do you?" She bent to examine a piece of torn lace hanging from the hem of her gown.

"I must get into the ballroom."

She glanced up at him sharply. "Why?"

He hesitated. "Does it matter? I thought that since I helped you out of a difficult situation—"

"You bounder!" She straightened so fast he expected to hear her spine snap. "You used me!"

A disavowal hovered on his lips, but she continued before he could express it.

"I thought you were being chivalrous . . ." She pressed her lips together, as if she had betrayed a confidence. "Is that the only reason you aided me? To make me so grateful that I would help you get into the house?"

"Of course not."

"And what do you intend to do once you have gained entrance to my home? Steal the silver?"

"Bloody hell," he muttered, exasperated.

"I will bid you good evening, sir. And I will be sure to alert the servants that there is a trespasser on the grounds!" She spun away from him in a swath of upswept skirts and bouncing curls.

He grabbed her arm and pulled her to a stop, his own temper simmering. He had risked discovery to help her; his very life hung in the balance.

"You ungrateful wench," he growled. "I just saved you from losing your virtue to that strutting popinjay, and this is how you thank me? What would you do if I had saved you from drowning—toss me overboard?"

"Do not be ridiculous." She tugged at her arm. Unable to break his grip, she sent him a look of cold fury. "I would tie the anchor to your feet first."

He narrowed his eyes. "That mouth of yours will get you into trouble."

"Not as much trouble as you will have when I scream."

As she opened her mouth to carry out her

threat, Alex pulled her close and stopped the cry with a kiss.

The taste of her exploded through him, as exhilarating as standing barefoot on deck while a storm rocked his ship. He rediscovered the thrill of pitting his wits and his will against an impressive force of nature as he held this spirited young woman in his arms. With such a woman a man could be tempted to forsake even that most demanding of mistresses, the sea.

The idea so unsettled him that he jerked away from Diana as if she were the devil's own daughter. She stared at him with eyes the color of storm clouds. A flush graced her cheeks, and her lips, moist from his kiss, parted.

It was better for both of them if he disappeared from her life. He retreated behind the rakish facade that had always served him well.

"Now, that was surely a proper show of gratitude, my sweet," he quipped. "But despite your lusty eagerness, I must take my leave. Mayhap we will meet again." He ignored the shock that swept across her features and sketched a mocking bow. Turning away from her, he melted into the night.

Diana stared after him, straining to see some trace of him in the shadows. She found herself touching her throbbing lips with wondering fingers and snatched her hand away. She would tell her father about the intruder. And she would have the servants beat the bushes for him. With their muskets. Aye, and she would be gracious when they flushed him out like a frightened quail, and she would listen to his pleas for mercy.

She was, after all, a compassionate woman.

Lost in her fantasy, she wandered back into the ballroom. She smiled and passed through the guests, inquiring after her father's whereabouts. One of the servants mentioned that he had called for port to be served in the study. She left the ballroom and made her way to her father's private sanctum.

As she approached the study, her steps slowed. Her ire faded, to be replaced by chagrin. As angry as Alex had made her, he *had* helped her out of a dangerous situation. Did he really deserve to be shot for trespassing just because his mocking remarks had sparked her temper? After all, if he had intended to harm her, he could have done so while she lay helpless beneath him.

The memory of his kiss rose in her mind. His mouth had felt softer than she expected, and when his lips met hers she realized how truly dangerous he was. He was the type of man that a woman might beg to seduce her . . .

"Explain these documents to me at once!" Her father's voice thundered through the hallway, jarring her from her musings.

"Really, Frederick, at times your actions are of such a common nature." Chilton's high-pitched tones brought a frown to her face. She'd thought the man would have taken his leave by now. Would she never be free of him?

She edged closer to the door of the study, which stood open a crack.

The sound of rustling paper broke the silence. Then came Chilton's deadly hiss. "Where did you get these?"

"You know where I got them," her father answered. "Did you really expect to keep this from me?"

"You had no right!"

"I had every right!" Frederick Covington's answering roar could have rattled the pictures hanging in the hall. "These documents, written in your own hand, are proof of your dealings with Marcus. You know Sir Henry Morgan as well as I, Chilton. What would our esteemed lieutenant-governor think of your activities?"

"Morgan is hardly a consideration."

"Hardly a consideration!" Her father's voice rang with incredulity. "The man has made it his personal mission to rid the Caribbean of piracy. Every plundering wretch in the area has either turned himself in for pardon or taken himself into hiding for fear of Morgan's wrath. And you say the man is hardly a consideration? You are either extremely arrogant, Chilton, or else you are a fool."

"Who is the fool here, Frederick?" Chilton's silky tone made Diana think of a snake slithering through the grass. "You and I are partners. Do you really believe that Morgan would consider you innocent in this matter?"

"He will," came the immediate reply. "And had he not already left for the evening, I would prove it. I am known to be an honest man. My good name is my protection." He paused. "A pity you cannot say the same."

"I give no credence to the ranting of a lowborn wretch such as yourself, Frederick. You are not fit to utter the Markham name."

Half a breath from flinging open the door in defense of her sire, Diana froze when he spoke for himself.

"I may be a 'lowborn' wretch, Chilton, but my daughter is not. As you are well aware, my late wife was the daughter of a Scottish nobleman. Diana inherited great wealth through her, in addition to the substantial dowry I intend to bestow upon her. However, a man who associates with the likes of Marcus would not do as a husband for Diana. Kindly do not press your suit again."

Chilton spluttered in response, but Diana lost interest in the conversation. Only one thought blazed across her mind, and brought a wide smile to her lips. Chilton would no longer bother her.

She started back to the ballroom, so happy she wanted to dance. Chilton could no longer offer for her! Frederick Covington did not tolerate dishonesty, and if Chilton was indeed linked to the pirate Marcus, then he certainly lacked scruples.

Her father's sterling reputation could withstand a little tarnishing. But the Markham name had been sullied when Chilton's father committed suicide after gambling away the

family fortune. Only Frederick's belief that the
son should not pay for the sins of the father
made him take on Chilton as a partner.

She entered the ballroom, where the blaze of
lights and lilting music raised her spirits
higher. Once her father reported Chilton's activities to Sir Henry Morgan, the persistent nobleman would be punished for his crimes. He
would no longer seek her as his bride, and her
father would be lauded as the hero who exposed the villain.

Satisfied that her unwanted suitor would
plague her no longer, Diana tried to lose herself in the dancing. But beyond the garden
doors the night beckoned, seducing her with
the memory of a dark stranger's kiss.

Chapter 2

Moonlight slanted into the unlit room and fell across the paper-strewn desk. A figure slipped through the window, head and shoulders briefly gilded by the silvery light. Wraithlike, he melted into the darkness of the study.

The ominous snick of a pistol hammer echoed like thunder in the quiet room.

"Hold, lest I splatter the wall with your ballocks." The menacing words came from a man sitting near the desk. He gestured with the pistol, pale light playing along the gold and ivory inlay of the weapon. "Come over here where I can see you."

The intruder stepped into the shaft of moonlight, white teeth flashing in a grin. "Is this how you greet your friends, Morgan?"

"Blast it, Rothstone!" Sir Henry Morgan uncocked the pistol and shoved it into his belt. "How do you expect me to react when someone sneaks into my house? I heard you tramping through my shrubbery and thought 'twas a bloody thief."

"I meant for you to hear my approach. I had no wish to be skewered before you realized my identity."

"You were almost gelded, my boy." With a chuckle, Morgan reached over to light a nearby taper. The soft glow of the candle accented the lines that hard living had etched in his face. "Sit down, lad, and tell me what you are doing here. I thought you to be at sea."

"I was." Alex took a chair opposite Morgan's massive desk. "But I discovered something that I wanted to bring to your attention at once."

"Indeed." Morgan raised his eyebrows. "It must be urgent if you risked your neck sneaking onto my private estate. I'm surprised my men didn't shoot you."

Alex gave a quick grin. "One must first see a target before one can fire upon it."

"Ha! And you move like the wind when you have a mind to. Now, what is this news of yours? I assume it concerns Marcus."

"Aye." Coldness settled over Alex at the mention of the name. "Our elusive quarry does not work alone."

"What?" Morgan sat bolt upright. "Someone is helping that blackguard?"

"Chilton." Alex spat the name.

Morgan settled back in his chair, his sun-browned face growing contemplative. "I would not credit that simpering peacock with so dastardly a scheme."

"That 'simpering peacock' has a black heart."

"Chilton and Frederick Covington own Fleetwood Shipping. Do you suppose Covington is part of the conspiracy?"

"I do not know the man. My sources only indicate Chilton as the villain. But that does not mean Covington is not involved. Mayhap he is simply more clever than Chilton."

"Not a difficult thing, that."

"Agreed."

Morgan toyed with the tufted end of his mustache. "Things would not go well for Diana, should her father be hanged for piracy."

The name caught Alex's attention. "Diana?"

"Aye, Diana Covington. Frederick's daughter." A lusty gleam shone in the ex-buccaneer's eye. "Would that I were a score of years younger, my boy. That woman has a rare combination of beauty and spirit, and she is an heiress to boot. That red hair hints at passion that would burn a man alive."

"Indeed."

Morgan gave him a sharp look, then chuckled. "So you have met her, have you?"

"Aye."

The curt answer seemed to amuse Morgan even more. "She did not fall prey to that handsome face of yours, eh, Rothstone? If your interest lies in that direction, you had best batten down for stormy seas ahead."

"My interest lies with Marcus." Avoiding

Morgan's keen gaze, Alex studied the intricate carving on the arm of his chair.

"A man can have more than one interest." Morgan stood and went to the sideboard. "Wine?"

"Aye." Alex watched the lieutenant-governor splash the liquid into a pair of crystal goblets. "As I said, my only interest is to see Marcus dead."

As Morgan handed him the glass of wine, he gave Alex the look that had once made men cower before the deadliest buccaneer in the Caribbean. "Our agreement was that you capture Marcus, Rothstone. You are not to be his executioner. Marcus will stand trial for piracy and be hanged from the public gibbet like the rest of his brethren. You are to bring him back to Port Royal *alive*."

Alex flexed his fingers on the arm of the chair. "What you ask is difficult."

"We have an agreement." Morgan swirled his wine. "Marcus will be an example to all the lawless sea dogs in the Caribbean. Either they cease their thieving ways and come before me for pardon, or I will see their bones clacking in the wind."

"Marcus is different from the rest of them." Swallowing half his wine in one gulp, Alex stood. He paced the room, his fingers clenched so tightly around the delicate crystal that he expected it to shatter from the sheer force of his raging emotions.

"Easy, lad." He looked up to see Morgan

watching him with concern. "I know 'tis difficult to resist temptation, but you must let justice prevail. At least you will have the
satisfaction of watching him dance at the end
of a rope."

"He killed my brother," Alex snarled. He
flung the goblet at the wall. It shattered, scattering shards of crystal across the floor.
Stunned by his own explosion of temper, he
watched reddish brown wine drip down the
costly wallpaper like rivulets of blood.

Morgan broke the silence. "Damned expensive crystal, Rothstone."

"I can afford it." Rubbing one throbbing
temple, he slanted a wry look at Morgan. "I
am, after all, the Earl of Rothstone."

"But you are also El Moreno." Morgan
scowled at the broken crystal littering the floor.
"This does not bode well, Rothstone. I chose
you for this task because of your fine sailing
skills, not because of your brother."

"But I accepted because of my brother. Do
you think just any man would be able to play
the role of pirate?" Alex raked a hand through
his long hair. "Had I only wanted adventure,
I could have found that on my own."

"But you can sail the world no longer." Morgan leaned forward in his chair, his expression
ruthless. "William is dead, and now you hold
the title. You were only too happy to take advantage of the opportunity to become El Moreno, to sail the sea with the wind in your hair

and forget about your obligations to the earldom. Admit it, Rothstone."

"All right!" Two strides took Alex to Morgan's desk. He slammed his hands down on the mahogany surface. "You are correct, sir, when you say that I hate being bound by my title. But 'tis also true that I cannot shirk my duty. I am the last of the Rawnsleys. I bear the title. I cannot change that." He leaned closer. "But I can do something about Marcus. He killed my brother. And now I find that Chilton helped him do it."

Morgan rose slowly. "And so will he hang alongside Marcus for his part in these crimes. Have patience, lad."

"Patience!" With a harsh laugh Alex turned away. He sprawled into his chair and stretched his legs out before him with an arrogance that bordered on flippant. "The spirit of my brother cries out for vengeance, and I cannot be at peace until I satisfy that debt of honor. Look at me, Morgan. What do you see?"

Morgan glared at him, his mustache practically bristling with impatience. "I see El Moreno, scourge of the seas, rival of that bloodthirsty bastard Marcus."

"You see a man in mourning," Alex corrected. He indicated his dark clothing with a sweeping gesture. "I have sworn to wear black every day of my life until my brother's death is avenged. The fact that my clothing has become El Moreno's trademark is an ironic coincidence."

"But an effective one," Morgan replied, settling into his chair once more. "You make a credible pirate, Rothstone. Would that you had been one of my crew when I sailed these waters."

Alex paused, some of the anger draining from him at such high praise. "My thanks, sir."

"You can thank me later—after you help me clap Marcus and that primping popinjay Chilton in irons."

Alex slowly smiled as he envisioned that. "I have already set a man to watch Chilton, but tell me what you have in mind."

Leaning across the desk, Morgan told him.

"Now, lass, hold still!"

"Ow! Maude, there is no need for this. I am perfectly capable of brushing out my own hair." Seated at her vanity table, Diana watched in the mirror as her mother's cousin pulled the brush through her tangled red curls.

Maude Dunstan pursed her lips. "A fine thing that, a lady o' your station brushin' her own hair! Your mother would skin me alive if she was here to see it."

Diana chuckled at the image of her gently bred mother doing such a thing. Maude, on the other hand, seemed quite capable of skinning someone alive. She was a dour-faced woman with a heart of gold and the protective instincts of a lioness. A spinster cousin who lived on the charity of Diana's grandfather, she had chosen to accompany Diana's mother from Scotland upon her marriage. When a fever took the life of Margaret Covington, Maude became Diana's caretaker and confidante.

"Did you enjoy yourself this evenin'?" Maude asked, disrupting Diana's thoughts. Her tone seemed innocent enough, but Diana knew that her companion planned every word as carefully as a general did a full-scale battle.

Wary, she answered the question. "I did indeed."

"I wasna certain. I saw you tryin' to avoid that . . . eh, Lord Chilton. It's the likes o' him that made your father order you not to be goin' about on your own." She paused, then continued, "Seein' as we're on the subject, miss, would you care to tell me where you disappeared to for a good half hour?"

An image of the black-garbed stranger rose in Diana's mind, his dark eyes dancing with mischief and his lips tempting her with that wicked grin. If Maude discovered the truth, Diana knew she would be guarded more closely than the queen's own jewels in the future.

"How would you know if I went anywhere?" she shot back in an effort to distract the other woman. "You were surrounded by members of the Assembly. Did no one ever tell you 'twas unseemly for a woman to argue politics?"

"Dinna play your games with me, missy." Maude tapped Diana's shoulder with the back of the brush. "Answer the question now."

Diana sighed with impatience. "I was in the garden."

"In the garden? At night? On your own?" Maude jerked the brush hard through the snarled curls. "Are you daft, bairn? You could have came to some harm."

Diana winced and gave Maude a baleful look. "I may yet come to harm right here in my own bedchamber."

"Dinna interrupt. You ken the rules right enough, Diana Margaret. Your father told you never to wander about on your own. There's too many lusty scoundrels about now-a-days."

"I know. I shall not do it again." Since Maude could lecture on behavior for more than an hour, Diana searched for a new topic of conversation. "Tell me, have you heard anything of interest in the marketplace lately?"

"I dinna ken what you mean."

"Now, Maude." Diana bit back a laugh as she saw a flush creep into Maude's cheeks. "You have heard something, haven't you?"

"Perhaps," came the soft reply.

"Please tell me." She folded her hands in her lap and presented her most cajoling smile. "I promise not to be unduly influenced by what you say."

Maude placed the brush on the vanity table. "It's not right for a lass o' your station to be so taken with the likes o' El Moreno."

"El Moreno." Diana savored the sound of the words on her tongue. "Even his very name is exciting. 'Tis said that he is trying to earn his fortune so he may wed the lady he loves."

"Earn a fortune, is it? Stealin' is what I call it." Maude signaled for Diana to rise, then unlaced her gown. "In Scotland such a way o' life would earn a body naught but a hangin'."

Diana slipped off her dark green silk overdress and stepped from the matching underskirt. Then she stood patiently while her companion unlaced her corset. "I am sure El Moreno did not choose to be a pirate."

"Piffle," Maude snapped. "He's as bad as that Marcus. The two o' them go about attackin' other boats, takin' captives, and collectin' ransoms. If that's not a pirate I dinna ken what is."

Diana rolled her eyes as Maude helped her out of her layers of petticoats. "You think all pirates are the same. You don't even trust Sir Henry Morgan, and he was appointed lieutenant-governor by the king himself."

"Brigands, the lot o' them!"

"Sir Henry Morgan is hardly a brigand, at least not anymore," Diana insisted. "But Marcus is simply a cold-blooded killer. And as for El Moreno, 'tis common knowledge that he always puts his captives ashore at the next port. I think that gold lures him, not blood. And I think *you* dislike him simply because he is Spanish."

"Aye! Spanish!" Maude shook one of the undergarments in her vehemence. "No decent woman would as much as look at a scurvy Spaniard!"

Clad only in her shift, Diana sat down to strip off her stockings and garters. "Maude, I understand your dislike of the Spanish, but please try to remember that the war has been over since I was a babe. Besides, given what I have heard about El Moreno's looks, I have no doubt you would give the man a second glance yourself."

"You've an ill tongue, miss." Maude stalked across the room to fetch a night rail from the wardrobe. "I dinna ken where you learnt such talk."

"Why, from you, of course."

Maude muttered something and came back with the nightgown, gesturing for Diana to stand. "It's not right for a lady like yourself to say such things. The man's a criminal."

"I have heard that he is of noble blood," Diana argued as she stripped off her shift.

"Noble blood? That one? Not likely," Maude scoffed. She helped Diana into the virginal white night rail, guiding her arms into the sleeves. "Nah, lass. The man's naught but a pirate and a scoundrel."

"A handsome scoundrel. And a bold one. And so deadly with a sword that none dare challenge him!" She brandished an imaginary blade as Maude struggled to pull her hair out of the neckline of her night rail.

"Piracy and murder," Maude lamented. "A fine thing for a young lady to be talkin' about! What would your father say if he heard you talkin' about El Moreno like he was a suitor

came to court you? I'd tell you what he'd say.
He'd demand me to leave his house since I
canna control one impetuous girl."

"Oh, Maude." Diana sighed as the exuberance drained out of her. She moved to stand
by the open terrace doors and stared out at the
dark beauty of the sultry Jamaican night. "My
maidenhood cannot last forever. Someday soon
my father will arrange a marriage for me. I will
never sail the world or see far-off places. I will
honor Papa's choice of husband, whoever he
be, with good grace and dignity. But in the face
of this mundane future, do you not consider it
my due to indulge in such romantic fantasies
while I may?"

"Then dream on this," Maude relented.
"They say El Moreno's in Jamaica this verra
minute. Perhaps he means to steal the earbobs
from Henry Morgan himself!" With this pro-
nouncement she withdrew from the room,
leaving Diana staring after her.

El Moreno was in Jamaica. Once more the
stranger in the garden crept into her mind. As
her fantasy took shape, El Moreno and the
mysterious Alex merged into one man. She
touched her mouth and wondered for an instant if she had indeed tasted the kiss of the
Black Spaniard. Then she dismissed the idea as
foolish.

All her life she had longed for one adventure, one thrilling memory to take with her into
her boring future. She had found it in the kiss
of a handsome stranger.

She cast one last, wistful look at the starry night before turning back to her room. Before climbing into her bed she paused to blow out the candle, holding her hair out of the way of the flame. Darkness settled over the room, and she lay back against the pillows.

Never again would she look at the pale moon against the midnight sky without remembering Alex's wicked smile.

The sound of a footstep woke her.

Diana opened her eyes just as the mosquito netting around her bed was ripped aside. A glimmer of moonlight pierced the darkness an instant before the shape of a man blocked it out. Before she could open her mouth to scream, a rough-skinned hand smelling of filth and ale clamped hard over her lips. She clawed at the man's shadowed face. He caught her wrists and restrained her, snickering at her frantic struggling.

"Hold her," he rasped.

Diana tried to roll away as a second man climbed up on the bed. Taking her wrists from the first man, he straddled her, his legs clamping hard around her thighs.

"Take your time," the man atop her sneered. "I'm likin' this."

"Don't like it too much," the first man answered in his harsh voice. "The captain wants first poke at 'er."

Fear shot through her at the words. She struggled harder to dislodge the man on top, her screams muffled behind the hand over her mouth.

"I think she likes me." The lascivious laugh along with the unwashed stench of the man above her sent terror rippling down her spine. She jerked her hips in an effort to unbalance him. "Hurry up and tie her, mate," he sniggered. "The wench is eager to have me."

The hand moved away from her mouth. Diana sucked in a deep breath to scream, and a wad of foul-tasting material was shoved between her lips. She tried to push it out with her tongue, but another strip of cloth was pressed between her teeth and tied behind her head to hold it in place. She shrieked her frustration behind the gag. The two men laughed.

"She's a hot piece, eh?" came the abrasive voice of the first man. "I wouldn't mind havin' a taste o' her myself." He roughly wrapped thin, coarse rope around her wrists, binding her hands together.

"We'll all have a turn when the cap'n's done." The man atop her ran his hands over her thinly clad body. "I just hope he leaves enough for a bit o' fun."

Fury and fear lent her a strength she did not know she possessed. As the first man moved to tie her legs, she bucked her hips and swung her bound hands at the head of the one who straddled her. The double movement sent the unsuspecting brigand to the floor.

Swearing, the first man dove for her. She raised both legs and slammed her feet into his stomach. He cursed, his harsh voice becoming more so as he stumbled backward and struggled for breath. Diana rolled off the bed and ran.

"Bitch!" A hard yank on her hair halted her flight mere steps from the door. The man she had pushed to the floor whirled her to face him. "Bitch!" he snarled again. Drawing back his hand, he cuffed her hard on the side of the head.

Pain exploded in her skull. She whimpered, hanging limply in his grasp, and he slung her over his shoulder like a sack of flour. As the blood rushed to her head, the throbbing from the blow increased. Her vision blurred. Dimly she grew aware of hands on her ankles, binding them together with more coarse rope.

"Hurry up, mate." The man holding her shifted his burden, sending a new wave of pain washing through her brain. She groaned.

"'Tis done," said the first man, his harsh voice augmented by his labored breathing.

"Then back to the ship for us." A slap stung her bottom, and the ruffian's hand lingered. "And with you as well, milady."

Despite Diana's struggle to stay coherent, the laughter of her captors started to fade to a distant buzz. A cool breeze tugged at her nightdress, and she realized she had been carried out to the terrace. She caught a glimpse of the stone balustrade. Her vision wavered, then swirled into a cloud of black . . .

Chapter 3

T he iron manacles hanging from the wall cast eerie shadows in the candlelit room. Shuddering, Chilton looked away from the gruesome sight and picked up his goblet of wine. Other tortuous devices decorated Marcus's cabin, but Chilton had learned long ago that his comrade's activities were best ignored by those who could not stand the sight of blood.

"You did not tell me she had red hair."

At the words, he glanced across the table at Marcus. The pirate's blond good looks and melodious voice gave lie to the evil and perversion in his soul. At the moment Marcus stared with peculiar fascination at Diana, who lay bound and unconscious on the bed.

"You never asked what she looked like," Chilton answered, sipping fine burgundy pilfered from some unlucky French vessel. "As a matter of fact, you were most annoyed when I asked you to abduct her."

"But red hair." Marcus reached for the silver

goblet containing his wine and caressed it. "I adore redheads. They have pale, delicate skin that bruises so well. And most of them are so very stubborn." He lifted his goblet, drained it, and wiped his mouth with the back of his hand. "I love breaking the spirit in a woman."

Chilton curled his lip at Marcus's crude table manners. "At this point I don't care what you do to her. Just don't kill her, for I still intend to wed the bitch." He glared at the unconscious woman. "She will pay for cuckolding me."

Marcus looked at him, his piercing green eyes glittering with amusement. "Peter, only a husband can be cuckolded."

"She betrayed me. She knew I wanted her to be my bride."

Marcus leaned back in his chair and raised his eyebrows. "You don't suppose she took you in dislike?"

His sarcasm rubbed salt in the raw wound of Chilton's pride. "She is but a woman and does not know what she wants."

Marcus grinned and picked up a jeweled dagger lying on the table. "I could teach her respect."

"Be my guest. Just do not leave scars where anyone might see them. I will not have tongues wagging about the future Lady Chilton."

"You surprise me, Peter." Marcus jabbed the point of the dagger into the gouged and burned wood of the table, leaving it stuck there. "I always thought you to be more squeamish."

"Mayhap you underestimated me." Chilton gulped his wine.

"Then you will stay for the entertainment?" Marcus rose and chose an iron from the brazier in the corner. Examining the poker, he cast a jubilant smile in Chilton's direction. "I will make her scream your name if you like."

Chilton shuddered. "My thanks, but no. I would not dream of infringing on your enjoyment."

Marcus lowered the poker. "Why, Peter, I am touched by your generosity. Allow me to respond in kind." The irons clattered as he replaced the one he held with a careless motion.

"How?" Wariness crept over Chilton. When Marcus was this happy, someone usually died.

"I shall save you a lock of hair! Is that not an excellent suggestion?" Marcus rattled the chains on the wall and then picked up a cat-o'-nine-tails. His exuberance as he handled the instruments reminded Chilton of a lad set loose in the confectionery.

"Leave her hair alone. I will not tolerate a bald bride."

"Not *that* hair." Chuckling, the pirate put down thumbscrews and cracked his knuckles. Muscles in his chest and arms bulged beneath his white cambric shirt. "I will begin as soon as she awakens."

"Why not now?" Chilton swept a hand at the helpless woman. "She is at your mercy."

"Peter, Peter, Peter." Marcus shook his head.

"Anticipation is half the game. Besides, she will suffer more if she is awake."

Chilton finished his wine in one gulp. "I care not how you do it, as long as there is no visible damage. Just keep her alive long enough for me to enjoy my wedding night."

"I have hope for you." Marcus laughed, a robust sound that sent dread rippling down Chilton's spine.

"I will inform Frederick of his daughter's fate," Chilton said, pushing the fear to the back of his mind. "After he gives us those ledger pages, I will marry Diana and take control of her dowry."

"That reminds me, Peter." Marcus came to the table and yanked the dagger from the wood. "About that ledger you were keeping . . ."

The wine turned sour in Chilton's stomach as he stared at the gleaming blade. Then someone pounded on the door to the cabin, breaking the tension. Chilton fell back in his chair as Marcus stalked to the portal and threw it open.

"What the devil do you want, Scroggins?" he snarled.

The scrawny seaman didn't even blink at the pirate's irate tone. "We're ready to set sail, Cap'n."

"Excellent." Marcus turned to look at his guest. "Well, Peter, as you have heard, the ship is ready to depart. Unless you intend to come with us, you must disembark."

"Very well." Chilton pushed away from the

table and moved toward the door. "I will contact you when I have the ledger pages."

Marcus sketched a mocking bow. "Have no fear for your future bride. I will be certain to leave her healthy enough to say the marriage vows."

"See that you do. I need her wealth."

A moan came from the bed. Marcus's face lit with pleasure.

"Ah, she wakes." Marcus pricked Chilton's hand with the dagger, drawing a drop of blood. "Off with you, Peter, and leave the master to his work."

Chilton paled at the trickle of crimson that threatened to stain the bright yellow silk of his coat sleeve.

"Good night, my lord." Marcus flung the dagger across the room, where it embedded itself in the scratched wooden table with a powerful thunk.

Chilton made a hasty exit, fleeing the ship and Marcus's laughter as if he were escaping the bowels of hell itself.

She heard voices.

Forcing herself to surface from the black void of unconsciousness, Diana struggled to make sense of the jumbled conversation that awakened her. Memory flooded back, and fear with it, as she recognized the raspy voice of one of her abductors.

"She sure be a comely piece, Cap'n."

"She is indeed, Scroggins." The man who

answered was not the one who had captured her earlier. His voice was richer. Deeper. Smoother. Almost aristocratic. From the familiar creaks and splashes that came to her ears, she realized that she was aboard a ship. The gentle rocking of the room confirmed it. She knew that she lay on a bed and that her hands were still bound. Her legs, however, were not. Tamping down the urge to flee, she continued to feign unconsciousness.

The bed dipped as if someone sat upon it. A hand ran through her hair, lifting it and letting it fall back against her cheek. "A red-haired virgin. She is much too fine for the likes of that fool Peter."

Despite its beauty, the deep voice chilled her. She had the fleeting thought that the devil must speak like this, his tones dulcet yet deadly.

"So lovely," the owner of the voice murmured. Hands smoothed down her body, forcing her to swallow her revulsion. "Mayhap I should see what charms the lady can offer." He ripped open the lacy bodice of her nightgown.

Diana shrieked behind the gag. Her eyes flew open to reveal a large blond man bent over her, his brutal hands clenched around handfuls of lace. He jerked his head up. His stunning good looks matched the loveliness of his voice, but what she saw in his gaze frightened her.

"She be awake, Cap'n," said the wiry, scarred man standing at the foot of the bed.

"I can see that, Scroggins." The villain's eyes narrowed with lust. Before she could blink he yanked the gag from her mouth, tilted her chin up, and forced a bruising kiss on her tender lips.

She whimpered, almost gagging as he pushed his tongue into her mouth. She strained against her bonds, disgust giving her strength. At last the knave raised his head.

"I love a woman with spirit."

The words sent fear snaking down her spine. She searched the room desperately for a means of escape. Instead, what she saw only terrified her more. Scattered about the room, all the more horrible for the casual way they had been left about, lay instruments of torture. Most of the frightening apparatus she did not recognize, but one or two she did. A well-worn cat-o'-nine-tails rested on a table. Heavy iron manacles hung from the wall. Pokers thrust menacingly out of a black brazier.

"I see that you are admiring my playthings, my dear. Mayhap you will join me in a game or two?" Her captor laughed at his own jest.

"Who—" Diana wet her parched lips before asking the question that would confirm her suspicions. "Who are you?"

"My dear lady." His eyes widened in astonishment. Placing a hand over his heart, he sketched a brief bow. "I am Marcus, king of the seas. And you are my captive."

* * *

The *Vengeance* sliced through the calm sea like a sword through silk. Alex braced his arms on the rail of the quarterdeck and watched the white foam dance back from the hull like the petticoats of a flirtatious maid. Even as he gloried in the caress of the salt air on his skin, he lifted his gaze to search the horizon for Marcus.

After his meeting with Morgan he had returned to his ship, where he found the man he'd ordered to follow Chilton waiting for him. Along with the news that Diana Covington had been taken captive by Marcus, Alex had also been given the location of his enemy's vessel.

At last he would have his revenge.

"Good evenin' to you, Captain."

Alex turned at the familiar Scottish burr and saw Birk Fraser, the ship's surgeon, climbing up to the quarterdeck. He grinned at the brawny Scot's reddened eyes and pained expression.

"Why, Birk, I do believe you are sober."

"O' course I'm bloody sober," came the acerbic reply. "You're takin' us into battle, chasin' after some wench that's been snatched from her bed. Do you expect me to pull pistol balls out o' your carcass from the bottom o' a bottle?"

Alex shrugged and faced the sea once more. "You've done it before. And Diana Covington is no 'wench,' Birk. She's a lady of good family, an innocent girl."

Birk joined him at the rail. "A bloody sainted virgin, eh?"

"I realize you are unfamiliar with the breed," Alex scoffed.

"I steer clear o' the lot o' them. Virgins can lead a man to the altar, and Birk Fraser is no' a man to be married." He shook his head. "It's your bloody honor that has you determined to rescue the lass, isn't it?"

"The thought of her purity being warped by his perversity turns my stomach."

"Aye, no woman deserves that kind o' abuse. I saw what he did to the wench on Tortuga, and it's a mercy the lass died. I took a whole bottle to bed with me that night."

"Everything seems to be cause for the bottle in your opinion, Mister Fraser." Alex gave him a level look.

Birk met and held his gaze. "You ken I have good reason to drink, Alex."

"I know, my friend. But I hate watching you destroy yourself."

"Who, me?" Birk threw back his head and laughed. His black hair blew wildly in the wind, giving him the look of a madman. "I'm not the one sailin' about callin' himself a pirate."

"Step carefully, Birk," Alex warned.

"Dinna use that cold tone with me, Alex. We've kent one another too long."

"That doesn't give you leave to address me with disrespect."

Birk lowered his voice so that it would not carry to the rest of the crew. "You might be a bloody earl now, but dinna think I canna beat you in a fair fight."

Alex chuckled despite himself. "How about an unfair one?"

Birk slapped him on the shoulder. "That's the best kind."

A moment of companionable silence stretched between them. "Birk, how long have we known each other?"

"Ten years." Birk gripped the rail as a swell rocked the ship. "It's a long time to put up with your stubbornness, I'll give you that."

Alex tried to look stern at Birk's irreverent words, but failed. "Has it been that long?"

"Aye, and a fair trial it's been keepin' you out o' trouble."

"Keeping *me* out of trouble? Who saved your neck from Lady Burston's irate husband?"

"It wasna my neck in danger that day, Alex. Many a wench has remembered you in her prayers for savin' the manhood o' Birk Fraser."

"Now that I recall, Lord Burston did seem intent on gelding you."

"It was worth the risk to have bedded Arabella Burston." Birk said the name as if he savored the taste of it on his tongue. "Now, there's a wild wench. The hottest piece o' goods in England."

"A wild wench? 'Tis a fine name for the wife of so powerful a man as Lord Burston."

"Aye." Birk rubbed his chest. "I still carry the scars from that she-cat's claws."

"And I still carry the memory of you racing

across the countryside with Burston firing his musket at your naked arse."

"It's a blessin' for the lasses the old fool was a poor shot," Birk said with his usual lack of modesty.

"Sail ho!"

The cry from the crow's nest snared Alex's immediate attention. On the horizon he caught sight of a tiny white blur that represented the sails of a distant ship. He pulled out his spy-glass.

"There he is." His heart pounded like a battle drum. Through the glass the blurry white image sharpened into a clear view of Marcus's ship *Marauder*, her sails swollen with a fair wind. "At last I have him right where I want him."

Lowering the glass, he called out, "Clear the decks!"

Men jumped into action. Some scrambled to clear all obstacles out of the way, while others scattered sand on the decks to prevent slipping.

A clatter of footsteps on the ladder preceded the arrival of the first mate. "Orders, Captain?"

"Loose the guns, McBride, and prepare to board to windward."

"Aye, Captain." The red-haired Irishman slipped back down the ladder. Seconds later his voice echoed across the decks, spurring a thunderous cacophony of sound as pairs of men unchained the cannons and rolled them into place at the gunports.

Birk sighed and turned from the rail. "I'd best get below and set out my tools. Watch your back, Alex."

"I will." As Birk left the deck, Alex focused on the horizon. The *Marauder* loomed larger as they closed in on her.

He thought of Diana Covington. Her proud bearing had proved an irresistible lure for someone like Marcus, a murderer who reveled in destroying innocence. With the flat of his palm, he snapped his spyglass closed.

He hoped he was in time.

Diana stared at her captor in mounting terror. She had heard stories of Marcus and his horrible crimes. Theft. Ravishment. Murder. Enslaving his captives as doxies for his men. In each tale, the victim died a painful death.

And she was next.

Bile rose in her throat as she looked into his glittering green eyes. "What do you want of me?"

He slipped his hand into the bodice of her torn nightdress and squeezed her breast with cruel meaning. "I think you know."

She froze, her entire body rebelling at the touch of his callused hand on her flesh. She actually thought she might lose the contents of her stomach. Then he gave her nipple a hard pinch that jolted her from her shock. She jerked away from him and rolled toward the edge of the bed. His hand snaked out and caught a piece of her nightgown.

"That was not very effective, was it?" Smiling, he yanked her back across the bed with one hard pull.

Scroggins snickered. Marcus wrapped her nightdress around his hand, slowly pulling her upper body off the bed. Grasping the back of her neck in a punishing grip, he ground his mouth against hers. He seemed to want to invade her, to take over her will and subjugate it to his.

Without thought to the consequences, she sank her teeth into the pirate's lip.

Marcus jerked back from her, blood trickling from his mouth. He stared deep into her eyes. Then a slow, pleased smile stretched across his face.

"I see you have decided to play my game."

He released her head with teeth-rattling abruptness and straddled her. She struck at him with her bound hands, but he clasped her wrists in one hand and stretched them above her head. With the other he took hold of the tattered lace and tore open the nightdress from neckline to hem.

She screamed and squirmed. He restrained her easily, his eyes gleaming with frightening enjoyment. He forced her thighs apart. Scroggins stepped forward, peering past his captain for a better view. Marcus yanked open the buttons of his breeches.

Suddenly a horrendous explosion rent the air. The ship listed hard to the side, causing the brazier to tip over with a clatter of pokers.

Shouts erupted on deck. Marcus snarled a vicious oath and glared at Scroggins.

"Get up there and find out what is happening!"

A fist pounded on the door before the mate could take a step. "Cap'n!" someone shouted. " 'Tis El Moreno!"

"El Moreno!" Marcus shoved Diana aside, almost toppling her from the bed as he leaped to his feet. "This time I shall skin the miserable cur inch by wretched inch!" He fastened his breeches as he stormed from the cabin, Scroggins scrambling after him.

The door remained open in invitation.

Diana wasted no time. She rolled off the bed, stumbling for an instant as the ship rocked again. She looked around the cabin and found what she sought in the form of a jeweled dagger stuck in the table. She pulled it free with her bound hands.

Seating herself on the floor, she held the dagger between her knees and sawed at her bonds. The rope fell to the floor in pieces. Clutching the dagger in her hand, she stood and looked for something to wear, since her shredded nightdress hung from her body in useless tatters. Her gaze fell on Marcus's sea chest.

The ship rolled again as she made her way to the wooden chest. Smashing open the lock with one of the pokers, she wrinkled her nose in disgust as she grabbed the first garments she laid her hands on. Though she loathed the thought of wearing the clothes of the man who had almost raped her, escape would prove impossible while stark naked.

She dressed quickly in a white shirt of fine silk and a pair of brown velvet breeches. The legs, which would normally be knee-length on a man, modestly covered her to the ankles. Finding the waist too wide, she knotted the rope that had bound her wrists and used it as a belt.

She tucked the overlong tails of the shirt into her pants, then grabbed a black leather vest to conceal her breasts. Twisting her hair into a loose knot atop her head, she jammed one of Marcus's hats over it, effectively concealing her femininity from all but the closest of glances. Then she took up the dagger.

With one last, repulsed look at the bed, she fled the cabin.

"Fire!" Alex roared.

Cannons boomed, sending acrid smoke drifting up from the gunports. He watched with deep satisfaction as the shots hit their targets. Cries of alarm rose up from Marcus's ship as the yellow fog of the smoke bombs spread across the main deck of the *Marauder*. A lazy sea breeze carried the putrid smell of sulfur to Alex's nose.

His helmsman controlled the ship with the tender deftness of a mother handling her babe, so easily did the *Vengeance* narrow the space between the two vessels. In minutes they were close enough for his crew to launch the grappling irons. The clawed irons snagged in the *Marauder's* rigging, binding the two ships together. Some men swung over the small expanse of ocean on the grappling ropes, while others simply dove over the side to climb like spiders onto the enemy ship.

Alex called out orders and paced the quarterdeck, scanning the battle as his men engaged Marcus's crew with the joy of true warriors. Shouts of pain and triumph rose as the fighting escalated. Cutlasses flashed in the light of the rising sun. Alex watched, waiting for the first sight of Marcus, his hand itching to take up the sword that hung at his side.

The discordant screams of the wounded rose above the clashing of steel. Against the eerie cloud of sulfur smoke, the combatants appeared to be gruesome shadows dancing with death in the orange light of sunrise. Most of the fighting was in the waist of the ship, the main deck. The upper decks appeared deserted, but a sudden movement caught Alex's eye. A small figure—a cabin boy, perhaps—darted across the quarterdeck of Marcus's ship, heading for the side. A blond man with a bloody sword in his hand bounded after the lad.

Alex strode to the side, gripped the rail, and stared intently at the blond man. His pulse pounded as he recognized him. Clenching his hands into fists, he jerked away, demanding a grappling rope. Someone shoved one into his hand. Battle fever raged through him as he plotted the trajectory for the grappling hook. All the while he kept his gaze on the blond man, who was about to corner the smaller person on the quarterdeck.

Marcus. At last.

The sea was her only option.

Diana reached for the rail, her fingers curling around the smooth wood with desperation. Jamaica loomed dark on the horizon, beckoning her to freedom. Footsteps sounded behind her. It had to be now. She could dive over the side and swim for shore, escaping both pirate vessels. And if she drowned, or if the sharks got her . . .

Any fate was better than the one Marcus planned.

"Leaving so soon?"

Diana froze in the act of climbing the side. The hated voice resonated through her. She lowered her foot to the deck and turned to face Marcus. He looked well pleased with himself, and though he stood a few feet away, he was still close enough to grab her should she decide to follow through with her plan.

Regret pierced like cold steel through her heart. After emerging through the hatch on the main deck and fighting her way through the battling pirates, stumbling through foul-smelling smoke that stung her eyes and burned her throat, she'd been stopped here, mere seconds before she made her escape.

She would die soon. Marcus's smile, pure

evil in the early morning sun, promised that much. First he would play with her, as a cat did a mouse before devouring it. While her own plan had courted death, at least the choice had been hers. Marcus gave no quarter.

The pirate raised his bloodstained sword and stepped closer, taking in her appearance from head to toe. "Is this a woman before me or a pretty lad?" he mused. A flick of his blade sent her hat over the side, and her hair tumbled over her shoulders. "I almost did not recognize you, my dear. Surely you do not seek to deprive me of your company? We have yet to finish our game."

"I have." She hid her revulsion as his greedy gaze skimmed her body. "There are alternatives to submitting to you." She pressed back against the rail as she spoke.

"You would kill yourself over me?" A delighted smile spread across his face. "How touching. However, I must protest. I am not finished with you."

"I would take my chances."

He clucked his tongue like a teacher disappointed with his student. "No doubt there are sharks down there, hungry for a tasty morsel such as yourself. I shall have to convince you to stay." He used his sword to lift a fiery curl from her shoulder, then brushed her ear with the flat of the blade.

She shuddered as cool steel, sticky with blood, touched her flesh. Refusing to let him see her fear, she glared at him instead. "Kill me by sword or by sea. It matters not. At least I shall be free of you."

Marcus stared at her with startled admiration. "You are truly worthy of me, my dear. And a redhead as well." One slash of his blade tore her shirt open. His greedy gaze took in the swell of her naked breasts. "I shall enjoy hearing your cries for mercy."

"And I shall enjoy depriving you of that pleasure," she spat. Though every instinct screamed that she jerk the garment closed, she refused to reveal any weakness. She lifted her chin and met his eyes. "Well? How shall I die?"

Silence ticked by as Marcus appeared to contemplate the question. Lowering his sword, he watched her with the unblinking concentration of a snake about to strike. "I have decided . . ."

A rush of air drowned out the rest of his words. The impact of a hard male body against her back coincided with a brawny arm curling around her waist; then she was jerked off her feet. She was swept through the air, dangling in nothingness but for the strong arm clamped tightly under her ribs. A scream of surprise ripped from her throat, and she clung to that arm with both hands, the only thing between her and broken bones on the deck below. She turned her head to glance at her rescuer, but her unbound hair whipped across her face, preventing her from identifying him. The scents of sandalwood and sea enveloped her, teasing her memory as to who so recklessly swept her from death at Marcus's hands.

Suddenly her feet touched the deck once again, several yards away. Gasping for the breath that had been squeezed from her lungs, she swiped aside her hair and looked up into the dark eyes of her savior. Recognition made her jaw drop.

"You!"

Chapter 4

～～◯◯◯～～～

Alex grinned down at Diana, his blood pounding with the thrill of battle. "A pleasure to see you again, my sweet." He pried loose her fingers where they clenched his black cambric shirt. "Do try to control your lusty impulses until we have more privacy."

Outrage darkened her gray eyes to smoke, but a furious yell grabbed his attention away from her. He turned to confront the rage twisting Marcus's face as the pirate flew at him with sword flashing. Shoving Diana behind him, Alex drew his own sword and met steel with steel. He gave Marcus a derisive smile as they remained poised in a punishing position: shoulder against shoulder, swords crossed, muscles straining.

"El Moreno, you filthy swine! You have finally shown your cowardly face!" Marcus's eyes bulged as he leaned his strength into his shoulder to force Alex off balance.

Alex bent his knees and then shoved the pirate with the power of his entire body. Marcus stumbled back, breaking them apart. Sucking in a cleansing breath, Alex relaxed into a more traditional stance, sword extended. "You pox-ridden bastard, I'll see you in hell this night!"

Marcus's laughter echoed out over the water as he, too, took up the dueling position. "Give the devil my regards. You shall meet him before I will." He attacked.

The scrape of metal striking metal was like music to Alex. He beat back Marcus's sword and made a thrust of his own. The pirate nimbly avoided it. An unholy smile stretched across Alex's face. "After I kill you, I'll scuttle your ship and use it for kindling," he promised. Then he threw himself into the duel.

Diana pressed herself against the side of the ship, her trembling fingers clenched on the rail as if it were a lifeline as the two men slashed and dodged mere paces away from her. Her mind spun with the implications of what she had just learned.

'Twas no dream—the bold rogue who had kissed her last night was none other than El Moreno, the infamous pirate.

Steel clanged against steel as the two men battled. Diana was unable to take her gaze from Alex, her own fantasy come to life. For each vicious thrust and swipe of Marcus's sword, Alex knew the correct maneuver to either avoid or return the blow. The muscles of his thighs bunched and relaxed with each leap away from the blade. His sinewy shoulders rippled beneath the black material of his shirt

every time he swung his weapon. She caught
her breath over and over again, each time certain his life was about to end. But somehow he
always avoided death with mere seconds to
spare. He smiled as he parried Marcus's at-
tacks, making it clear that he reveled in the
fight. His teeth gleamed in a feral smile as the
two blades flashed.

A toss of the ship sent Diana staggering.
Bracing herself with the rail of the quarterdeck,
she slowly sank into a sitting position. She
pulled up her knees and rested her chin on
them, wrapping her arms around her legs. The
fear from her confrontation with Marcus had
sapped the strength from her limbs.

A furtive movement to her right caught her
attention, and she turned to see Scroggins,
creeping up the ladder from the deck below.
He did not see her sitting just to his left, for his
eyes were fixed on Alex's back. The wickedly
sharp dagger between his teeth proclaimed his
intention.

Diana knew the exact instant when Marcus
spotted Scroggins. The pirate sneered and gave
a brutal thrust, causing Alex to jump back.

" 'Tis a beautiful morning to die," Marcus
hissed. "Any last requests?" Not by the flicker
of an eyelash did he betray the man creeping
up behind his opponent.

Alex parried the next thrust. "My only request is to see your bones rattling in the wind!"

Marcus laughed. The sound sent a shudder
down Diana's spine. After a deep breath to

calm her pounding heart, she pulled out the blade she had stolen from Marcus's cabin. She clenched her fingers around it as the shadow that was Scroggins crept past her hiding place. She braced herself; then, with a cry of alarm, she leaped at the seaman.

Alex glanced over at the commotion. Diana stood toe to toe with a scarred member of Marcus's crew, waving a bloodstained dagger before the stunned seaman's eyes. The cur was swearing and clutching his arm to his chest. Blood trickled from between his fingers.

A stirring of air alerted Alex as Marcus took advantage of his momentary distraction and slashed at his midsection. Alex whirled away, but a hiss of pain escaped his lips as the pirate's sword sliced across his ribs. The wound burned, but at least he still lived. He came out of the turn to meet Marcus blade to blade.

Diana kicked away the henchman's dagger, sending it skittering across the deck. She winced as the blade pricked her bare foot, but she never took her eyes from Scroggins.

"Ye poxy slut! Ye cut me!"

"And I'll cut you again, so don't test me." She held the dagger at the ready for emphasis.

Scroggins narrowed his eyes. "Ye're just a wench," he sneered. "Ye need a man to show ye who yer master is!"

He lunged at her and grabbed both her wrists. A cruel twist made her fingers spring open, and she gave a moan of denial as the knife tumbled to the deck.

Scroggins laughed. Fear spiked up from her gut, and her pulse thundered in her ears. As she saw the triumph that glimmered in his squinty eyes, she knew Scroggins thought she was trapped. Something cold and unemotional settled into her soul. Not taking her gaze from his, she grabbed his sleeves for leverage and slammed her knee between his legs.

His yowl of pain echoed like a dying thing as he released her and fell to his knees. She kicked him in the chest, and with a pitiful cry, the seaman crashed to the deck. He curled into a ball, his hands cupped protectively at the juncture of his thighs.

Diana stepped away from him and scooped up her dagger. Scroggins still lay where he had fallen, apparently stunned. She silently thanked her father for teaching her how to defend herself. Keeping her dagger ready, she moved toward Alex.

The two pirates continued their battle. Marcus fought like a madman, his slashing sword a weapon of fire as it reflected the hues of the rising sun. Alex parried each vicious blow, but every one cost him a step backward until he bumped the rail of the ship. Marcus surged forward. With a clang of steel, the two men grappled for the advantage.

Diana put her hand to her throat as each strained to win, blades locked, Alex trapped against the railing of the ship. She took a step toward them with the idea of helping Alex. Then Marcus stumbled backward, propelled by the force of Alex's booted foot in his stomach. She smiled as she saw how her rescuer had used the ship's railing for leverage to accomplish the maneuver. As Alex regained his footing, he winked at her. Then Marcus's roar of rage reclaimed his attention.

Marcus rushed Alex. Seconds before Marcus's sword would have pierced his flesh, Alex dodged to one side. Marcus slammed against the rail. Before the pirate could regain the breath that had whooshed from his lungs, Alex grabbed him by the shirt and seat and shoved him over the side.

A moment later a wail and a splash reached their ears. Alex turned from the rail, his black hair damp with sweat and falling in a tangled mass to his broad shoulders. He lowered his sword and approached her with a cocky grin.

"Your taste in men has not improved. Must I ever rescue you from your bad judgment?" He sheathed his sword and nudged the fallen seaman with the toe of his boot. "Though this was very nicely done."

"Thank you so very much," she retorted, redirecting all her fear and frustration onto his arrogant head. "I cannot tell you how much your praise means to me."

"How can you be so shrewish at so early an hour?" he asked with interest.

"I have had a terrible night."

"Well, your morning will be much better. Come, let's away."

She pulled her elbow from his guiding grasp. "I'm not going anywhere with you."

Folding his arms across his chest, he raised an eyebrow. "You are the most ungrateful female I have ever met. This is the second time I have rescued you, only to feel the bite of your tongue for my efforts."

"As before, sir, I was about to extricate myself before you appeared."

"Indeed." Male indulgence underscored his words.

Diana fumed at his patronizing tone. "You need not speak to me as if I were a child, Alex. Or shall I call you El Moreno?"

"Call me what you wish. And give me that." Before she could protest, he took her dagger and tucked it into his own boot.

"How dare you? I saved your miserable life, yet now I cannot be trusted with a blade?"

"Your tongue is sharp enough. And any woman who would not leave Marcus's ship is indeed a fool."

"I did not say I would not leave the ship. I only said I choose not to leave with you."

"You are not given a choice, my sweet." Directing his attention to the decks behind her, he put two fingers in his mouth and gave a shrill whistle. Then he grabbed her hand and pulled her with him to the rail of the quarterdeck.

"What are you doing?"

"Hush, woman." His dark gaze touched on her lips before he raised his eyes to hers. "Lest I find a way to silence you."

His sensual promise awakened a tremor of response in her untried body. Well did she remember the power of his kiss. She did not think she could handle the confusing emotions he inspired on top of everything else that had happened. Out of self-preservation, she slowly nodded.

He turned to face his crew.

Alex looked out over the lower decks of the ship. His men had gathered in response to his signal, having incarcerated the surviving members of Marcus's crew in the hold. They looked up at him in expectation.

He stood silent for a long moment, then drew his sword and speared it into the air. "Well done, my friends! Marcus is ours!"

A rousing cheer answered his words. John McBride, Alex's first mate, pushed a seething, dripping Marcus to the front of the crowd.

"Captain!" McBride called out. "We fished a little somethin' out o' the water. Even the sharks won't eat it!"

Roars of laughter echoed across the decks. With rope binding his wrists in front of him, Marcus glared as if he would strangle every man there. Alex smiled with deep satisfaction as he met the hate-filled gaze of his enemy.

"Clap him in irons, McBride. Let him enjoy

the hospitality of his own rats in his own hold."

McBride tried to lead Marcus away, but the pirate shook off his hold. "This is not over yet, El Moreno!"

Alex leaned over the rail. "It is for you."

Marcus once more resisted McBride's determination to see him away. He looked at Diana. His lips curved in a slow, terrible smile. "We will meet again, my dear. Believe it."

Alex expected her to quail. To his amazement, Diana stepped forward and addressed her abductor. "If we do," she said in a clear voice, " 'twill be at your hanging."

Marcus sketched a little bow, then looked at Alex. "Enjoy the whore, you Spanish bastard. Just remember—I had her first."

With a wave of his hand McBride signaled to two burly men, who grabbed the pirate and dragged him away. Marcus continued to glare at them until he disappeared belowdecks.

Alex glanced at Diana. "You are a brave woman," he murmured, impressed.

"I was terrified."

"An intelligent woman, as well." He grinned and shook his head. "But we really must do something about your affinity for such disagreeable companions."

"Absolutely." She swept him from head to toe with a meaningful look and then turned away.

He chuckled. "You must admit, I am a better choice than Marcus."

She shrugged. "One pirate is the same as another."

Her casual insult chafed like a splinter beneath his skin. It was bad enough that he was so attracted to her when he couldn't afford the distraction. But he had saved her life, and she treated him as if he were the one intent on harming her.

Shoving his sword back into its scabbard, he reached for her. "Come with me."

"Where are we going?" she demanded, resisting as he tried to lead her to the ladder.

"Must you plague me with questions?" Alex jerked her forward. She fell against his chest, grabbing his shirt for balance. The garment, slashed from his battle with Marcus, tore open to expose the bare skin of his midsection. Still clutching the strip of black cambric, Diana stared up at him, her expression a picture of maidenly horror.

"Ah, Diana," he teased. "Your lusty appetites astound me. I would gladly have disrobed had you but asked."

"Oh!" Diana dropped the material as if it burned her. "As if I would ever ask such a thing!"

For an instant he could see it vividly in his mind—both of them naked in his bed and straining for release. Then he banished the erotic image.

"Perhaps you might," he answered shortly. "Someday." He took her arm. "Now you may walk with me to my ship like the lady you are, or you may share quarters with Marcus in the hold. 'Tis your choice."

"You are vile." Her nose raised in haughty disdain, she preceded him to the ladder. Chuckling despite his thwarted appetites, he followed.

They descended to the lower decks, where McBride awaited him in the waist.

"Orders, Captain?" The mate fell into step behind his captain as Alex led Diana across the deck.

"Take a few men and secure the ship," Alex replied. "Leave Fernandez in command here. I need you back on the *Vengeance*."

"Indeed I will, sir."

"And cut loose the grappling ropes as soon as you can," Alex added. "A storm's blowing up, and I don't want the *Vengeance* dragged under by this barge if it hits."

"To be sure." With a nod, the wiry Irishman hurried across one of the planks balanced between the two ships.

Alex made to follow, but Diana brought him up short. Her gray eyes widened with apprehension as she stared down at the sea below them.

"Don't be afraid. I won't let you fall."

"I cannot tell you how much that reassures me," she snapped.

He cocked an eyebrow at her. "There is always the alternative. I am certain Marcus would be glad of the company." She gave him a look of disgust, and he laughed. "That is what I thought. Now come." Tugging her behind him, he mounted the plank.

Diana burned with chagrin as Alex led her like a spaniel on a lead. She wanted to protest, but dared not test him further. He seemed to win every challenge.

She followed him across the plank with small steps, and her stomach rolled as she viewed the choppy water beneath them. She looked up with haste and fixed her gaze on his broad back. How could he stroll such a narrow board with such confidence? He seemed totally in control of his environment, certain that he could handle any problem that arose.

So where did that leave her?

It had not occurred to her to be afraid of him, since he had once before refused the opportunity to do her harm. But that had been in the garden of her home, where one cry from her would have brought armed men to her rescue. Fear trickled along her spine. What was to prevent Alex from abusing her now? On his own ship, no one would stop him.

The thud of his boots hitting the deck of the *Vengeance* jerked her from her musings. He helped her down from the plank, his strong hand the only security in the precarious situation. Then he led her across the main deck and up the ladders to the quarterdeck. McBride already waited there.

Alex gave her a hard look as he released her near the outside rail overlooking the ocean.

"Stay here and cause no trouble. My men are not the sort of lily-livered buffoons you are used to. If they see a woman unattended, they will act according to their baser natures. Do you understand, or must I say it in less respectable terms?"

"I comprehend you quite well. It is what I expected."

"No doubt." With one last warning look, he crossed the deck to confer with the first mate.

Even wounded, the man moved with the grace of a tiger. As Diana watched him, a fluttering sensation sprang to life in her stomach to echo the erratic skipping of her pulse, born when he had taken her hand. This man had a wild, untamed side that both frightened and intrigued her. He glanced up from his conversation and met her eyes for an instant. The contact lasted only a brief moment, but its effect lingered in her trembling limbs. Then he returned his attention to the first mate.

Disturbed by the intensity of her response, Diana turned her attention to the open sea. She had no interest in the low-voiced conversation going on a few feet away. Instead, she occupied herself with plans for escape.

Alex glanced at Diana again and frowned. Her contemplative expression made him uneasy as she stared out to sea. He would wager his ship that she was plotting something. From her fearless demeanor, one would think she was abducted by pirates every day.

"Bloody hell," he muttered.

"Captain? Did ye say somethin'?"

He frowned at McBride, who regarded him with a puzzled expression. "No." With effort, he pulled his thoughts away from Diana Covington. "Did we profit well from the contents of Marcus's hold?"

McBride chuckled. " 'Tis true we lightened his load a bit."

"Excellent. Divide the shares, then, but none for me. I claim the woman as captain's share. That should keep the peace amongst the men."

"Agreed. They will not be missin' a woman when their pockets are full o' gold."

"That is my intention. I have no desire to punish any member of my crew whose lust might overwhelm his common sense. But if I have to, I will." Himself included, he thought wryly.

"There's not a man aboard who would dare touch the captain's woman," McBride said. " 'Tis not worth the risk o' losin' a hand."

"Or any other body parts," Alex added dryly. He stretched and then hissed in pain as the slice in his side protested the movement. Rubbing the wound, he asked, "Is all well with the *Marauder*?"

"It is. I've six men aboard to sail her back to port. If we need more, we have them."

"Excellent. And Marcus?"

"Locked in his own hold with his own irons."

"Good." He paused, torn between the neces-

sity of seeing to Diana's welfare and the desire
to ensure the security of his captured enemy.
Necessity dictated he make a show of charming Diana, lest he be forced to punish one of
the men for molesting her. "I'll attend to him
later, then. Those irons will keep him well
enough."

"Indeed," McBride concurred.

"Set sail for Port Royal," Alex said, his eyes
on Diana. "I have a matter to oversee."

"That ye do," came the reply.

"I suppose I must play the pirate here," Alex
muttered to himself, in no hurry to deal with
the tempting, red-haired baggage. "The more
afraid she is of El Moreno, the less trouble she
will cause. Then I can return her to her father
none the worse for wear." He sighed. "Let's
get this over with." With determined strides,
he approached Diana.

Chapter 5

White sails bloomed as wind filled the sturdy canvas, guiding the *Vengeance* toward Port Royal with the *Marauder* trailing behind. On the horizon, iron-gray clouds gathered in anticipation of the coming storm.

Alex expected a storm, too, as he came to stand beside Diana. Any other woman would have collapsed with the vapors by now, but not this termagant. No, her face reflected a fierce pride and determination that would wreak havoc aboard his ship if he did not take steps to stop her.

"So, you are captain of this vessel?" Her calm words belied the spark of challenge in her eyes.

"I am."

"Then it is to you whom I should speak." She clasped her hands, her aristocratic demeanor defying the ill-fitting pirate's garb that adorned her slender frame. "I would know my fate, Captain. I am certain you are aware that my father is a wealthy man. He would be more than happy to reward you handsomely for my safe return."

"That prospect did occur to me." He watched as she struggled to control her temper. Her flush deepened, and she twisted her fingers together. He smothered a laugh. Bloody hell, but he enjoyed baiting her. He could not seem to help himself. "I have not yet decided whether I will return you to your father. I am considering other alternatives."

"Considering other alternatives?" Abandoning her ladylike pose, she propped her hands on her hips and glared at him. "Just what might those be?"

"I could sell you into slavery. In the East, red hair is quite rare." He stroked a lock with his finger. "You would fetch quite a price. Far more than your father could ever pay."

Her mouth fell open. "Sell me? You wouldn't dare!"

He shrugged. "A pirate's goal is profit."

"You are beneath contempt." Curling her lip in disgust, she turned away from him to stare out at the ocean.

Alex allowed a small smile to escape, then pressed his lips together so she would not see how much she amused him. "Or I could keep you for myself," he suggested.

She whipped her head around so fast that the ends of her hair brushed his face. "What did you say?"

"You would make a fetching addition to my bed."

"How dare you!" Anger sparked in her eyes like new steel reflecting the sun. He wondered if she would respond with such passion in his arms.

"I dare anything, my sweet." When she turned her back on him again, he moved behind her and pressed his lips to the top of her head. " 'Twould be quite a simple matter to make you my mistress."

"Never," she whispered. Her breasts rose and fell rapidly in her agitation.

"The idea has merit," he mused aloud, slipping an arm about her waist. He pulled her against him so that her buttocks pressed against his thighs. His new position gave him an interesting view of her semi-exposed bosom and warmed his blood more than a little.

"No, it does not have merit." She tried without success to remove his arm. "I *demand* you return me to my father."

"With a temper like that, I doubt he would want you back." He chuckled, holding her close against him as she struggled for freedom. Desire twisted in his gut as she wriggled in his arms. "Mayhap he would pay me to keep you."

"My father would relinquish his entire fleet before he would leave his only daughter to the mercy of a lying, lowborn Spanish sea scum!"

Alex grinned, unable to contain himself any longer. "Then more the fool he. I see where you have inherited your bad judgment."

She gave a frustrated growl and struggled

harder to break his hold. Her elbow slammed into his midriff, whether by chance or design he did not know. He cursed as his wound throbbed, and he tightened his grip. "As a matter of fact, you might be too difficult for the slave market. I suppose I have no choice but to keep you for myself."

"I thought you said profit was a pirate's goal." She turned her head to glare at him, tendrils of fiery hair blowing across her face. "There is no profit in keeping me here. I demand you return me to my father."

He burst out laughing. "This is my ship, my lady. No one makes demands but me. Should I choose to keep you, there is naught you could do about it."

She bared her teeth, and he moved his hand just in time to avoid being bitten. "I will make your life miserable," she vowed.

"Of that I have no doubt." He turned her to face him. "I should let the slave traders teach you some manners. But even they do not deserve such punishment."

"I would prefer slavery to lying with a jackal like you!"

He arched one dark brow. "Your judgment fails you once again, my sweet. 'Tis an honor to share the captain's bed."

"Such honor would gain me naught but dishonor. Again, I reject your offer."

" 'Twas not an offer but a command." He traced one finger along her ear. "You are mine."

"The devil I am!" She slapped his hand away.

He grabbed her wrist and held it in a grip she could not break. "You have little choice, hellion. Marcus claimed before all and sundry that he took your innocence. Whether he lies or not, he will be believed. Unless you wish to whore for my men, you will do as you are told."

"He lies, and well do you know it!" she spat.

"I know nothing of the sort." He looked her up and down as if considering the matter. "And neither do my men."

"What sort of captain cannot control his own men?"

"I can control them ... if you give yourself into my keeping."

She gaped at him. "You are truly despicable."

He mockingly bowed his head. "Thank you."

"I see you do not deny it."

He raised an eyebrow. "Never. However, I would not give you to the men. But if I let you roam this ship unprotected, it would not be long before one of them took what he wanted. At least as my woman, you will have my protection."

"I cannot fathom this! You would not stop them, should they attempt to ... to ..." She jerked her hand from his grasp, and he let her go. "This would never happen on one of my father's ships. Any man who even looked at me wrong would be flogged within an inch of his life."

Alex scowled. "Your father is not here. And I am not in the habit of punishing my crew for acting like the men they are. The only protection I can offer you lies with the position of a mistress."

"I will not share your bed."

"Oh, but you will."

Considering the matter settled, he turned away. McBride lurked nearby, awaiting further orders. Alex was halfway across the deck when her voice rang out loudly enough for the whole ship to hear.

" 'Twill be a cold day in hell before I share any man's bed against my will, Captain. Your commands mean naught to me."

Alex halted and turned to face her. She stood with her hands on her hips, her hair whipping about her like a wild thing as the wind kicked up. A triumphant smile played about her lips as she tilted her chin in defiance.

Disbelief at her foolishness quickly turned to anger. By challenging his authority, the blasted woman risked the very treasure she would guard. He could not be everywhere at once, and without the protection afforded the captain's woman, she would soon find herself on her back with some horny fool taking his pleasure between her thighs.

His temper rose like a hungry beast seeking its prey, stirring his lusty impulses into a boiling stew of emotions. She had forced his hand.

With a certain perverse pleasure he approached her, his strides measured, aware that all ears and eyes on the ship were focused on them. Her smug smile faltered as he drew even with her.

"So you will share no man's bed against your will, eh, my sweet?" He stood close enough to see the frantic pulse beating in her neck. "Well, then, I will simply have to make you willing."

His seductive words ignited something primitive deep inside her. Part of her wanted to flee, but the other half was drawn to the sensual spell he cast. Frightened at the strength of her emotions, once again she took shelter in the anger that had always protected her.

"You will not succeed," she answered with bravado, eyeing him as if he were a snake about to strike. "Better men than you have tried."

"I will," was his soft response. With a contemplative expression, he took a lock of her hair between his fingers as if to test its softness. She yanked her head back, but he held tightly to his prize. Tears formed in her eyes at the sting of her scalp. She reached up and snatched the hair from his hand.

In lightning-quick reaction, he took her chin in his hand and tilted her face, studying her features with careful scrutiny as if inspecting horseflesh. She pulled herself loose of his grasp, only to have him wrap his arm around her waist.

"What are you doing?" she spat, squirming to escape his embrace. She strained away from him as he cupped her cheek.

"You're a hot-tempered morsel," he commented. Then he pried open her mouth and made a show of looking at her teeth.

A strangled sound of fury escaped her throat. What was he doing? She was no slave to be picked at and pawed! She snapped her teeth, hoping to catch his finger, but he was too fast for her.

"Good teeth," he announced, as if she had not just tried to relieve him of a finger. Ignoring her growl of outrage, he continued, "Nice skin. No pockmarks. Soft hair, but that blinding color . . ." He shook his head.

"You lily-livered excuse for a—"

Alex clamped a hand over her mouth and sent an amused look across the deck. Diana followed his gaze and realized that every crewman aboard was watching the entertainment.

"She has a sharp tongue," he announced, his voice carrying easily to the leering audience. "But even the sharpest tongue can be put to good use!"

Shouts of laughter answered his bawdy comment. Diana stiffened as rage flooded her body. Though she did not know the exact meaning of Alex's remark, she did understand that he mocked her. Without thought to the consequences, she kicked her captor hard in the shin.

"Bloody hell!" Alex inhaled sharply and released her to grab his leg.

"Who gave you leave to touch me?" she demanded. "I am no slave to be—"

"Silence." Fury dripped from the word. Straightening, he gripped the back of her neck and forced her gaze to his. "You are whatever I say you are, you bloodthirsty wench! And from this moment forth, I say you are mine, God damn me for a fool."

Despite her growing fear at the anger that blazed in his eyes, Diana responded, "You are mad. I belong to no man."

"On that we disagree, my sweet." He took a step back and swept his gaze over her body, from her bare feet curling into the deck, over her borrowed clothing and torn shirt, and up to her face. "You are a beautiful woman. *My* woman."

Before she could protest, he whirled her around and pulled her back against his body, as if displaying her for the crew's enjoyment. Stunned, she stood frozen as he slid his hand from her shoulder and past the side of her breast to rest warmly on her hip. His long fingers splayed over her sensitive belly, the heat of his caress making her tremble even through the soft, velvet breeches.

Alex enjoyed the surge of desire that throbbed through him as he staked his claim on her. It had been too long since he had been with a woman, and this one fit against him as if she had been made for him. Boldly, intimately, he ran one hand possessively down her curves while he anchored the other around her waist to hold her against him. Ignoring her struggles to avoid his touch, he cast a commanding look across the ship. Every man on board understood his actions, but he spoke to reinforce his authority.

"Captain's share, lads! Which leaves more gold for the rest of you!" A boisterous shout went up at his words. Alex allowed himself a slight smile. Now no man would dare trespass on what was his.

Diana was horrified. Captain's share? Was this her fate? To be doxy to a pirate? She jerked from Alex's relaxed hold and came around swinging. Her fist connected with his jaw with such force that his head snapped hard to the side. He stood frozen like that for a moment, as if he could not believe that she had actually struck him. Diana rubbed her stinging knuckles against her thigh as he slowly turned his head back to face her. She dared not move when she saw the look in his eyes.

The laughter of the watching crew faded to silence as they all waited to see what their captain's reaction would be.

"McBride!"

His voice cracked out like the lash of a whip, and she flinched.

The first mate appeared as if from the air itself. "Captain?"

"Set the course we discussed." Alex grasped Diana's wrist. "I'll be in my cabin."

"Very well, Captain."

Alex turned toward the hatch, intending to

haul Diana along with him, but she dug in her heels and refused to be led. With a shrug he reached out and lifted her, tossing her over his shoulder like a sack of grain. Her shriek of outrage incited snickers from the watching crew, and lewd suggestions flew after them as he stalked across the deck.

"Aye, Cap'n! Show the wench who her master is!"

"Teach the uppity piece her place!"

"She'll be walkin' bowlegged for days when the cap'n's done with her!"

The laughter added fuel to Diana's temper. Bouncing ignominiously on the captain's shoulder, she began cursing, casting aspersions on his dubious parentage and questionable masculinity. He descended with her into the bowels of the ship like Hades carrying Persephone into the underworld.

Reaching his cabin, he opened the door and strode into the room to drop her unceremoniously on the bed.

Diana bounced once on the mattress and came up fighting. Leaping to her feet, she glared at him as he shut the door. "How dare you tote me about like a cask of rum? I'll see you hanged for this humiliation!"

"Indeed." With a little smile, Alex turned away, apparently ignoring her threat.

"Oh!" Furious at his casual dismissal, Diana clenched her fists and whirled away from him, struggling to get her temper under control. She looked around the cabin and saw . . . the bed.

The walls of the cabin seemed to shrink as she stared across a sea of red coverlet to the elaborately carved headboard. While logic dictated that the bed could not be as huge as it seemed, especially given the size of the cabin, nonetheless it seemed to dominate the room. She looked away—at the dining table, with its carved armchairs. At the desk covered with neatly rolled maps and charts. At the flickering shadows dancing on the walls, cast by the candles that had been left burning.

Against her will, her gaze slid back to the bed. It seemed even bigger than before, like a dragon lying in wait for its next victim.

Unnerved by the silence, Diana glanced back at Alex. The expression in his dark eyes shook her to her core. No man had ever looked at her in such a way. So . . . hungrily. He made her feel as if he could see inside of her, as if he knew everything about her. Flutters of excitement danced in her belly, and she sought to squelch the shameless reaction. She could not possibly feel this way for such a man. He was a rogue. A thief. A pirate. He was the wrong sort of man altogether.

And she found him dangerously attractive.

"Put this on."

She looked up just in time to catch the robe he tossed at her. The black silk slipped through her hands like water, and she marveled at the exquisitely embroidered flowers that twined along the back. It had obviously come from the Far East. She wondered if he had been there, or if the robe had come into his hands by illicit means.

"You can't stay in that rag." With a wave of his hand, he indicated her torn shirt. "Until I find you something to wear, my robe will have to suffice."

"You are too kind," she sneered.

He glanced at her, taking in her appearance with obvious appreciation. "You should be grateful that I decided to garb you at all." His tone was as smooth as silk and simmered with seduction.

She trembled, literally trembled, at the rumble of desire that darkened his voice. Her redhead's complexion betrayed her once again as heat crept into her cheeks. For an instant she could only stare at him, lost in those dark eyes where forbidden fires burned, her heart pounding like that of a rabbit trapped by a wolf.

No, not a wolf. A cat. A jungle cat like the one she had seen once, the pet of a foreign nobleman who had done business with her father. That creature had moved as smoothly as Alex did, its obsidian fur so sleek that her hand had itched to stroke it. She had even reached out to do so when the cat had turned its jeweled eyes on her, green eyes that reflected the emeralds and diamonds in the collar around its throat. There was something untamed in that gaze, though the cat appeared docile, that had made her withdraw her hand and back away.

And she should back away now, she thought, as the tension stretched between them. But there was nowhere to go. Ignoring the trembling in her limbs, she took up her shield of bravado and used it to defend herself against his potent allure.

"I am only too happy to be rid of these vile clothes. Now please have the decency to turn your back."

His laughter echoed throughout the cabin, the attractive sound making her pulse skim faster through her veins. "Decency? In a pirate? My dear, my reputation would never survive such a slur."

She sent him a look of scorching annoyance. "Hang your reputation! And hang you, too!"

He raised one eyebrow. "A very likely possibility, my dear." As if he had suddenly tired of the game, he turned away and opened one of the cabinets built into the wall. Ignoring her completely, he poured some brandy into a silver goblet.

Using the brief respite to change her clothes, she moved behind one of the high-backed chairs and turned her back on the rogue. With great relief, she shed Marcus's shirt and quickly shrugged into the robe. For modesty's sake, she left on the breeches.

Alex turned around just in time to see her smooth feminine back disappearing into black silk. He noticed that the only garment she had shed was the tattered shirt. For a moment his hand tightened on the goblet as he considered reaching beneath that robe and relieving her of those damnable breeches as well. Then he relaxed his grip and moved to hand her the brandy.

"You have had quite an ordeal this night. Drink this; it'll warm you."

Diana stared at the amber liquid and wrinkled her nose at the pungent smell. "I don't drink spirits."

Alex stepped closer, intentionally brushing her body with his. "Drink. Or mayhap you would prefer that I warm you another way?"

After one glance at his face, she took the cup from his hand. She took a hesitant sip, then choked and quickly handed the goblet back to him.

Alex took the cup from her hand, enchanted by the becoming flush pinkening her cheeks. His body hardened as he considered how she would look wearing nothing except the rosy hue of that blush. Tightening his fingers around the goblet, he tossed back a healthy portion of the brandy, then deliberately ran his tongue over the rim of the cup.

Diana stared in rapt fascination as his tongue touched the spot where her mouth had been. In that instant, with his black clothing, white teeth, and pink tongue, he reminded her more than ever of a jungle cat. He played with her now, and she couldn't help but wonder if he planned to devour her as well.

She fought to keep her voice calm. "What do you intend to do with me?"

He slowly traced the rim of the goblet with one finger as he appeared to contemplate the question. "What do you expect me to do with you?"

"What all pirates do," she answered with a flippancy belied by the pounding of her heart. "Hold me for ransom."

"That is a possibility." He gazed steadily at her, his expression unreadable.

"I thought that was the purpose of piracy." She met his enigmatic look with one of her own. "To steal from others to make a profit. Gold is what you want, isn't it?"

His eyes took on a predatory gleam. "You have no idea what I want of you."

"On the contrary, you vile cur, you have made it quite clear that you want me in your bed. Well, I will fight you until the last breath!"

"Will you?" An amused smile playing about his lips, he placed the goblet on the table. "Are you so certain, then, that I want you in my bed? Mayhap I have something else in mind."

"After that lewd display for your crew? Hardly!"

"Some might consider it lewd . . . but you liked it." He moved closer to her, crowding her backward. "You are a passionate woman behind that shrew's tongue, my dear. A man would count himself lucky to have you in his bed."

Her legs bumped the chair behind her. She was trapped. And still he approached.

He placed his hands on her shoulders and forced her to sit. Then he leaned over her, gripping the arms of the chair with either hand and caging her with his body. "Why don't you tell me what you want me to do with you?"

His quiet words immobilized her. She watched him warily as her mind scrambled for a response to his audacious question.

He gave a slight smile at her confused silence. "Have you no suggestions?"

The husky purr of his voice slipped into her mind and conjured forbidden images to tantalize her. Out of her vivid imaginings, the memory of his kiss in the darkened garden loomed larger and clearer than all the others. She opened and closed her hands in her lap, remembering how it had felt to touch his muscular body while his mouth had moved on hers. She licked her lips to banish the disturbing memory.

"Let me go," she whispered.

"Ah, my sweet. That is something I cannot do." He stroked his hand across her cheek. "You are mine. And I intend to keep you."

Chapter 6

"**Y**ou cannot keep me against my will."
He pushed her hair back over her
shoulder. "I could make you *beg* to stay with
me."

A quiver shot through her, sensitizing her
body from head to toe, making her acutely
aware of him, of his scent, his heat. The
thought of surrender seemed more a pleasure
than a price.

"What were you doing at my home last
night?" she challenged in a hoarse whisper,
clutching at composure.

He brushed a finger along her moistened
mouth. "I was looking for someone."

At the gentle touch, her thoughts threatened
to scatter. She struggled to keep her words coherent. "Who? Lord Chilton, perhaps?"

"Perhaps." Abandoning her mouth, he
glided the backs of his fingers down her throat.
"If I were seeking Chilton, I certainly found
him, did I not?" He teased the edge of the robe,
his fingertips just brushing the upper curve of

her breast. "You seem to be well acquainted with my lord Chilton."

"He is my father's business partner," she whispered, barely aware of what words she spoke. Her entire being focused on the sensations bursting to life in her body. Her breasts tingled and grew heavy, the nipples tightening. Her heartbeat quickened. She pressed her thighs together as heat bloomed between her legs.

"Obviously your father values him, else he would not be a suitor for your hand." His fingers glided up and down the edge of the robe, each movement causing the garment to open a fraction further.

Something penetrated Diana's consciousness that his words were not quite right, but sensations lapped over her like ocean waves. She couldn't think.

"Well?" The robe fell partially open, catching on the tips of her breasts. He traced a finger down one soft, white mound, stopping just short of touching the nipple hidden beneath the black material.

"He is nothing." Her voice came softly and quickly. "He seeks to marry me . . . but . . ."

"I can understand his eagerness. You are very beautiful." Brushing aside the material, he cupped one naked breast in his palm and caressed the puckered nipple with his thumb.

She gasped as heat streaked through her. She opened her eyes to find his face inches from hers, his dark eyes hot with need and something else. Something more deliberate. She glanced down at the hand cradling her breast, strength against softness, dark skin against light. What was he saying? Chilton. Chilton and Marcus. Dear God. Her father.

Clarity exploded in her brain. Her temper quickly followed, fueled by frustrated desire and the sting of knowing that Alex had been using her body's responses against her.

"You bastard!" She shoved his hand away and jerked the edges of the robe closed. "You are trying to seduce me in order to gain information!"

"Not precisely." Alex clenched the hand that had so briefly caressed her softness and straightened, smiling sardonically. True, he was guilty of the charge she leveled. Yet his seduction had uncovered something else, as well.

Though Diana had claimed that Marcus had not raped her, Alex hadn't been sure. However, she had not responded to his touch as a woman abused, but as one encountering her own sensuality for the first time. He breathed easier at this further evidence that she had escaped Marcus untouched.

Still, his sense of honor stung, that he would stoop to such levels. Worse, he had enjoyed it. He had thought his own considerable experience would give him enough control to stop short of bedding her. Now he was not so sure.

He glanced at her, her skin so fair against the dark material of his robe. Unable to face her accusing glare, he turned away and reached for the goblet of brandy. Even now he wanted to touch her again. And never stop.

Diana watched him turn away, a sliver of pain piercing her heart. *He hadn't wanted her at all.*

She leaped from the chair, unwilling to spend another moment in the position of what might have been her ultimate humiliation.

"You do not even deny it," she accused, disgust heavy in her voice.

"No." He swallowed the last of the brandy.

She hissed out a breath. "You are no better than Marcus. At least he never lied about his motives."

"Is that so?" Alex set aside the empty goblet. In two strides he stood before her. Gripping her arms, he pulled her to him.

"I warned you once before not to compare me with him."

Too late she heard the dark passion in his voice, even as her skin warmed in response to the touch of his hands. She licked her lips nervously. "Don't do this."

His gaze fixated on her mouth. "You feel it, too, don't you?"

"Please." It was all she could say. Her voice trembled. She knew she should pull away from him, but her limbs seemed oddly heavy. "Please," she said again, unsure if she was begging him to stop . . . or pleading for him to continue.

Cupping the nape of her neck in one hand,

he gently touched her mouth with the other. Desire shot like a cannonball to her stomach, melting her knees and leaving her shivering.

"You're so responsive," he murmured.

Caught up in a sensual haze, she tried to recall that she had been stolen from her home, that the man holding her was a pirate. Confusing emotions surged through her. In reckless response, she caught the tip of his caressing finger in her teeth.

Something untamed flared in his eyes. He speared his hand into her hair, holding the back of her head in both hands now, his actions jerky, as if he had no control over them. He tilted her face toward him and lifted her to her toes.

Something hot and exciting coiled in her. She had no idea what had possessed her to bite him, but as she felt his strong hands gently cradling her head and watched his mouth descend toward hers, she suddenly understood. This was passion. This was freedom.

This was life.

And despite his unscrupulous motives, she was not about to let this opportunity to taste it slip away.

His mouth closed over hers, stunning her with the hunger of his kiss. She hadn't remembered his lips being so soft. Ensnared in a silky web of need, she reached up to clutch his wrists, her fingers curling into his flesh as her knees threatened to dissolve.

He broke the kiss, gliding his tongue over

her lower lip before slowly raising his head. She stared helplessly into his dark eyes, his mouth still inches from hers. She leaned closer to him, turning her face up to his in a silent plea.

Suddenly he set her away. She frowned in confusion, then realized that what she had thought was the pounding of her heart was actually someone rapping on the door. They stared at each other, gasping for breath, as the knocking continued.

"Bloody hell!"

His harsh curse severed the tension between them with the sharpness of a blade. Shaken from her sensual spell, Diana closed her eyes as a second wave of humiliation swept over her. Fight him to the last breath? Why, she had practically crawled into his bed and begged him to take her—just as he had claimed she would. Mortified, she raised a shaking hand to her mouth, her face hot. Alex stormed to the door and threw it open.

The wooden portal bounced off the wall. "What?" Alex roared. "I gave orders . . . Oh, 'tis you."

"Well, now. In a wee bit o' a temper, are you? Is your wound painin' you so much, then?" A tall, brawny man with dark hair and the face of a fallen angel bounded into the room. He stopped short upon seeing Diana. Glancing at Alex, he said, "Are you aimin' to introduce me to the bonnie lass, Captain? Or do you mean to keep her to yourself?"

"Birk, this is Diana Covington." Alex closed the door, noting with male satisfaction that the flush of passion still lingered in her cheeks. "My sweet, this rascal is Birk Fraser. When he can see straight, he serves as our surgeon."

"Surgeon!" Birk huffed. "Dinna be blackenin' my name like that, man. I'm no bloody barber! I'm a physician, highly educated and wastin' my talents on the likes o' you." He slammed his satchel of medicines down on the table. "And I'm no stumblin' sot, either. I just enjoy my ale, that's all."

"And everyone else's," Alex quipped.

"The devil take you." Birk brushed aside the insult and sent Diana a beaming smile. "Dinna be listenin' to him, lass. It's the truth he gets a bit ill-tempered when he's not feelin' fit."

"Indeed?" Sarcasm dripped from her words. "I thought 'twas his natural disposition."

Birk barked with laughter. "There's a lass." He turned to Alex. "Now I'll be seein' to that wound, Captain."

Alex frowned and glanced down at the slice across his ribs. The brandy had long ago dulled the pain. Truth be told, he had forgotten about it. " 'Tis just a scratch."

Birk snorted. "It's the bite o' a viper. Now set yourself down and let me take a peek at it."

"If you insist." Alex stripped off his shirt. From the corner of his eye, he saw Diana's mouth fall open. Shock crossed her face before she could hide it, and her gaze swept over his naked torso with maidenly fascination.

Amused, he gave in to the urging of his male vanity and asked, "Is something amiss?"

She closed her mouth with a snap. "Have you no manners at all, disrobing before a lady?"

"First decency, now manners. You have strange expectations of a pirate, my dear." Alex rubbed a hand through the light dusting of hair on his chest and watched her eyes follow the movement. "If you have not seen a naked man ere now, 'tis high time you broadened your education."

"I have no need of any education you might provide," she retorted.

Alex smiled and sat down in a chair, sprawling his legs out before him. "So you say. But perhaps this innocence of yours is a good thing. After all, I do not need a wench big with Marcus's bastard strolling my ship."

"I . . . why, you . . . oh!" Diana's face grew as red as her hair. "You vile cur!" Fists clenched, she advanced on him. "You poxy son of a dockside whore!"

"Such language, lass." Birk's tone was one of admiration as he poured water into a basin.

"You lily-livered bastard!" Diana kept coming, and Alex stood his ground. His attempts to subdue her had done little. She was still far too reckless.

"Diana," he warned.

"You plague-ridden spawn of Satan!"

"Enough!" Alex's roar shook the cabin. He surged to his feet, towering over her. "If you wish to be regarded as a lady, you will cease at once."

She jutted her chin. "And if I do not?"

He took that stubborn chin in his hand. "A trollop's mouth has many uses. Mayhap I should teach you one or two."

"I am no trollop!" She jerked her head away.

As fast as she pulled away, Alex grabbed her arm. "Then do not behave as one."

"I am no trollop," she insisted again. "No man has ever touched me."

"Indeed." Alex cocked a brow and glanced down at the robe she wore. "I cannot help but remember your attire when you first boarded my ship, my sweet. It seems you were ill-used at some point during the night."

"Marcus tried to force himself on me, but your attack interrupted him." She yanked her arm from his grip. "I bear no man's bastard."

"Yet." He bared his teeth in a mocking grin, and felt Birk's heavy hand clamp down on his shoulder.

"Enough now." With a hard look at Alex, Birk turned his attention to Diana. "The two o' you can stop squabblin' like a couple o' bairns long enough to let me do my work. Lassie, set yourself down in the chair there and keep your bonnie mouth shut."

Diana hesitated only a moment. Throwing Alex a haughty look, she stormed over to the chair farthest from him and sat down, her back ramrod straight, her face turned away from them.

"At least one o' you has sense." Birk nodded once in approval before turning back to Alex. "Set yourself down, Captain." As Alex complied, Birk continued, "I need to be stitchin' up that slice in your side, and I'll thank you not to be bellowin' at the lass the while. If you take the notion to be leapin' out your chair, then I'll not be responsible for what portion o' your body ends up stitched."

Alex's lips twitched. "Understood, Mister Fraser. But when you are done, I shall bellow as I like."

"Captain, when I'm finished, you can do whatever you bloody well please."

"Just so we understand each other."

"I'm understandin' things quite well," Birk muttered. Then, without another word, he set about treating the wound. First he cleaned the gash with water, wiping away the dried blood and bits of thread. "It's a fair simple cut, Captain. Clean but a wee bit deep. I'll need you to be still."

"I'm well accustomed to the procedure," Alex remarked with amusement.

Birk fed the needle with silken thread and bent to his work. He jabbed Alex with it, making him jump. "Why do you prick the lass like that?" he murmured. "She's surely been through enough this night."

Alex winced as sharp pinches of the needle bit through his flesh. "She challenges me at every turn," he said, pitching his voice so that only Birk could hear. "The wench doesn't know when to concede the battle."

"And you think you do? You stamp and snort like a stallion, tryin' to prove to that bonnie mare that you're worthy o' her." Birk shook his head, a smile tugging at his lips. "You dinna even ken what you're doin', do you, laddie?"

"She is too proud," Alex hissed, flinching at yet another stab of the needle. "She needs to be taught her place."

"And who better to teach her than a man with more pride than she? Alex, your temper is cloudin' your vision. You want the lassie. It's lust, not anger, that guides you."

"She is spoiled," Alex insisted. "She thinks to order me about like a pup. But I'm no lapdog, and I will not be led about by a woman."

"It would seem your loins have a different opinion." Birk snapped the thread, having finished the stitching.

Alex cast a glance down at the telltale bulge in his breeches and gave a rueful smile. "The wench is yet innocent and not given to noticing such things."

"Should you bide in that state, she'll not be innocent for long." Birk stood and slapped Alex on the back, the crack of flesh on flesh drawing Diana's attention. "I suggest you walk about the deck, Captain, so your side doesna stiffen." He bent closer to Alex to murmur, "And maybe the night air will cool both your temper and your loins."

"A sound suggestion, Mister Fraser." Alex stood and tested his arm experimentally, wincing at the pull of the stitches. His eyes touched on Diana for a moment before he turned to Birk. "I want you to examine her for any injuries she may be hiding," he ordered in a low voice. "She acts unharmed, but she is too damned proud. I know Marcus and his games, and no woman has ever escaped his clutches unhurt."

"Indeed, Captain." Birk cast a meaningful look in the direction of the door. "Give my regards to the watch."

Alex nodded. Not even bothering to don a shirt, he swung about on his heel and left the cabin.

Birk gave a hearty sigh as the door slammed behind Alex. "It's the devil's own temper he has." He smiled at Diana. "The two o' you are like flint and steel, strikin' sparks off each other."

"I have no desire to 'strike sparks' or do anything else with your captain." Scowling at the closed door, she added, "I am naught but a captive."

"Nay, lass. Dinna judge the captain so harshly." Birk smiled, the corners of his blue eyes crinkling. "Things are verra often not what they appear."

Diana snorted. "In this respect, Mister Fraser, I believe things are exactly as they appear. I was abducted from my home by Marcus, then taken yet again by your captain, a vile, wretched pirate—" She flushed and pressed her lips together.

Birk sighed. "Lass, I think there's things you should ken."

Diana regarded the handsome physician with skepticism. He had a pleasant manner about him, and his blue eyes were kind. His Scots burr had a calming affect, reminding her of both her mother and Maude. Yet he sailed under El Moreno's command, and she was wary of trusting him. Still, she needed so desperately to trust someone. She looked down at the hands in her lap.

He seemed to comprehend her dilemma. "Lass, I am a physician, sworn to heal folk, not hurt them." He sat down in the chair Alex had vacated. "Maybe I can shed a bit o' light on your situation."

After a moment's thought, Diana raised her eyes to his. Alex's departure had cooled her anger. She hadn't realized until this moment that her temper had been the only thing keeping apprehension at bay.

" 'Tis a frightening thing," she admitted softly, "to have no control over a situation."

Birk nodded, his expression sympathetic. "Indeed it is. Tell me, lass. Have you any idea how you came to such a pass?"

Diana hesitated before answering, having already deduced the reason for Marcus's abduction. She knew it had to have something to do with Chilton, and the conversation she had overheard in her father's study. Obviously

Chilton and Marcus had taken her captive in an attempt to force her father to relinquish the incriminating ledger pages. Thanks to Alex, they had not succeeded. Yet she could still be in danger. Even though her instincts encouraged her to confide in Birk Fraser, she elected to keep the knowledge of the ledger pages to herself for the time being.

"Did I bring on bad memories for you, lassie?" Birk's soothing tone once more urged her to trust him. "You say Marcus didna harm you. Still, if you got as much as a splinter aboard that devil's ship, I want to be hearin' about it."

"I am unharmed, Mister Fraser. Really."

"To be certain, I would like to examine you, if you wouldna mind."

Slowly, she nodded. "All right. But first tell me what you know of how I came to be here."

"So that's to be the way o' it?" Birk chuckled. "Verra well, lass, have your own road. You're acquainted with a man called Chilton?"

"Yes." The name conjured up memories of Alex's attempt to seduce information from her. Ice dripped from her words. "I am well acquainted with Lord Chilton. The man is a greedy snake."

"Aye, so you ken the true man and not the noble face he shows to the world. Then you willna be surprised to hear that the blackguard is involved up to his fancy earbobs with Marcus. Cut from the same cloth, they are."

"That wretch!" Well aware of the facts just revealed, Diana continued to maintain her pretense of ignorance. "How he must have laughed at us."

"It was Chilton that had Marcus snatch you," Birk continued. "Have you any idea what he might have done that for, lass?"

Diana kept her counsel. Chilton wanted those ledger pages badly, and her father had threatened to take them to Morgan. How better to force her father's hand than with a threat on his daughter's life?

"Lass? Have you remembered something?"

Diana blinked at him. "Chilton," she said. "He wants to marry me. I believe he covets my fortune."

Birk looked doubtful. "There's no other reason?"

She shook her head, her expression innocent. "None that I know."

"Hmmm." Birk rubbed his chin. "He was certain there was more to it than that."

Diana leaned forward in her chair. "Who was? Alex?"

"Alex, is it?" Birk hooted with laughter. "The lad must be in his dotage to have made such a slip as that. When did he tell you his name, lass?"

She bit her lip and avoided his shrewd gaze. "It doesn't matter. Just tell me what Alex has to do with Chilton."

"It isna Chilton. It's Marcus. Alex has sworn to see the bastard brought to justice."

"Why is that?" she asked, intrigued despite herself.

"I'm not at liberty to say. Believe me when I tell you that Chilton is a means to an end. Alex means to see Marcus hang . . . and all his cohorts with him."

"You mean Chilton."

Birk gave her a look. "All his cohorts. Every last one o' them."

Apprehension seized her. "Even if Chilton is as guilty as you say," she said in a strained whisper, "you must believe that my father had nothing to do with any of this."

Birk shrugged and rose, glancing away. A long pause preceded his words. "Whether he has or no, I canna say. But Alex means to capture Marcus and see him swing. Any that aided the cur will bend the gallows with him."

"Not my father." She came to her feet and grabbed his arm when he would have turned away. "Mister Fraser, please. My father is an honest man. I am certain he knew nothing of this."

Birk patted her hand. "It's Alex you have to convince."

Her mind raced. "Tell me, how did Alex come to discover Chilton's dealings with Marcus?"

Birk just looked at her. "Alex makes it his business to ken *everything* about Marcus."

Diana stared after the physician as he moved away from her. "My father is innocent," she repeated.

"Then your father will certainly have some proof o' his innocence, lassie." Birk took up his

medical bag. "Everything will work out as it
should."

Proof. The word seared into her brain. Her
father had the proof of Chilton's dealings with
Marcus. But could that same proof also implicate him by association? She hadn't considered
that until now. Perhaps that was why he had
postponed giving the pages to Morgan. It had
to be.

Birk gestured to her robe. "Come on, then.
We'll have a look at you."

Distracted, she obeyed without a murmur of
protest. Somehow she had to help her father
outwit Marcus and Chilton, without being implicated himself. Her choices were few. Indeed,
there was only one.

Alex was the only man she knew who might
actually be able to clear her father. He had already captured Marcus. All that remained was
Chilton. If she could convince Alex of her father's innocence, perhaps he could bring the
two to justice without involving her sire.

He was her only hope to save her father's
life. And whatever the price . . . she would pay
it.

Chapter 7

〜〜∽◯◯∽〜〜

Alex leaned against the rail of the quarter-deck and watched his ship slice through the ocean. The impact of water on wood sent a fine mist of sea spray shooting upward, the salty scent tickling his nose. The sky loomed dark and forbidding as a prelude to the impending storm.

He had already given orders to batten down both ships, for Caribbean storms had been known to take many a crew unawares. Now there was naught to do but wait, to forge ahead to Port Royal and turn in their hard-won captive.

He inhaled deeply as satisfaction rushed through him. At last he had captured the bastard who had murdered his brother. After more than a year of pursuit, his quest was finally over. He had checked on his prisoner less than an hour ago, and remembered with a grim smile how the pirate had looked, bound with his own chains in his own black and stinking hold. Marcus had spewed his usual venom, but

103

the look in his eyes had been that of a trapped animal. Alex had left him imprisoned aboard the *Marauder* with his cutthroat crew, secure in the knowledge that the villain would pay for his crimes. All he had to do now was to bring Marcus to Morgan and let the lieutenant-governor apprehend Marcus's allies.

He was certain that Chilton was involved, but not as sure about Frederick Covington. He hoped for Diana's sake that her father had been merely a dupe in a dastardly scheme.

Diana. God's blood, but she was beautiful. She was the type of woman a man dreamed of when he'd been too long at sea. Unblemished skin, fiery hair, and those smoky eyes clouded with passion . . . she was his most sensual fantasy brought to life.

Even now he could taste the sweetness of her on his lips. Both times, putting his mouth to hers had ignited the passion that he kept so carefully banked inside him. For over a year, no woman had succeeded in distracting him from his quest for vengeance. Indeed, nothing had. Yet this lovely temptress had the ability to make him forget everything.

It wasn't just her beauty. It was the way she moved. Her spirit. Especially her spirit. Her temperament matched his own and excited him in a way few women ever had. She threw down the gauntlet at every turn, as if daring him to do his worst.

And he wanted to. He wanted to take her to

his bed and keep there until neither of them could walk.

But he couldn't. The girl was a maid still, and he steered clear of innocents. He had a woman on Besosa who saw to his needs. Rosana was a hot-blooded Spanish wench who nearly exhausted him whenever he visited her. So why did he feel this craving to tumble his lovely captive into the nearest bed? She was well bred, and so was he. He could not in good conscience take from her that which should go to her husband.

God's teeth, there was no excuse for his behavior in the cabin. He had been provoked, true, but never in his life had he treated a gentlewoman so. Had he been chasing Marcus so long that he was becoming like him? Had he indeed become El Moreno, the black-hearted scourge of the Indies? No! He was the Earl of Rothstone, and this pretense would end when he gave Marcus over to Morgan. As appealing as an adventurous life at sea might seem, he had a duty to uphold. Until the time arrived when he would take on the title and all the responsibilities involved, he would play out the charade with as much honor as possible. And that included keeping his lust to himself.

A boot heel scraped on the deck behind him. He turned his head as Birk joined him at the rail. "Well, Birk? How fares our guest?"

"The lass has a nasty-lookin' bump on her head. She says one o' the bastards clouted her when they snatched her. Apart from that, she's fit enough."

"Someone struck her?" Alex clenched his hands on the rail.

Birk quirked a brow. "Och, man, you've got it bad. The lass is in better shape than many we've taken from Marcus, yet a lump on the head has you ready to fight a duel."

"She should never have been involved in this."

"That's neither here nor there," Birk said. "You have to decide what you're goin' to do with her now that you have her."

"What's there to do? We sail for Port Royal and turn Marcus over to Morgan. And Diana will go home to whatever awaits her."

"And do you mean for her to arrive there yet a maid?"

"Of course." Alex shrugged off the encroaching guilt of lingering desire. "'Tis true that I want her. Were she any but who she is, I would no doubt indulge myself."

"You talk o' her like she's the bloody queen." Birk snorted and leaned his back against the rail. "She's just a woman, Alex. I'm thinkin' there's more to your feelings than you suspect."

Alex scowled. "Do not speak to me of love, Birk Fraser."

Birk barked with laughter. "Love! I'm the last man to be prattlin' o' love. I'm sayin' that your well-meanin' ideas come more from what your wife did to you than from your own sense o' honor." He held up his hands. "And I'm not sayin' you're not honorable," he added hastily.

"Bianca has nothing to do with this." Saying her name was like choking on a fish bone. "She is long dead, and my feelings for her died with her."

"I'm not sayin' that you're pinin' for your wife, either."

"Blast you, Birk, then what *are* you saying?" he snapped. "Cease your rambling and say the words."

"My point is that you have not so much as glanced at a lassie o' Diana's class in all the years I've kent you. The wenches you take to your bed are more o' Rosana's ilk. I'm thinkin' that Bianca ruined you for marriage."

"Marriage!" Alex spat the word. "Do not speak to me of marriage, Birk. I have no intention of taking a wife."

"You dinna have a choice, man. You're the earl now. You need to marry and sire an heir to carry on your title. As you said before, you're the last o' the Rawnsleys."

"Then the title will die with me."

Birk barked out a laugh. "You think you can escape your own fate, do you? If you dinna choose a wife o' your own, the Crown might do it for you. And dinna be forgettin' your mother. If the king disna saddle you with some milk-and-water miss, then your mother will. Face it, Alex. You must wed. Sooner or later you have to find yourself a woman o' your own class. Like the lassie."

"Are you suggesting that I marry Diana Covington?"

"Dinna sound so surprised. You want the lass. She's bonnie and well off and all that. She's the right class to be a countess. Granddaughter o' a duke, she is."

"Is that so?" Alex arched a brow. "And how did you come by such information? 'Twas my knowledge that her father was a common seaman who hoarded his wealth."

"She told me herself." Birk smirked. "Her mother was the youngest daughter o' a duke. A Scottish duke," he added with relish. "Her family is just as powerful as yours."

"So for that reason I should take the wench to wife? My thanks, Birk, but I put my neck in that noose once before. The bruises have not yet faded." He turned away to contemplate the growing unrest of the ocean.

"Bloody hell, Alex! You didna kill your wife."

Alex whirled on the physician so fast that the bigger man fell back a step. "I did," he insisted. "She was running from me, Birk—me. I killed her as surely as if I had reached out and pushed her down those stairs."

"It wasna your fault."

"It was." Alex turned back to the sea, absently noting how the wind had kicked up. "It was."

"It was an accident. Blamin' yourself winna bring Bianca back. It's best that you get on with your life. You need a wife, Alex, and who better than the lass? The two o' you go at one another like a couple o' cats in heat." He paused, but Alex remained stubbornly silent. "Bloody hell, man!" Birk burst out. "You canna keep hidin' behind El Moreno. Soon enough Marcus will hang, and you'll have to go back to your life as the earl."

Alex remained silent for a long moment. Birk's words made him face what he had been doing: hiding. As El Moreno, he didn't have to worry about estates and titles and heirs. And wives.

He didn't want another wife. But he knew Birk was right. Eventually he would have to take one, whether he wanted to or not. 'Twas a bitter draught to swallow.

He spoke softly, but with words honed sharper than any blade. "There are times, my friend, that I regret sharing that bottle of whiskey with you. Had I not been so sotted, I would never have told you about . . . her."

" 'Twas bound to come out sooner or later," Birk said. A booming clap of thunder nearly drowned out his words.

Alex turned his face into the gusting wind and eyed the black and swollen clouds above them. "Best batten down, Birk. 'Tis going to be an ugly one."

"I plan to settle in with a bottle I've been savin'—" Birk's words were cut off by another crack of thunder.

A cry of alarm came from the crow's nest. Alex turned to see what had happened. Shouts reached his ears, all but indistinguishable through the howl of the wind and the boom of thunder. Then he saw it. The *Marauder* had broken from its course and was drifting away from them.

"What the devil are they doing?" Alex cursed. Rain-swollen clouds had blocked out most of the sun, making it hard for him to distinguish the forms of the men he had left aboard. Any moment, he expected the skeleton crew to regain control of the vessel and bring her back around.

He couldn't lose her. Not with Marcus aboard.

"McBride!" he shouted. Down in the waist of the ship, the first mate raised a hand to his ear. "Keep pace with her," he called. McBride acknowledged the order with a wave.

Alex fixed his gaze on the *Marauder* again. Something was not right. He felt it in his gut. He clenched his jaw and decided to follow his instincts. Turning on his heel, he strode to the edge of the quarterdeck and barked orders to the crew.

"Clear the decks! Loose the guns! Prepare to fire on my order only!" The clatter of chains announced the release of the cannons from their confinement. Alex turned his head and stared at the *Marauder*. Something was very, very wrong.

"Alex?"

The *Marauder* drifted along innocently enough, yet it edged farther and farther off course. The *Vengeance* kept pace. Everything looked peaceful and quiet . . . as if the *Marauder* were a ghost ship.

A ghost ship.

Sweet Jesu, let it not be true.

Alex straightened with a suddenness that made Birk jump back a step. "Come about!" he barked. "Hard to port!"

The helmsman obeyed his command, sending the *Vengeance* tilting with the sharp turn.

Life exploded on the other ship. Dozens of men, many more than the crew Alex had left there, swarmed the decks of Marcus's vessel, shouting and whooping. Cannon fire exploded from the *Marauder*, the shots falling where the *Vengeance* had been only moments before. Alex swore and damned himself for a fool. He should have expected this. He should have known.

Groups of men swarmed to the sides of Marcus's ship. One by one, each group tossed something heavy into the water. As the bulky objects rose to the surface Alex realized they were the bodies of the crew he had left aboard the other ship. And only one still moved. His men. Guilt bit at him like an adder.

Morgan's edict be damned! This time the bastard would pay for his crimes.

"Mister McBride!" he roared. "Fire at will!"

Birk laid a hand on his arm, but Alex shook it off. "Get below," he ordered. "There will be blood this day."

"Be sure it's not your own." The physician

gave him a hard look. "Or Marcus's." He stalked away.

The cannons exploded in punctuation with Birk's warning, and smoke drifted across the deck. Alex cursed as the shots fell short of their target, blown off course by the shifting wind.

"McBride! Again! Fire!"

The ship listed violently, water spewing up in her wake. Alex clenched his hands on the rail and watched as his shots missed once more. Suddenly the *Marauder* came about, heading right for them at full speed. At her angle, she would be within firing distance in seconds.

"Come about, come about!" Alex barked. The ship heeled sharply again as the helmsman obeyed the order. Water sluiced across the waist and drained away again through the scuppers. A boom of thunder echoed the sound of the cannons as a flash of lightning split the sky. Alex's gaze was riveted on a figure standing alone on the quarterdeck of the *Marauder*. The figure raised a sword in salute.

Marcus. Goddamn his soul to hell.

The *Marauder* came about again.

"McBride! Prepare to fire!" Alex roared. "Helm, drive the bastard into the wind, at my mark!" He waited, sweating with every second that ticked by.

"Helm! Now! McBride, fire!"

As the *Marauder* came at them, the helmsman jerked the *Vengeance* practically into her path. She came about hard to avoid it and ended up with her nose in the wind. As Alex knew would happen, the wind hit her sails from the wrong direction and Marcus's ship was pushed backward.

The guns boomed. Smoke drifted up from the gun deck. A loud crack announced a hit as the *Marauder*'s bowsprit crashed into the sea. A shot to the hull would have been more effective.

"Bloody hell!" Alex slammed a fist against the rail.

The *Marauder* recovered her wind and came after them. She fired. One shot cracked the mizzen, sending the top of it crashing to the deck. Another landed dangerously close to the hull, sending water splashing everywhere.

"Scuttle the bastard!" Alex ordered.

He was answered by the roar of his guns. Something bright flared on Marcus's ship, and cries of alarm rose as smoke drifted up from the main deck.

She was on fire.

Alex slowly smiled. He saw Marcus pointing and yelling, but the fire spread quickly. He would have to abandon the ship.

Alex had him right where he wanted him!

The *Vengeance* moved quickly, intent on the kill. Alex leaned forward on the rail, as if his will alone could push the ship to a quicker pace. Soon Marcus would die. Honor would be satisfied.

Revenge tasted sweet.

Thunder roared and lightning flashed—and

the black clouds finally gave up their burden. Rain poured down, hissing against the deck and pelting Alex's bare torso with needle-like pricks like a thousand tiny daggers.

The fire aboard the *Marauder* petered . . . and slowly went out.

"*No!*" He shook with the force of sweet satisfaction so close and now snatched away. "No," he whispered again in disbelief.

The *Marauder* recovered quickly, and came at them at full speed. Clearly she meant to ram them.

"Come about!" Alex cried, but it was too late. With a splintering crash, the *Marauder* smashed into them, tearing a hole in the hull just above the waterline. She continued past them, so close Alex could see the smile on Marcus's face. He clenched his hands into fists as the pirate laughed and saluted him.

"Gunner!" Alex bellowed. "Blow the bastard out of the water!"

The guns fired, belching smoke. One shot caught the *Marauder*'s mainmast, splitting it in half. Two others ripped the rigging apart. It slowed her, but didn't stop her. She sailed past, moving farther and farther out of firing range.

"After her!" Alex commanded.

"Captain."

He whirled to find McBride standing behind him. "What is it?"

"We can't be goin' after her, Captain. We're takin' on too much water." The first mate shouted to be heard over the rain. "She got us good. 'Tis a lucky thing she didn't hit the powder room."

"The damage?"

"Too close to the waterline, Captain. I have men workin' to patch the hole, but we can't be goin' after the bastard."

"What about the guns?"

"They're dry enough."

Alex looked after the *Marauder*. He knew Marcus intended to turn back and blow them to pieces—because that's what he would do. He smiled slowly. "Fire at will, McBride. Take whatever you can of her."

McBride grinned. "That I will, Captain."

The mate hurried from the quarterdeck, leaving Alex to contemplate his nemesis. As he had expected, the *Marauder* changed direction and closed in to finish off the wounded *Vengeance*. Closer and closer she came, almost flaunting the fact that she had full power while Alex's vessel took on water. Rain poured down, soaking everything.

The guns thundered once more. Water spewed upward from shots that missed. One took a piece of the *Marauder*'s hull, though not enough to slow her down. The guns barked again. Rigging tore loose and fluttered to the deck of Marcus's vessel. Another explosion sounded from the gun deck. With a loud crack, the *Marauder*'s mainmast split in half. Midcharge, she heeled and changed directions. Beneath the cover of the driving rain, she limped away.

Every instinct he had urged Alex to follow and close in for the kill. But his own ship was in danger of sinking unless he put in for repairs. Port Royal was out of the question now.

Bitterness washed over him. He had come so close to reaching his goal . . . so bloody close. And now he had several men dead, a wounded ship, and a beautiful captive who had distracted him from his objective. *Damn it to hell*. If he had not been so fixated on Diana and the confusing emotions she incited, he might have foreseen this. His men would still be alive. His ship would be whole. Diana would be on her way home to her father. And Marcus would be swinging from the gallows.

He clenched his jaw as he watched Marcus disappear into the storm. It would not happen again. He would start at the beginning, track the bastard down, and see him hang for his crimes. *Nothing* would distract him.

And no one.

"Bring up the bodies," he ordered. "I saw at least one survivor. Then set sail for Besosa." With a grim expression, he left the deck.

Chapter 8

~~~⟶◯◯⟵~~~

Diana picked her way through the debris littering the floor of the cabin and reached her objective, the cabinet from which she had seen Alex take the brandy. For a moment she stood there, resting her forehead against the smooth wood of the tiny door, trying to regain control of her jangling nerves. With a shaking hand, she pulled open the cupboard and withdrew the brandy bottle.

Her palms hurt from gripping the headboard of the bed so tightly. She had clung there like a child to its mother's bosom as the ship rocked and cannons exploded and she prayed she would live another day. She stared down at the bottle and combed her fingers through her tangled hair. Though she normally did not indulge in spirits, nothing about this situation was normal. She had just survived her first battle at sea, and now she needed to convince El Moreno, scourge of the Caribbean, to help her prove her father's innocence.

Definitely not normal.

Still she hesitated, but the way her hands shook convinced her. She had to be completely in control when she faced Alex. A pounding heart and trembling fingers would hardly aid her cause. Biting her lower lip, she twisted the cork from the bottle. Not bothering with a goblet, she closed her eyes and drank.

Fire streaked to her gut. She gasped, wine dribbling out the corners of her mouth and down her chin. She swiped the back of her hand over her face and neck.

The door clicked open.

Diana froze and slowly turned to meet Alex's sardonic gaze. He paused in the doorway, his bare torso and wet hair stopping her breath and sending her pulse skipping. He eyed the brandy bottle and raised an eyebrow.

"It seems you are indeed the granddaughter of a duke," he remarked. "That is my best brandy."

"I was just . . ." Flushing, she shoved the cork back in the bottle and replaced it in the cabinet. She must look like some tavern bawd as she swilled brandy straight from the bottle, hair all tangled and his robe her only garment. But she had to forget that, remain in control, not let him fluster her. Her father's life depended on it. "I was thirsty."

"Oh?" He stared at her, unsmiling.

"Yes." She held her ground, her carefully rehearsed speech hovering on her lips. "I am glad you came back. I want to speak to you."

"Not now." He turned his back on her and

headed to the sea chest at the foot of his bed. Diana stared after him, aghast at his rudeness, as he bent over to dig a fresh shirt out of the chest. She came up behind him.

"What do you mean, not now?" The words came out sharper than she intended, since she found herself distracted by his tight buttocks. For an instant she had the compelling urge to reach out and touch them . . . He stood up and turned to face her. She forced her gaze upward, but his mocking smile told her he knew where she had been staring. Heat surged to her cheeks.

"Not now. I am too busy for your idle pratter."

"Idle pratter!" With effort, she ignored the attractive way his muscles bunched as he donned the shirt. "What I have to discuss is extremely important!"

"To be sure." The disdain in his expression also echoed in his voice. "My ship requires my attention just now. You will have to wait."

"I don't want to wait. I want—"

His head snapped up. In his eyes burned something terrible.

"What you want means nothing," he bit out.

She wanted to back away. She wanted to run to the bed and cower beneath the covers until he left the room. She wanted to cry and scream at all the confusing emotions warring inside her.

But an image of her father with a noose

around his neck rose in her mind, and she did none of those things.

"I can see that you are not in a good humor," she forged on.

"Not in a good humor?" Each word dripped with sarcasm. "My dear Mistress Covington, I have just come from battle, and my ship is damaged. Now you would plague me with your rantings—a spoiled little girl who hasn't the sense when to keep her pretty mouth shut. I have more important things to do."

Stung, she said, "Like what? Counting your ill-gotten gold?"

"No," he snapped back. "Like recapturing Marcus!"

They stared at each other for a long moment. She could see the frustration in his expression, the rage of a man who had obtained his goal, only to have it ripped away again. His chest rose and fell with rapid breaths. Tearing his gaze from hers, he turned away to stand with his back to her. His shoulders sagged slightly.

"Marcus has escaped?" she asked softly.

"Aye." Still he didn't look at her. He lifted one hand and rubbed the back of his neck.

She twisted her fingers together. Part of her wanted to comfort him. She was frankly surprised that the bold and dashing El Moreno would show such vulnerability in front of her. In her daydreams, she had always thought of him as strong, confident, and unbeatable.

Now she saw he was just a man.

"I'm sorry," she said quietly, remembering

Birk's words about Alex wanting Marcus brought to justice. "I know how long you have been chasing him."

He glanced at her then, his mouth twisting in a cynical smile. "Do you, now? What would you know of such things, my sweet innocent?"

"More than you think. Mister Fraser told me some of it."

"Bloody hell." He raked a hand through his long hair. "That bloody Scot has a tongue that rivals any gossiping woman's, drunk or no."

"He wanted me to understand. I was very frightened."

Alex watched her with those haunted eyes and smiled. "Perhaps your instincts were correct."

"Perhaps. But I dislike being afraid." She swallowed. "I am sorry that Marcus escaped you. But perhaps what I have to say will help."

He faced her, hands on his hips. "I see you would have your way even though I told you I have no time for such nonsense."

"Perhaps you will change your mind. I can help you trap Chilton . . . perhaps Marcus as well." She held her breath for his reaction.

He laughed. "Indeed?"

"Yes." She straightened her spine. "Before I was abducted, I overheard something that would be of great interest to you in your quest to gather evidence against Marcus."

He stopped laughing and stared at her. "You had best not be jesting with me, my girl."

" 'Tis no jest." She twisted her fingers together, then determinedly dropped her hands to her sides. "But before I tell you anything, I would have your promise that you will see my father left out of it."

"I make no promises."

She shook her head. "I will have your word on it, else I will tell you nothing."

"This is no child's game," he hissed. He came to her and took her face in his hands. "Tell me."

Her skin warmed from his touch, but she blanked the pleasing sensation from her mind. "Your word," she insisted quietly.

His fingers tightened on her face for an instant, never hurting but just the slightest bit dangerous. Then he released her and stepped away. "I need no proof of Marcus's perfidy. I will kill him with or without you."

Her heart sank. Her only hope lay in telling him all of it. Perhaps he would be grateful. "The night we met, I overheard Lord Chilton talking to my father. Papa had discovered that Lord Chilton was an accomplice to Marcus and had some sort of proof of it in his possession. Lord Chilton became quite angry."

"Proof?" His stance took on a stillness that reminded her of a wolf scenting prey. "What proof?"

"Some pages from a ledger that Lord Chilton kept. Apparently he wrote down all his dealings with Marcus."

"He wrote down everything?" Alex gave her a skeptical look. "I find it difficult to credit even Chilton with such foolishness. Where are these ledger pages now?"

"I don't know. I believe Papa has them, and that is why Marcus abducted me. He wants them."

"Is there anything else?"

"Just that Papa told Lord Chilton he could not marry me. I'm afraid that I was too happy about that to consider much else." Even as she said it, Diana realized she sounded like a feather-witted child. "That is, I didn't realize the significance of those ledger pages until much later."

Alex crossed his arms and frowned at her. "You mean to tell me that you didn't know who Marcus was at the time?"

"Of course I knew who he was . . ."

"Or his reputation?"

"Everyone knows of his reputation!"

"And you mean to tell me that you ignored all this in face of the fact that your father had forbidden Chilton to press his suit?"

"Well . . . yes."

"It never occurred to you that your father could be in danger because of this?"

"I told you that I wasn't thinking of that!" She had been spoiled and selfish. She knew that now, but did Alex have to remind her of it?

"Yes, yes, you were too overwhelmed by the prospect of losing Chilton as a suitor to com- prehend the implications of anything else." Giving her a considering look, he asked, "Are you certain there was nothing else?"

"I have told you everything." She bit her lip as a sinking feeling slithered through her. He should have been excited by the information she had just given him. Instead he was entirely too calm. "Don't you understand? My father is in possession of some evidence that will see Marcus hanged and Lord Chilton with him! My fear is that Papa will be wrongly implicated because he and Lord Chilton are business partners."

His eyes narrowed. Suddenly she realized how her statement must sound to him.

"My father is innocent," she asserted, challenge in her stance.

"Of course he is," Alex answered, his tone silky.

"He is!"

"Without a doubt." He raised a brow. "Just because he and Chilton are partners in legitimate business is no reason to suspect that they are also partners in these dark dealings."

"That is exactly what I am trying to tell you. Why do you mock me?"

"Mock you? Why, dear lady, what ever gave you that idea?" He smiled, but the hard look in his eyes did not fade. "It never entered my mind that your father might be involved."

She clenched her fists at her sides. His derisive gaze belied his charming tone. She knew how far-fetched her tale must sound to him, but she had to find some way to make him believe her. "It is the truth," she said, almost desperately.

He gave her a look of innocent inquiry. "You do not suppose—and this is just a thought, mind you—that your father might have been blackmailing Chilton?"

"Certainly not!"

"Hmmm." He appeared to think over the matter. "It never once occurred to you that your father might have been dissatisfied with his arrangement with Marcus and Chilton and sought to increase his profits by blackmailing Chilton with his own foolishness?"

"That is absurd!" Diana lifted her chin. "My father is a good man with an honest reputation. He would never do such a thing."

His smile turned cold. "My point exactly, my sweet. Everyone knows of the scandals in Chilton's past, though he has managed to recoup some wealth and respectability these past few years. Even the slightest whisper of his association with Marcus would destroy that. However, your father might have been counting on his own reputation as an honest businessman to make people believe that he was not involved."

She gaped at him. "He would never do that!"

He shrugged. "Some men will do anything for wealth."

"My father is already quite well off. He has no need of such underhanded tactics."

"Some men never have enough gold."

"Do not credit my father with the same motivations as yourself, *El Moreno*," she snapped.

"Do not be so blinded by your love for your father that you think he can do no wrong," Alex sneered. "He is a man like the rest of us, and quite capable of acting on his baser instincts."

"He has not done anything wrong," she insisted.

He strolled over to her and touched her cheek. "What profit would there be for me in saving your father's life?"

"What is it that you want?" How she hated the desperate tone in her voice.

"There is no price you could name," he said softly, "that could steer me from my goal to see Marcus swing."

"And my father with him?"

Alex shrugged. "If he is guilty."

"There must be something." Her mind worked. Gold would not sway him, of that she was sure. A personal motive drove him; therefore, perhaps something personal might make him relent. She looked him in the eye, pride straightening her shoulders and strengthening her resolve. Whatever the sacrifice, she would perform it gladly to see her father live. The idea whispered through her mind that what she was considering might not be so much a sacrifice as a pleasure. She pushed the thought away.

"There is *nothing*, Diana. Let the matter rest."

"I cannot." She met his eyes squarely, then

reached with quivering fingers for the sash of the robe. "I will do anything to save my father's life."

An expression crossed his face that stilled her hands for an instant. She couldn't quite define it.

"Don't even think about it." He closed his hand over hers before she could discard the robe. For a moment she could have sworn that his fingers trembled on hers, but she dismissed the notion as unlikely. She could clearly feel that Alex's grip was firm and commanding. What reason had he to tremble?

She was simply so confused by his refusal that she imagined vulnerability where there was none.

"You do not want me? I don't understand. All my life men have been trying to lure me to their beds, including you. And I am willing to accommodate you as long as you promise to help my father." Too late, she heard the conceit in her own words.

"My dear girl." He surprised a shiver from her by stroking one finger along her jaw. "You are indeed most beautiful. But I don't need to make bargains to lure women to my bed. Indeed, they come there most willingly."

"I am certain they do." She drew back from his touch, her face hot with both embarrassment and arousal. He had neatly handed back the same arrogance that she had just displayed. So she knew she was beautiful. So what if men had been falling at her feet for most of her life?

This man would not. This man was as beautiful a man as she was a woman.

Slowly she retied the sash. "Alex," she said quietly, "you must believe me when I tell you that my father is innocent. And you are the only man who can help him."

"Lovely Diana." He lifted her chin with his finger so that she met his gaze. "I wish that I could. But if he has fallen in with Marcus and Chilton, then he must pay for his crimes."

"You don't believe me. You think my father is guilty, and that I am trying to protect him." Her eyes stung with the onset of tears that she fought to hide. "If it is the last thing I do, Alex, I *will* convince you."

"You are welcome to try."

He turned away from her and went to the door. Pausing with his hand on the latch, he glanced back at her. "Go to sleep, my girl. Mayhap you will think more clearly after you have rested."

She frowned as he left the cabin. Think clearly, was it? She was thinking perfectly clearly! 'Twas he who needed to see things as they were. But one thing he said had made sense: she needed to sleep. It had been a harrowing night and an even more nerve-wracking morning. She needed all her wits about her to win this dangerous game.

As she climbed into the big bed and pulled the coverlet over her, she made a vow. She *would* make him believe her. No matter what it took.

* * *

Alex stood just outside the door to his cabin and listened to the sounds of Diana climbing into his bed. Part of him wanted to climb in there with her . . . the wrong part. But well did he remember the consequences of following the prompting of his loins and not those of his head. He had sworn that no one would distract him from his goal. That included the tempting Diana.

But oh, how he wanted her.

He lifted a hand and laid it flat against the portal. "Ah, sweet lady," he murmured. "Had we only met in another time and place, I would have accepted your offer most willingly. But as it is, that very offer has only made this easier."

He removed his hand from the door and rubbed it over his face. He knew the only reason she had offered herself was to save her father's life, not because she truly wanted him. And he would be damned before he'd ever again have duty bring a woman to his bed. Bianca had taught him all too well the consequences of that.

He glanced once more at the door, noting the silence that had fallen within the cabin. How easily Diana had accepted his suggestion that she rest. No doubt she was relieved that she had been spared from sacrificing herself to duty.

"If you ever come to me again, my lovely, 'twill be because you want me. Not because duty bestirs you."

Putting his disturbing captive from his mind, as she had so clearly put him from hers, he headed abovedecks to tend to his ship.

Frederick paced the floor of his study. Covington Hall had been in an uproar since daybreak. Maude stood nearby, her eyes reddened from tears, the skirt of her dark brown, serviceable dress wrinkled from her wringing her hands.

"My bairn," she whimpered over and over again. "My poor wee lassie!"

Frederick clenched his teeth and tried to ignore the litany. "Maude, do try to calm yourself."

"Calm myself?" Maude shrieked. "How can you expect me to calm myself when my poor innocent Diana is nowhere to be found? Stolen from her bed? In the hands o' some monster?"

"Please try," Frederick insisted. "I am trying to think."

"This is what comes o' makin' a pirate the lieutenant-governor o' the island," Maude railed, shaking a finger at him. "All pirates are o' the same cloth and mean no good to decent folk."

"Woman, this is not the time for politics."

She laughed harshly. "Indeed it is. Dinna be goin' to Henry Morgan with tales o' your daughter's disappearance," she warned. "The Brethren o' the Sea stick together like honey on bread. The Assembly was right to send the governor to England to get Morgan removed.

Do you ken, Frederick? They were right!"

"Enough!" Frederick bellowed. "Cease your ranting! Can you not see that I am trying to concentrate?"

Maude looked stricken for a moment. She pressed her trembling lips together. Then she buried her face in her hands and began keening and wailing, her accent so thick that Frederick couldn't understand a blessed word she said. He gave a disgusted sigh.

"Leave me, Maude. I shall inform you when I have word." Maude babbled a response and stumbled toward the door. Just as she reached it, the portal opened to reveal Walter, one of the house servants. Maude streaked past him, nearly knocking down Frederick's visitor in her haste.

"Lord Chilton to see you, sir."

"Chilton! What in bloody blazes does he want?"

Before Walter could respond, Chilton himself stepped forward, a buffoonlike figure in black and crimson. "Now, Frederick. Is that any way to speak of your business partner?"

Frederick glared at Chilton and signaled Walter's dismissal with a wave of his hand. The servant bobbed his head and left the room.

Frederick eyed Chilton with ill-concealed revulsion. "Now that you have chastised my manners in front of my servant, what the devil do you want, Chilton?"

"Frederick, Frederick." Clucking his tongue, Chilton sauntered into the room and settled into a chair. "I was merely seeking to edify you in the ways of a gentleman. I should have known it was a fruitless exercise."

Frederick clenched and unclenched his hands. "I have a rather urgent matter to deal with. Walter will show you out." He indicated the door in a gesture of dismissal.

Chilton sat back in his chair and critically examined the toe of his shoe. He pulled a lacy handkerchief from his ruffled cuff and dabbed at a speck of mud.

Frederick snorted in disgust and headed for the door. "Good day, Chilton."

"I suppose, Frederick," Chilton drawled in languid tones, "that this 'urgent matter' refers to Diana's disappearance?"

Frederick shut the door with a soft click and slowly turned to face his uninvited guest. "What do you know of Diana?"

"More than you do, apparently." Chilton surveyed the heavy rings adorning his thin fingers. "You should not have crossed me, Frederick."

Frederick slowly retraced his steps until he stood just in front of the nobleman. Alarm crept down his spine as he noticed how pleased and confident the fop appeared. A man who was a breath away from being arrested for piracy should not look so calm.

"What do you know of my daughter, Chilton?" he demanded.

"Do not sound so ominous, Frederick. She is quite safe." Chilton raised his eyebrows and gave Frederick an amused smile. "Actually, 'safe' is not quite the word. I believe 'twould be more accurate to say that she is alive. Yes, that is much closer to the truth."

"Just what is that supposed to mean, Chilton?" Frederick snapped. "What do you know about Diana's disappearance?"

"Everything, of course." Chilton leaned back in his chair and withdrew an elaborate snuffbox from his coat pocket. Flicking open the lid with a practiced gesture, he drawled, "I arranged the whole thing. Your daughter, my dear sir, is being held by my associate until such time that you turn over the pages of my ledger to me."

"Associate!" Frederick shook with fury as Chilton pinched a bit of snuff and inhaled it with fastidious care. "What associate? You can't mean—"

"But I do." Chilton flipped the snuffbox closed before pulling forth a second handkerchief from his other cuff. He sneezed into it. "Marcus is holding Diana until he receives word from me that all is well. I have no fear that he will kill her, though she may return to you slightly damaged—"

"*You bastard!*"

Frederick's roar echoed through the room. The snuffbox went flying as Frederick toppled the chair in which Chilton sat. He closed his hands with merciless accuracy around Chilton's throat.

Chilton gasped for breath, clawing at the

hands cutting off his air supply. His eyes bulged; his face reddened.

"You bastard! You bloody, primping, prancing bastard!" Frederick slammed Chilton's head over and over against the floor. "I'll kill you! By all that's holy, you shall die this day!"

Chilton grabbed one of Frederick's wrists with both hands and pulled. He sucked in a breath. "Can't . . . kill . . . me," he gasped. "You'll . . . never . . . find her."

The logic of his words cut through the blinding haze of fury. With a blistering curse, Frederick yanked his hands from Chilton's throat, dropping the man's head to the floor with a thud. While Chilton groaned and fingered his abused throat, Frederick rose from his perch on the man's abdomen. He took great gasps of air, trying to calm his searing rage. Chilton slowly picked himself up off the floor.

Rubbing his bruised neck, he glared at Frederick. "You will regret that, Frederick," he rasped. "In the meantime, there is no need to discuss terms of release. You know what they are." Sweeping his crumpled hat from the floor, he perched it atop his precariously tilting wig.

"You will indeed discuss terms, Chilton." Frederick's voice dripped with menace. "You have three days to produce my daughter. If you do not, the pages of your ledger go to Morgan. And I will come for *you*."

Chilton paled at the blatant threat. "Three

days is impossible," he objected. "She is not on the island."

"A week, then," Frederick amended. "You will return my daughter within seven days' time. And there had better not be a mark on her."

"You are not in a position to issue threats, Frederick," Chilton said with bravado. "If you give the pages to Morgan, you may implicate yourself as well."

"And you are not in a position to test me, Chilton. If I must give my life for my daughter's safe return, then so be it. Now get your skinny arse from my home, lest my boot show you the way!"

Chilton curled his lip and departed with as much hauteur as he could muster. The slamming of the door behind him echoed like a cannon blast in the room.

Frederick's shoulders sagged. He looked heavenward and clenched his fists. "Though it may cost my own life, I will see you home safely, Diana. This I vow!"

Chapter 9

Diana opened her eyes. At first she lay disoriented, confused by her unfamiliar surroundings. Then she remembered. She had been abducted by Marcus and stolen from him by Alex. And Alex was El Moreno. She was asleep in Alex's bed, in his cabin, aboard his ship.

But where was the man himself?

She abruptly sat up as another thought occurred to her. If she was sleeping in his bed, where had he slept? She glanced anxiously around the room, but saw no evidence of any other bedding. The pillow beside her showed no impression that his head had rested there.

Footsteps echoed in the companionway. She stared at the door as it slowly creaked open. With white-knuckled fingers, she pulled the coverlet to her chest.

"Good mornin' to you, lass." Birk entered the room, balancing a tray. Her empty stomach growled as she caught sight of the food he had brought her. The Scotsman laughed. "I can see you're hungered. It's a good sign."

136

"I feel as if I haven't eaten in a week." Pulling the sash of Alex's robe tighter, she slipped from the bed and went to sit at the table as Birk put down the tray. The hot tea and day-old bread looked like a feast, and the bananas were a treat. Fruit rarely lasted more than a couple of days once at sea.

"Aye, the sea has a way o' wakin' the hunger in a body," the physician answered. He watched her, amusement in his eyes, as she tore into the bread. "Did you sleep well, lass?"

She flushed and reached for the tea. "I slept soundly."

"I canna say the same for the captain." Birk seated himself and grinned. "He kept me awake most o' the night with his tossin' and turnin'."

Diana chewed a bit of bread and washed it down with a sip of tea. "He spent the night with you?"

"Och, aye." The twinkle in Birk's eyes belied the innocence of his expression. "He came to my cabin last night and asked me to spare him a bit o' space. So I bade him take his rest on the floor."

Diana put down the bread and stared at him. "You made the captain of the ship sleep on the floor?"

"That I did." Birk folded his arms behind his head. "He might be the captain to you, lass, but to me he is just a man. It's near ten years we've kent one another, and a better friend a man canna find."

"You know him well, then."

"Nobody kens him better. Not even his own mother." Birk shook his head. "You shouldna have gone to him like you did. He'd be the last man to bed a woman against her will or because o' duty. It would have served you better to just seduce the man and be done with it."

Heat surging in her cheeks, Diana grabbed a banana and began to slowly strip the skin from the fruit. "I don't know what you're talking about."

Birk laughed. "Dinna play the innocent, missy. Dinna you ken I'm tryin' to help you?"

She couldn't deny the truth in the face of those knowing blue eyes. "As much as I appreciate your suggestion, Mister Fraser," she said, "I doubt seducing him would have done much good. He seemed to resist my charms most easily."

"That's because you're listenin' to what he tells you and not to what your eyes are tellin' you. Alex wants you right enough, that's easily seen."

"Mister Fraser!" Flustered by his bluntness, she bit a piece of banana.

He chuckled. "Forgive my boldness, lass, but I thought you might be better off kennin' the situation as it is."

" 'Tis you who does not see clearly, sir. Alex has made it most clear that he has no interest in me. I am just another woman to him."

"If that was the truth, lass, he would have passed the night with you instead o' keepin'

me awake with his tossin'." Birk grinned. "He
didna take to your bargain, that's all."

She couldn't look at him. "He would not accept my gold. And I need his help."

"Aye, he told me the way o' it. As for myself,
I can see that your father could well be innocent o' any ill-doin'. But you must ken that
Alex is obsessed with capturin' Marcus. He can
be a wee bit hard-headed in that respect."

She jerked her gaze to his. "You believe
me?"

"I'm just sayin' that the possibility's there.
There's equal chance that your father's as
guilty as the rest o' the brigands."

"He is innocent!"

Birk held up his hands. "I'm not the one you
have to convince, lass."

Her shoulders sagged. "I know that. Alex
will not even consider the possibility that my
father is innocent. I asked him to help me, and
he refused. Nothing I offered would change his
mind."

Birk chuckled. "Aye, you got yourself in a
swither, didn't you? Truth be told, lass, Alex is
a reasonable man when it comes to anything
but Marcus. But he's a man that wouldna make
a promise he couldna keep."

"I don't understand."

Birk paused, as if weighing his words. "Despite what it seems, Alex is a man o' honor.
He'll not make a promise he's not sure he can
keep, nor will he take from you anything he
disna have a right to."

"A pirate who is a man of honor? I have never heard of such a thing!"

"Pirates have honor amongst themselves. Alex more than most."

"So you are saying that he did not accept my . . . offer," she said, blushing, "because he wasn't sure he could help my father?"

"That's part o' it." Birk glanced away, causing Diana to wonder what the other part was.

"But I believe he is the only man who can help Papa," she continued. "What should I do now?"

"As for that, I believe I told you what to do. Seduce the man."

"Oh, for certain," she scoffed, indicating her appearance. "I am the very picture of seduction." But the idea gave her pause.

"You can be. If you set your mind to it." She rolled her eyes, and he laughed. "I'll help you, lass." He got up and went to the sea chest. After a few moments of rummaging, he produced a set of woman's clothing: a saffron-yellow skirt and matching bodice trimmed with black lace, and an underskirt in a paler shade of yellow. "Wear this. It will look bonnie with your fine red hair."

"It's beautiful."

"Nothing is too good for the captain's mistress, if you ken my meanin'."

Where once the term 'mistress' had made Diana cringe, now she discovered an advantage to the title. She smiled slowly. "I believe I do." She glanced back at the gown. "Whose is this?"

"The captain meant it as a present for some-body, but he says you need it more."

She hesitated, wondering whom he had in-tended the dress for. "I don't know if it is right for me to wear something he meant as a gift," she said finally.

He let out an exasperated sigh. "Wheesht, woman! Do you think to entice the man while wearin' Marcus's breeks?"

She wrinkled her nose at the reminder and reached for the clothing. "Very well. Give it to me."

He handed it to her, then reached again into the chest to produce a silver-backed brush and a handful of ribbons.

"There are no petticoats?" she asked, exam-ining the gown. "No corset or chemise?"

Birk tossed a plain white chemise on the bed, then put his hands on his hips, still holding the brush and ribbons. "That's all there is, though I dinna ken what you would be needin' that for when you'll only take it off again."

She blushed to the roots of her hair. "Mister Fraser!"

"Lass, you canna bring a man to his knees wearin' six petticoats and a whalebone chastity belt!" He handed her the brush and ribbons, then strode to the door. "Call me when you're finished. Then I'll take you to the captain."

Diana blinked as he slammed the door, then looked at the yellow satin in her hands. She longed to get out of the borrowed clothing she had worn since early yesterday morning, but she knew that once she donned these garments, things would never be the same.

It was one thing to talk to Birk of seducing Alex, she thought as she laid the satin raiment across the bed. But now that the plan required action, she found herself hesitating. She had no qualms about sacrificing her innocence to save her father's life. Yet she had always expected that when she gave herself to a man, he would be her husband, someone to whom she had made a commitment.

She sighed. Slowly she untied the sash of Alex's robe and let the garment fall to the floor. She was attracted to Alex. Admitting that to herself made her task a bit easier. Yet to actually lure the man to her bed in exchange for services rendered smacked of harlotry. He had named her his mistress before all the crew, and now she would become so in truth.

She stepped out of Marcus's breeches and kicked them aside with pleasure. Naked, she ran her fingers through her tangled hair and then looked down at her unclothed body. She knew she was beautiful. Yet was she attractive enough to entice Alex? She smoothed her hands over her hips. There was only one way to find out. She picked up the chemise. From this moment on, everything would change.

She managed to dress by herself, though the lack of a corset made the garments fit uncomfortably. The laces in the back of the bodice would not meet, and the ones in the front were false laces, for decoration only. The skirts hung long without the petticoats to hold them up. Still, anything was better than Alex's robe. Even though she couldn't lace up the back, she felt proud of herself. Never before had she gotten dressed without Maude's help. She tried not to breathe too deeply for fear of losing the bodice, and she left the laces dangling, thinking to ask Birk's help with that small duty.

Her hair proved a difficult task, and she now understood why Maude tended to mutter beneath her breath while dealing with it. She could not duplicate any of her normally fashionable hairstyles, but she managed to brush the tangles free and tie it back in some semblance of order.

Once finished, she stood a moment and contemplated what she was about to do. The moment she stepped out of the cabin, she would become a pirate's mistress. She would give up her virtue and her reputation without any misgivings, out of love for her father. Yet part of her feared what would happen when she sacrificed her virginity to El Moreno. Would he be gentle out of care for her maidenhood? Or would he rend her like a beast and devour her for his own pleasure?

She prayed that the flirtations she had learned from society would be enough to entrance him, that he might approach her as a lover and not a conqueror. But if it saved her father's life, she would endure even being conquered.

With a small sigh, she opened the door and stepped out to meet her fate.

Alex watched over the repairs with a critical eye. They would arrive at Besosa late tomorrow afternoon, where they would repair the hole in the hull . . . and put Diana ashore.

He closed his eyes to avoid thinking about his comely captive and her outrageous offer. Instead he inhaled the sea air and listened to the creaks of the timbers and the snap of the sails in the wind, reminding himself that this was his idea of heaven.

"Good morning, Captain."

His eyes flew open as Diana made her way across the deck, with Birk following her like a protective duenna. Daintily she sidestepped the men scattered about mending sail, apparently immune to the stares and leers of the crew around her. She had donned the dress he had meant for his mother, but it did not look quite as he had expected it to.

While the saffron silk looked wonderful with Diana's vivid coloring, and the black lace trim enhanced her very fair skin, the gown was cut lower than he remembered. Diana's bountiful bosom looked as if it would fall out of the top that she held to her chest with both hands. The breeze blew her skirts against her, clearly outlining her legs and announcing to all and sundry that the woman wore not a petticoat underneath. Knowing he had purchased the proper undergarments for the gown, he wondered what the devil she hoped to accomplish by marching about his ship half naked.

No doubt she sought to tax his willpower, damn her. And she might well succeed if he didn't put the idea from her head immediately. A man could only take so much torture.

He glanced at Birk, hoping for aid. His good friend shrugged and rolled his eyes, indicating his total helplessness in the face of Diana's will.

"Do you not even say good morning?" she chided as she came to a stop before him.

"When it is a good morning." He scowled, keeping his gaze with difficulty from the smooth breasts that threatened to slip free of the loosened bodice.

"I see the foul humor of last night plagues you still, Captain."

"Aye, there's a plague about—a red-haired plague."

She clucked her tongue. "Captain, how unkind." Her voice carried the teasing lilt he had often heard in ballrooms. She smiled, her gray eyes warm, and desire vibrated through him as if he were a harp string just plucked.

"Is there some reason you have chosen to honor me with your presence this morning, Mistress Covington?" he snapped, irritated by his uncontrollable reaction to her.

"Why, yes." She turned her back to him. "I believe I left my lady's maid at home. Would you mind?"

He looked at the garment before him, half laced and all but falling off her. He was un-

comfortably aware that only one layer of flimsy
cloth separated his hands from her bare skin.
He didn't want to touch her, so aroused was
he, but neither could he leave her half clothed.
Torquemada could not have created a better
torture. He looked up and glared at Birk.

"You couldn't have done this?"

"I've no wish to lose my hands for touchin'
the captain's woman," Birk said, all innocence.

Alex sealed his lips against the sharp retort
that hovered there. Too many ears listened,
and too many eyes watched them. With the
grimness of a man forced to perform an execution, he yanked on the laces, taking great
care to touch nothing else. He ignored Diana's
soft gasp as the garment tightened around her
uncorseted middle. He threaded the laces
through the holes with grim precision. Each
time his fingers brushed the chemise, he could
feel the warmth of her flesh beneath. He gritted
his teeth and kept going. When his knuckles
accidentally brushed her spine, she made a soft
noise, and blood rushed to his loins. The
woman was a menace, he reminded himself.
She was a spoiled, willful child.

If only she weren't so bloody beautiful.

Her hair curled over his wrist as he slipped
the laces through the last holes. Impatiently he
brushed it over her shoulder, only to have the
wind blow a few strands back at him. The er-
rant tendrils gleamed with lively fire and
drifted over his lips and nose like a spider's
web, bringing her scent with it. He'd be

damned if he'd let himself be ensnared, though. He performed this charade to protect Diana from his lusty crew, and for no other reason than that.

He certainly didn't enjoy it.

"There." He tugged the laces hard and tied them quickly, then stepped back from her. She turned to face him, a smile on her lips, and smoothed the skirts of her gown.

"Why, thank you, Captain. You are most kind."

Her saucy tone irritated him. "In that you are wrong, my dear. I am not a kind man."

She laughed, a melodious sound that clashed with the snap of the sails and the slosh of the sea against the hull. He had to keep her at a distance, lest she entice him with her siren's ways. Her society airs did not belong here. And neither did she.

"I believe you have wasted enough of my time," he said low enough for only her to hear. "Either amuse yourself elsewhere or you will pass the rest of the voyage belowdecks."

She stopped laughing, a flash of hurt streaking across her face before she concealed it. "Must you be so harsh, Captain?"

He leaned closer. "I know what you are about, mistress. And your coquette's wiles have no effect on me."

She tossed her fiery curls and propped her hands on her hips. "Indeed? I am beginning to believe that you are not interested in women at all!"

Alex stared at her. If the wench only knew how much control it took to keep from tossing her over his shoulder and carrying her off to his bed, she would not make such ridiculous assertions.

"You've the tongue of a lightskirt," he said.

She laughed in his face. "You must think me completely naive, sir. Pray do not forget that I grew up in Port Royal, one of the wickedest cities in the Indies. Or that I am the daughter of a blunt-speaking man. I am not so innocent of the world as you would believe me."

Birk finally recovered from his shock. "The captain's no bloody catamite!" he spluttered.

She eyed Alex from head to toe and arched her brows. "Perhaps."

Alex gave her a predatory smile, tempted almost beyond reason to prove her accusations false by deed. Instead he said, "Just because I do not see fit to bed *you*, my dear, do not assume that I neglect to enjoy women as much as any other man."

Her cheeks flushed. "I don't know what you are talking about."

He laughed and yanked her against him. Enjoying both her discomfiture and the slow burn of his own unceasing need, he slid one hand down her back to gently caress her bottom. She struggled, but he held her fast. "Now, now, my sweet. Let us not give the game away. You are supposed to be my mistress."

She would not meet his eyes. "Let me go," she muttered.

"I do not choose to." She jerked her gaze to his and glared. He laughed again, long and loud. "So fierce, my sweet? You would lure me with a girl's pouty looks and teasing comments, when 'tis a woman I want in my bed."

"All you will find in your bed is rats," she snapped. "Now release me."

He let her go so abruptly that she stumbled. "Only little girls tease a man and then pull away in virginal fear. Go play with your toys, little one, and leave the seduction to the women who can handle the reality."

She straightened her spine and raised her chin in challenge. "I am woman enough for you, El Moreno, if only you were man enough to take what is offered."

She turned her back on him before he could answer and took off in a flurry of yellow satin. Birk looked at Alex, shook his head like a man disappointed, and followed Diana's path.

"I am more than man enough for you," Alex murmured to himself, desire still raging in him like an angry sea. "That is indeed part of the problem."

"That man is entirely too involved with himself," Diana declared as she stormed across the deck. Birk caught up with her and took her arm, slowing her to a walk.

"Easy, lass," he murmured. "Keep your voice down now."

"I don't want to keep my voice down."

"If it gets about that you've quarreled with

the captain, you might find yourself in a bit o' difficulty."

"What are you talking about?"

Birk pulled her to a stop. Holding her gaze with his, he said softly, "You've brought a bit o' attention on yourself, lassie, not all o' it good. Not every man aboard is as honorable as the captain."

"I have my own opinion of the captain, Mister Fraser, and I assure you that it does not include honor!"

"Now, there, hen." With a gentle but firm hand, Birk guided her to a private place at the rail. "Dinna be so severe on the man. It's naught but your pride speakin'."

"He is so infuriating!" Diana clenched her hands on the rail and turned to look out over the ocean. "How can I seduce a man who does not want me?"

"He wants you, lassie. More than he would like."

She glared at him. "He called me a child."

"He disna like what you make him feel." Birk sighed. "He's not the same man that first went after Marcus. I've kent him many a year, and the change in him disturbs me."

She frowned. "How so?"

Birk's expression grew troubled. "He disna think beyond makin' Marcus hang for his crimes. He forgets that he has a life to live after that."

"A fine life indeed, if he does away with his

greatest rival," Diana scoffed. "The seas will be his to plunder."

"There's more to it than you ken," Birk murmured. "Still, an obsession can be a chancy thing. It consumes a man till there is nothing left."

"Your captain is well up to the task," Diana retorted.

"You're a hard-hearted lassie." Birk crossed his arms. "Can you not find a bit o' kindness in you for the man?"

She felt a twinge of sympathy, but her own goals remained firmly fixed in her mind. "The only kindness I can afford is for my father. Alex will not even consider the possibility that Papa is innocent. I need to make him listen to me."

She glanced across the deck at Alex. He stood with his feet firmly planted on the smoothly rocking deck, looking dangerously handsome in his black clothing. Sunlight gleamed off the mane of dark hair falling to his shoulders. She remembered how silky that hair had felt tangled around her fingers when he had kissed her yesterday. And how much his rejection had stung today.

The man could keep his kisses, damn him.

"You can make him listen, lassie. It might take a bit o' time, that's all."

"I don't have a lot of time." She tore her gaze from Alex to look at Birk. "Each day that passes brings my father closer to the hangman.

And El Moreno is the only man who can help him."

"There's no certainty in that," Birk reminded her. "You dinna ken what you're askin' o' him."

"All I wanted was for him to help my father," she whispered. "To at least try." He had deflected her attempt at seduction so easily. She felt so helpless, something she had never experienced before. She took a breath that ended on a sob, and regained control with effort. She was strong, she reminded herself. The hurtful words of one man would not defeat her.

"He thinks me a child. Well, I am no child." She began walking over to where the men mended sail.

Birk hurried after her. "Where are you off to?"

"I do not play with toys, Mister Fraser," she tossed back over her shoulder. "And no longer will I play games with your captain. From this moment on, you will find all of my time better spent."

Birk sighed as he caught up to her. "Leave it to a woman to toss pepper in the stew," he muttered.

"Did you say something, Birk?"

He gave her a look of total innocence. "Just a wee prayer, that's all."

"Say one for your captain," she retorted. "He needs it the most."

Chapter 10

Alex tried to avoid Diana for the rest of the day, but he only discovered how very *small* his ship was, and how difficult it was to steer clear of anyone for any length of time. Still, he made certain to go to his cabin at an hour when Diana would not be around. Yet her absence didn't help matters, since her scent haunted the room. He dared not look at the chair where he had attempted to seduce her, nor the bed where she slept. *His* bed, damn it all, and he wanted to share it with her for reasons that had nothing to do with sleeping.

He was just leaving the cabin when he came upon her in the companionway. For a long moment they stared at each other in the dim corridor. One of them would have to step aside, he knew, for both could not pass at once. He gave her a mocking bow and stood back, pressing himself flat against the wall to give her as much room as possible.

She hesitated, then came forward, gathering her skirt and easing past him. Despite her ob-

vious intention to make no contact, her lacing
caught on his belt buckle, trapping her against
him from chest to thighs. She looked down and
froze, and he saw that her breasts swelled precariously   above   her   bodice—which   had
plunged even farther, tugged down by the captured lacing. Her every breath gave him cause
to believe that total exposure was imminent.

He dreaded the thought of her breasts pop-
ping free of their constraints, even as his mouth
watered in anticipation.

She looked up at him with those big eyes,
awareness darkening the irises to smoke. Her
chest rose and fell with her rapid breathing,
and he leaned closer, hunger for her parted lips
driving all rational thought from his head. Her
gaze dropped to his mouth. She made a little
sound that sent the blood thundering straight
to his groin.

It would be so easy to shove her skirts aside,
pin her against the wall, and give them what
they both wanted. As captain of the ship, no
one would gainsay him.

Lust ripped at his insides, clawing to get out.
He lowered his mouth to hers, even as she
stretched up on tiptoe to meet him. Their lips
had barely touched before the ship listed, un-
balancing them. Her lacing tore free of his belt
buckle as she stumbled back against the opposite wall. Mercifully, her bodice stayed in
place.

He regained his balance, and his reason, before she did. With a muttered curse, he turned

and left her. He knew well the price she would demand for bedding her, and he was not willing to pay it. Not when it meant that one of Marcus's associates might go free.

Diana's father would answer for his actions, just like every other man living on this earth—and nothing his daughter did would delay that reckoning.

"Dat's a fine woman you got, Captain."

Alex slowly turned to face the speaker. He had to look up, since Mister James, the boatswain, stood nearly a head taller. The enormous black man watched Diana attempt to mend sail with the crew. His face reflected true admiration, and his dark eyes gleamed with respect.

"Thank you, Mister James," Alex said curtly.

"Real pretty."

"Yes, she is." Alex glanced at her, admiring despite himself the way the sun gilded her hair with fire. He was painfully aware of how lovely Diana was.

"And smart."

"I know."

"Sweet." Mister James smiled, revealing strong white teeth that gleamed almost as brightly as the two silver earrings in his left ear. He slapped Alex on the shoulder with one huge hand. "You one lucky man." Without another word, he turned and stalked off across the deck.

Alex surreptitiously flexed his shoulder to

ease the sting. Mister James was the third crewman to compliment him on his mistress. A mistress in name only, he thought sourly.

He scowled at the turn his thoughts had taken. Although he would rather have his genitals rot and fall off than allow duty to bring a woman to his bed, he still found himself responding to her physically. He wondered what would happen if she were to offer herself to him out of mutual desire. Would his convictions remain strong, or would they crumble beneath the power of his attraction to her?

Keeping an entire deck between them, he watched her laughingly hand the seamer palm and the needle back to one of the men. Though she had given it a mighty effort, she hadn't the physical vigor to push the huge needle through the heavy canvas sails. But she had shown strength of character in lowering herself from her higher station to sit with his men and try to forge a bond with them. And that, he realized ruefully, was much more attractive than any of the flirtatious mannerisms that she practiced with such skill.

Birk was there to lend an arm as she got up from the deck and shook out her skirt. Laughing, she waved to those still mending and strolled with the physician to where three men sat cleaning the fish that had been netted that morning. She watched with a smile of pure delight that he found curious.

He folded his hands behind his back. She seemed to sincerely enjoy what she was doing.

Her enthusiasm enchanted his battle-roughened crew. The old sailor whom she now spoke to treated her in a most respectful manner, never once even looking at her in the wrong way. So it had been with all the men.

Alex frowned. If he wasn't careful, he, too, would soon be ensnared in the spell of his own mistress.

"You take well to life aboard a ship," Birk observed.

Diana flashed him a smile and turned her attention back to the three crewmen efficiently filleting the morning's catch.

"I have always loved the out-of-doors," she replied. "Papa often allowed me on board his ships when I was a child, but as I grew older he decided it would be more prudent if I remained at home."

"Aye, I can see the wisdom o' that."

"As can I. But I do miss the privilege." She lifted her face to the sun and smiled as the breeze stirred her hair. Inhaling deeply of the salty, fish-scented air, she opened her eyes to meet the brooding gaze of El Moreno.

He watched her from across the deck, hands clasped behind his back, his face grim in the way of a man who considered a baffling puzzle. She held the eye contact for a moment, then deliberately turned away. Even with the ship between them, he could still make her tremble with little more than a look.

"I used to fish with my father when I was a

child," she told Birk, trying to ignore her body's unruly response to Alex's presence. "Indeed, I believe he oft mistook me for a son rather than a daughter."

"He wouldna make that mistake now," Birk said. "You're a fine woman, lassie."

She blushed at the sincere admiration in his voice. "You are too kind, Mister Fraser."

"Birk Fraser disna lie."

She gave him a wry smile. "Would that others shared your opinion."

Without giving him a chance to respond, she squatted beside one of the crewmen and admired the way he deftly cleaned a fish. He tossed the scraps in a nearby barrel and dropped the fillets into a basket to be brought to the galley.

"Watch yourself, now," Birk warned. "That's dirty work."

She grinned up at him. "This was always the best part, Birk. I wonder if I still remember how." She glanced at the seaman, a grizzled oldster with one eye and missing teeth. "May I?"

The sailor glanced uncertainly at Birk. Before the physician could answer the unspoken question, the captain's voice interrupted.

"Let the lady try." A mocking smile spread across Alex's face as he crossed the deck. He stopped several paces away. "She has an affinity for sharp objects."

She stiffened. His sarcastic tone indicated that he expected her to back down, or fumble with the blade. She raised her chin. Taking the proffered knife from the old man, she picked up a fish.

Her hands remembered the motions even as the memories crowded her mind. Her father and she had fished in the river near Covington Hall. She could feel again his large adult hands guiding her smaller ones as he taught her how to slit the fish from tail to gill and how to clean the guts from the cavity. With practiced strokes, she sliced upward along the head, down the length of the spine, and then deftly flipped the fillet over to slice the meat from the skin. She repeated the procedure on the other side of the fish, remembering the first time she had done it, and the mouthwatering flavor of her first catch. Though the fish had tasted delicious seasoned with lemon and precious pepper, she had savored her father's pride even more.

Her father meant the world to her. And the one man who could save his life refused to help her.

She flipped the fish scraps into the barrel and the fillets into the basket. Handing the knife back to its owner, she took the rag Birk handed her, wiped off her hands, and stood.

Alex arched a brow. "Impressive."

She smiled sweetly in return. "You said it yourself, sir. I am well versed in the use of a blade."

"That is well-known to those who have felt the prick of your sharp tongue, my sweet." He grinned like the pirate he was. "Of course, only I have experienced the pleasure you can provide as well."

She gasped, heat searing her cheeks, as the men roared with laughter. For a moment she could say nothing as chagrin—and longing—swept through her. But as she watched Alex laugh, how he threw his head back, the contrast of white teeth against tanned skin, a calm settled over her. She smiled at him, then slowly ran her tongue over her lips.

His laughter ceased, and his face tightened with desire. The men seemed to notice nothing amiss. Indeed, they probably expected such behavior from the captain's mistress. For the first time in her life, Diana realized she could do as she wished, with no one to hold her back, no one to remind her of the rules that governed a lady.

For here she wasn't a lady. She was El Moreno's woman.

Her heart started to pound. *El Moreno's woman.* She fancied the idea. With a slow, seductive smile, she propped her hands on her hips and tilted her head to eye him provocatively.

"Now, now, Captain," she teased in a throaty voice. "You know my . . . skills . . . are not for public airing."

She heard Birk snicker from behind her, but kept her eyes on Alex. His face showed stunned surprise before he narrowed his eyes. She could feel the intensity of his regard as surely as if he had placed his hands on her. She took a shaky breath as desire clenched demandingly around her loins.

"Are you telling me what to do?" he asked in a quiet, dangerous voice.

She glanced at the crew, then back at him. "Of course not, my captain. I save that for when we are alone."

The men hooted. To Diana's delight, a ruddy hue crept into Alex's cheeks. Her blood raced with a reckless abandon. She knew she teased a tiger; she just didn't care. After all, what could he do to her? She already knew that he would not harm her. And if he took her to his bed? She swallowed hard. Perhaps he would do just that. And perhaps she wanted him to.

She sauntered over to him, half expecting him to move away. But then she realized that such a maneuver would be construed as a retreat by his men. She had him right where she wanted him. Holding his gaze, she traced a finger down the front of his shirt, barely controlling the tremor of her hands as she savored the heat of his body.

"Do not fret, my love," she teased, keeping her tone light with difficulty. "I am certain your men still respect you."

He grabbed her wrist and held it still. She could see the pulse throbbing at the base of his throat and the way he clenched his jaw. He was not as unaffected as he pretended. Indeed, she had the feeling that he might snap at any moment and satisfy her maidenly curiosity in a most explicit manner.

Though she doubted she would still be a maid when he was through with her. The idea thrilled her even as it made her nervous.

"Do not play games with me," he murmured for her ears alone. "I have no patience for a little girl's flirtations."

She stroked his lip with her index finger, this time unable to quell its shaking as she felt his breath caress her fingertip. "This is no flirtation, sir. I only express my feelings."

"You only want me to help your father," he hissed through clenched teeth, his body stiff with tension.

"I do," she answered softly. "But that has nothing to do with this."

"The hell it doesn't."

"Look at me, Alex," she whispered. "Could I pretend the way my body reacts to you? Could I feign the way my pulse pounds, or the way I cannot seem to look away from you? Or this?"

Mustering her courage, she stretched and kissed him. It was a soft kiss, not fiery and passionate like the others. But it shuddered through her like lightning, and it was freely given. And that, she hoped, would make the difference.

He broke the kiss. "Perhaps we should discuss this further," he said with a silky tone that sent a ripple down her spine. "Let us retire to my cabin."

She knew he expected her to back down. "An excellent idea," she agreed, and was satisfied to see the surprise and then the hunger that crossed his face before he hid it. "I await your convenience, Captain."

"Now is convenient." He signaled to the physician. "Birk will escort you below. I will join you directly."

She took the arm the Scotsman extended. "Do not take long," she murmured, then allowed Birk to lead her away. She could feel Alex's gaze on her, but never looked back.

"Verra good," Birk murmured to her. "He looks like you clubbed him with a belaying pin."

"Good," she retorted. "We will soon see if I made a dent in that stubborn skull."

Birk left her at the door. Diana went immediately to the basin, poured water in it, and began to wash the scent of fish from her skin. Her hands were still shaking.

What had come over her? she wondered. Two days ago she had been an overprotected maid with dreams of El Moreno. Today she trembled in anticipation of sharing a bed with that very man.

How had it happened so quickly? Although she had feelings for Alex, she didn't want to accept the idea that she could fall in love with such an unsuitable man. There was no future in loving El Moreno. Chances of his survival were slim. If he didn't die in battle, then most probably the law would see him hanged for piracy. No, she could not admit to such feelings.

Better to lose herself in passion. Aye, her first feelings of desire for a man were more than enough to make her act so uncharacteristically.

With her father's fate a separate issue, she made a woman's choice to give herself to the man she wanted.

The door clicked open. She whirled around, her hands still wet, to see Alex standing in the doorway. He closed the door without taking his gaze from her.

"What game do you play with me, woman?" he asked softly. His voice brushed over her like satin over bare flesh.

The now-familiar ripple of desire shook her. "As I told you, I play no game."

He laughed. "Every woman plays a game, my sweet. Women are born plotting."

She raised her brows. "I do not know what sort of women you have encountered, sir, but I do not plot."

"Do you not?" He approached her slowly, as if he expected her to bolt.

Her breathing quickened as he stalked her, though not from fear. She could feel his nearness, though he had not yet touched her. Excitement surged through her on a wave of need.

"What you see before you is all I am," she insisted, her voice breathy with excitement.

"What I see before me," he mused, taking

her chin in his hand, "is a pretty child toying with a woman's schemes."

"I am no child, Alex." She met his gaze. "I am a woman. And I want you."

He moved his hand from her chin to brush his knuckles over her cheek. "So simple. You want me. Yet you know not what you ask."

"Why do you persist in thinking me some naive little girl?" She covered his hand with hers. "I know what goes on between a man and a woman. And I know what I want. Just because I have never lain with a man does not mean I cannot recognize honest desire when I feel it."

"Honest desire." He turned his hand to clasp hers and brought her fingers to his lips. "Would it not be crowded in my bed," he murmured, "with all three of us there?"

"Three?" Her eyes widened.

He laughed. "What a wicked mind you have, my dear. You, me, and your father."

"I told you, my father has nothing to do with this."

"He has everything to do with this!" Releasing her, he stepped back. "He is the reason you suddenly long for my bed. I remember you declaring, not a day ago, that you would fight me should I try to bed you. To your last breath, I believe you said."

"I was frightened," she replied. "I didn't know you. I didn't know what to make of these feelings you bring out in me."

"You still do not know me."

She gave him a confident smile. "I know more about you than you think."

"In that case, my dear," he said, reaching out to stroke his finger down her cheek, "you should be frightened indeed."

She took his hand and boldly pressed it to her heart. "You do not scare me, Alex. *This* is what you do to me. My body is not my own whenever you are near."

He stroked his thumb over the upper curve of her breast. Her heart skipped into double time. She watched his face, how his eyes narrowed in concentration until she could see little more than the gleam of desire through his long, thick lashes. His sensual lips parted as he continued to rub his thumb against her skin.

"Alex," she whispered, helpless in the storm of emotions that rushed over her. She wanted to glide her mouth over the tanned flesh of his cheekbones and curl her fingers into that silky black hair. Her palms itched to slide beneath the black cambric of his shirt and test the resilience of his muscular chest and shoulders.

"Easy, my sweet." He stepped away, taking the warmth of his touch with him. She wanted to cry out at the loss.

"Now who plays a game?" she asked, frustrated. Closing her hands into fists, she turned away from him.

"Diana." He came up behind her and placed his hands on her shoulders. She took a deep, shuddering breath as his touch sent her blood surging again.

"I don't know what you want from me," she whispered. "I have never felt this way before. You will have to forgive my clumsiness, since the rules of polite society do not dictate the correct procedure for this circumstance."

"You aren't clumsy."

"Innocent, then. Naive. I can't deny it." She reached up to touch his fingers with her own. "Yet I have always known there was more to life than my limited world allowed. And I want to experience it."

He sighed. His breath swept over her neck and sent gooseflesh rippling down her arms. "Diana, you are young. You have your whole life ahead of you."

"What life?" she scoffed. "I am like a pampered pet kept in a cage. Rules and conventions are my jailers. I am preened and primped to attract a suitable husband, though I have no voice in the choosing of him." She let her head fall back against his shoulder. "I much prefer your way of life."

"The sea is no place for a lady."

"But don't you see?" She turned to face him. "I don't want to be a lady. I want to be a woman free to make her own choices. Even a child has more options."

"You cannot change who you are," Alex argued. "You are a woman of good family, and you must live as one."

She glanced askance at him. "When I was a child, I had more freedom than I do now. I went where I wanted. I played. I ran. I filleted fish! Now my life consists of endless balls and routs, the purpose of which is to display me like prize goods at the market."

"You would rather be hungry? Homeless?"

"Of course not." She shook her head. "I merely want the freedom to make my own decisions. To live where I choose, go where I choose." She gave him a pointed look. "Love whom I choose."

He stepped back. "Do not speak to me of love, Diana."

"Passion, then. Is that a more comfortable word for you?" She came to him and slid her hands up his chest. Standing on tiptoe, she pressed a kiss to his lips, her heart beating wildly as she awaited rejection.

Miraculously, he returned the kiss, parting her lips with his and stroking his tongue urgently against hers. Then he pulled back with a harsh moan. "I can't do this," he said through gritted teeth. Raking both hands through his hair, he turned his back on her.

"Then tell me why. And tell me the truth. Is it because you simply do not find me attractive?"

He laughed and glanced over his shoulder at her. His look stopped her breath and made her tingle from head to toe. "No, my dear. That is not the problem at all."

"Is it my father?"

"No. I am starting to believe you, damn it." He bowed his head and sighed. When she saw him rub the back of his neck with a weary gesture, she couldn't stay away.

She moved up behind him and touched his arm. "This is the first decision I have made about my own life, ever, Alex. It may be the last."

"There are things you don't understand, Diana. Things I cannot explain."

"I know," she whispered. "How I envy you your freedom, Alex. I could learn to live this life all too easily."

He let out a disbelieving laugh. "The life of a pirate? I doubt it."

"You underestimate me, sir." She sighed. "I would love to feel the sun on my face, rather than tote a sunshade about lest I freckle. And I would love to be busy with tasks that need to be done, rather than being dragged about to balls and dinners."

"Most women would thrive in that sort of lifestyle."

"I am not most women," she retorted. "I would rather fillet fish than dance the minuet with some foppish lord, however *suitable* he might be. I would rather wear comfortable clothes, instead of the latest styles and all the restrictions that go with them. I would like to feel the wind blow through my hair, instead of having to be cautious of every carefully placed curl." She sighed and shook her head. "How lovely it would be."

"We are all prisoners, Diana. In one way or another."

Since he had not shrugged off her touch, she grew bolder and rubbed his shoulders with both hands. "Perhaps we both have things in our lives that prevent us from having true freedom. But can we not, just for a little while, take something for ourselves?"

"You tempt me, little one," he groaned.

"Alex, you have already declared me your mistress before the men. We would be merely making truth of a lie." She rested her forehead against his back. "No one would know."

"*I* would know." He turned and took her upper arms in his hands, pulling her against him. She closed her eyes at the pleasure of being in his embrace. Nuzzling his chest, she enjoyed the way his intoxicating scent sparked her senses and sent them reeling.

"Diana." His voice sounded hoarse. With a deliberate motion, he set her away from him. "I cannot do this."

She made a little sound of protest and reached out to him as she was denied the warmth of his arms. "Alex, please."

He backed away. "I cannot. There are things you don't understand, Diana. And I do not want to hurt you."

"You hurt me now," she said. She took a deep breath to hold back the tears that threatened. She would *not* cry in front of him.

"I would hurt you even more, perhaps beyond repair, if I were to give in to what I want." He sighed and reached back for the door latch. "It's better this way."

She shrugged and raised her chin, trying to ignore the howling needs of her overheated body. "As you wish, Captain. I am but your prisoner and have no say in anything."

He scowled. "Diana . . ."

"Go."

"If I could," he said, his voice taut with his own need, "I would take you to bed and never let you go."

"If you could," she retorted. "I did not realize, Captain, that you are more a prisoner than I."

"As I told you, we are all prisoners."

"Some of us of our own making," she snapped. "Now please leave, sir. I grow weary."

"As you wish." He opened the door and paused to look back at her. "But just so you know . . . I do want you. Too much."

He left, closing the door behind him. She took another deep breath, successfully holding tears at bay. "I believe you, Alex," she said to the empty room. "But there is obviously something you desire even more."

Chapter 11

Night approached with a speed that made Alex want to shake a fist at the setting sun. He had spent the day on deck, barking orders to his men in a voice that made all but Birk give him wide berth. He oversaw the repairs and brooded, watching with a frown as the sun sank lower and lower in the sky. Each hour had brought him closer to the night . . . and the thought of Diana sleeping in his bed.

Despite his will, night indeed fell, and he went belowdecks with a scowl on his face. He stalked down the companionway toward Birk's cabin, but found himself passing the physician's door and stopping outside his own.

Damn her. He laid a clenched fist on the door, tempted to knock, then slowly flattened his hand against it. Only this morning it had seemed so easy. But there was little defense against her honesty, and this afternoon her innocent candor had shaken his resolve more than her ballroom airs ever could have.

With effort, he turned away and backtracked

to Birk's cabin. He pounded on the door with enough force to rattle the hinges. Birk opened the door, saw Alex and scowled.

"You dinna have the sense God gave a goat," he declared.

"Just let me in."

Birk moved so that Alex could enter. "If you prefer the hard floor o' my cabin to the soft flesh o' the lassie, then I'll wash my hands o' you."

Alex ignored him. "Have you a bottle of something around here?"

"Och, mind who you're talkin' to." Birk fetched a bottle of whiskey and handed it to him. "She has you in a swither right enough. What's the lassie done now?"

Alex popped the cork and took a swig straight from the bottle. The whiskey slid down his throat with fiery smoothness, and he closed his eyes and waited for the liquor to soothe his savage emotions. It didn't work.

Birk took the bottle from his hand. Opening his eyes, Alex glared. Birk shook his head. "You'll not be gettin' this back till you've told me the whole o' it."

"You are far too hairy to be my mother, Birk. Now give me the damned bottle."

"You'll not waste my best whiskey on your demons, Alex." The physician settled into the only chair in the room, placing the bottle on the tiny table and keeping his hand on it. "What did the lassie do to get you all conflummoxed?"

"I am *not* conflummoxed."

"You are that."

"I am not!" Alex roared. "I know exactly what is bothering me."

"As do I." Birk reached for the bottle and took a drink. "Do yourself a favor, man. Take the woman to your bed, and to wife as well, if you've a brain in that empty head o' yours."

"She offered herself to me."

Birk stopped with the bottle halfway to his lips, then shrugged and took another swig. "You told me that already."

"No, not then. A while ago." Alex closed his eyes as his tumultuous emotions threatened to explode. "She offered herself—no artifice, no games. She wants me, goddamn it!"

"Sweet Mary and all the blessed saints." Birk shook his head. "Alex, you're the only man I ken that would see such a thing as a trouble and not a pleasure."

"You know my reasons." Alex raked a hand through his hair. "As long as she acted like Bianca . . . as long as duty was all that brought her to me . . ." He stopped and took a long, shuddering breath. "She is so bloody honest, Birk. She hides nothing. I can see the passion in her eyes."

Birk snorted. "I could have told you long ago that the lassie wasna a bit like your wife. Bianca wanted to give herself to the kirk, but her family made her give herself to you instead. She didna want a man in her bed." He grinned and pointed a finger. "That one, now.

She can match you, in bed and out."

"You think I don't see that?" Alex paced the room. "But there are other reasons. She is a virgin, Birk. I cannot take from her something that should go to her husband. Her reputation would be ruined."

The Scotsman laughed. "Her reputation is already soiled, Alex. The first hour she spent on Marcus's ship saw to that. It disna matter that the lassie is yet a maid. Her people will consider her damaged goods and wed her to the richest lecher they can find. Either that or some horny knave will take her as mistress."

Alex stopped pacing. "Her father would protect her."

"Aye, for certain. But you forget about Chilton. That bastard wants her for himself. I'd wager my best whiskey that he'll be spreadin' tales o' her abduction with an eye to bein' the only man willin' to wed her after all is said and done."

"Chilton will never wed her," Alex said with a smile of satisfaction. "He will hang with Marcus."

"Aye, but he disna ken that. He thinks he's got Covington right where he wants him. And maybe he does."

His smile faded. "Damn. I had not considered that."

"You'd be doin' the lass a favor," Birk continued. "The man that weds her willna ken that she's a virgin still. The blackguard might hurt her for certain."

"You paint a bleak picture, my friend."

"You have the power to change the woman's future, Alex. Bed her now, then wed her later."

"You know it's more complicated than that." He shook his head slowly, still amazed by the emotions Diana engendered in him. "She trusts me, Birk. What other woman would have the courage to approach a man like El Moreno and offer herself with such sweet simplicity?"

"She's a Scot," Birk announced with pride in his voice.

"Aye." He began pacing again. "But there is more to it than that. I like her, Birk."

Birk held out the bottle. "Then drink up, man, and celebrate."

Alex took the bottle. "Celebrate what?"

"Your resurrection."

Alex arched a brow. "I do not recall having died, my friend."

"Your body didna pass on, only the soul o' the man I kent before Marcus killed your brother. Revenge had bled the life from you, Alex. I was wonderin' if you felt anything anymore."

"I feel plenty."

"And I'm glad to see it." Birk motioned with his hand. "Are you goin' to drink or no?"

Alex drank. "I have always had feelings," he said after swallowing.

"Aye. Anger. Frustration. But never anything softer. The lassie is good for you, Alex."

"I feel anger and frustration with her, too,

Birk," Alex said, amused. "A more exasperating woman I have never met."

"She's a hot-tempered morsel. But she's a fine match for you. I say wed her, bed her, and beget a dozen bairns . . . not necessarily in that order, mind you." Birk toasted him with the bottle and tossed back a healthy draught.

Alex entertained Birk's suggestion for a moment. To his surprise, the prospect of wedding Diana did not seem as distasteful as before. But there was yet an obstacle between them.

"What of her father, Birk?" He watched the jocularity leave the Scotsman's expression. "You know as well as I that Covington could be involved with Marcus. If he is, he must pay for his crimes. And I will have been the one to bring him to justice."

"Aye, it's a fair coil. Perhaps the lassie has the right of it, and her father isna involved. Maybe he's a victim as well."

"It matters not," Alex said with a sigh. "You know as well as I, Birk, that 'tis Morgan's decision on who will live and who will die. Even if I were to attempt to help her father, I cannot guarantee Morgan's word. I won't make promises I cannot keep."

"Talk to her," Birk urged. "I think the two o' you can come to an agreement."

"But—"

Birk rose from his chair. "Go! Out with you." He shoved Alex toward the door with his free hand. "Take the woman to bed, before your black humor causes a mutiny."

Alex opened his mouth to protest, but Birk gave him another hard shove between the shoulder blades.

"Out! And if that woman is still a virgin in the mornin', then I give up on you. You can blast yourself to hell in pursuit o' Marcus, and I willna stop you."

Alex paused on the threshold. "I don't know if I should do this."

"Stop thinkin' so much, and start feelin'! Your instincts willna fail you." With a mighty shove, Birk sent Alex stumbling into the hall.

"Birk—"

The door slammed in his face. Alex stood looking at it for a long moment. Then he glanced at his own door down the hall. *Wed her, bed her, and beget a dozen bairns*. At the moment, Birk's advice didn't seem so far-fetched.

Birk's words had also shed new light on the matter of her reputation. She was already ruined, and once returned to her family, she would no doubt be sold off to the highest bidder. Either that or forced to live as a spinster in her father's house for the rest of her life.

Slowly, he started down the hall to his cabin. *Wed her, bed her, and beget a dozen bairns ...*

He hesitated at the door, then pushed it open and slipped into the darkened room. The lantern that hung in the hall cast enough light for him to make out Diana's sleeping form in his bed. His blood surged as he noticed the way her hair spilled across his pillows like a fiery waterfall. He imagined how it would feel against his skin. Desire made his hands shake as he closed the door.

With the ease of long practice he made his way to the desk and found the tinderbox and lit the candle there. The flame flickered to life, casting a soft glow about the room. He took a moment to pull off his boots and stockings. Barefoot, he moved to the side of the bed and looked down on her.

She looked like a child, peaceful and serene in sleep. But he knew well that she was no child. She had proven herself all woman when she had so eloquently admitted her feelings. She wanted him. Simple. To the point. No games, no duty. Just a man and a woman and a mutual need.

He sat on the edge of the bed. Reaching out, he stroked the back of his fingers over her cheek. It never ceased to amaze him how soft and unblemished her skin was. So many women had pockmarks or poor complexion from too much powder and rouge. Not Diana. Her flesh glowed with youth and vitality.

Her lashes fluttered. He watched her eyes slowly open and focus on him. Smiling, he traced one finger over her lower lip. The sleepiness in her eyes faded, replaced by awareness.

"Diana." Just her name. But it was enough. She took his hand in hers and kissed it, then nuzzled her cheek against his palm. His breath caught at the natural, affectionate gesture.

"We have to talk," he said softly. She nodded and sat up in bed, revealing that she still slept in his robe. As she raised her arm to push her hair out of her face, one pale breast peeked out, then retreated when she lowered her arm. He gripped the coverlet to keep from reaching for her.

"What did you want to talk about?" The huskiness of her voice sent his pulse pounding. She licked her dry lips, and he almost lost control right then and there.

"You are so bloody beautiful." Unable to resist, he took a handful of her hair and fingered the silken locks.

Her eyes widened, then grew smoky with passion. He couldn't resist. Cupping his hand around the back of her head, he pulled her close.

"One taste," he murmured against her lips. He kissed her gently, loving the way her inexperienced mouth trembled against his. Breaking the kiss, he rested his forehead against hers, eyes closed, his hand stroking her hair.

"Alex." Her breath grazed his lips. He opened his eyes and looked into hers, only two inches away. The pure need in her gaze swept away the last of his resolve.

"This is about us," he said, moving to kiss her cheek. "Nothing else."

"Yes." She tilted her head to give him better access.

"I will try to help your father," he continued, gliding his lips over her jawbone to her neck. "But I can promise nothing."

"All right."

"I mean that." He raised his head to look her in the eye. "If your father is guilty, he hangs. If he is innocent, I will do my best to see that he is proven so."

"Thank you." With a sweet smile, she took his face in her hands and pressed a kiss to his lips.

He made a sound in the back of his throat as her innocent touch set his blood aflame. "Do you know what you are doing?" he asked hoarsely. "You are chancing your future for this."

"No," she said. "I am stealing a moment of happiness, despite the consequences." She traced her fingers down his face. "In the worst of times, I will always have this to look back upon. Make love to me, Alex."

He took a deep breath. His heart pounded until he expected it to burst from his chest. His shaft had grown harder than a belaying pin, and he had to find some discipline. This was her first time. He wanted it to be a memory she cherished forever.

"Alex." She threatened to blow holes in his fragile control as she traced his ear with her finger.

"Yes." With effort, he asked, "Do you want me to snuff the candle?"

"No." She smiled with innocent seductiveness. "I want to see you. I have no intention of missing *anything*."

"You won't," he said. "That I promise you."

"Show me."

"Yes," he murmured, then kissed her.

Diana clutched his shoulders with desperate hands as passion surged within her like a hungry beast. The strength of her emotions might have frightened her if it hadn't been Alex who touched her.

He held her tenderly, yet with an experience that was reassuring. His mouth on hers made her moan with newfound emotions. Excitement rose on a wave of pleasure as he tangled his fingers in her hair and pulled her head back to expose her throat. The slow, gentle glide of his mouth from ear to collarbone made her whimper. She gladly lost herself to his touch.

He moved to toss aside the bedding that covered her legs, then gathered her against him and kissed her with a slowness that maddened her. Very gradually he deepened the kiss as he held her tightly and stroked her back with long, languid caresses. The silk absorbed the heat of his hand, leaving a tingling path behind.

Her breath caught as he brushed the sensitive spot between her shoulder blades, then smoothed his fingers down to curve over her bottom. He reversed the course. Up. Down. Up. Down. The unhurried pace drove her wild. Each time he reached her shoulders, he pulled the robe open an inch or so more, never touching her bare flesh. She anticipated the moment, longed for it. The waiting stretched, building tension, until the expected touch came, and desire streaked higher.

He brushed his lips over her forehead, her cheekbone, the contact so light she could barely feel it. Her belly clenched with each caress of his mouth, each tickle of his breath over her skin. Barely touching her, he aroused her slowly, letting the passion build.

Her mind awhirl, Diana reached out to smooth the rippling muscles of his shoulders. He made a small sound of pleasure and bent his head to nuzzle her neck. She pressed her hands down his chest, stroking over his nipples and down his sinewy rib cage. He pulled his shirt over his head, and she repeated the movement over his bare flesh.

"Diana," he whispered, his dark eyes hot with need.

"I know." Clinging to his shoulders, she lifted her head to kiss him. His mouth lingered on hers as she pulled back.

"Slowly," he murmured, staring into her eyes. "We have all night."

"Slowly," she repeated, then eagerly sought his mouth again. His kiss echoed the unhurried sensuality of their movements, his lips molding to hers, then retreating, only to return again. Hunger spiked into urgency.

She trembled when he caressed her sensitive lower lip with his tongue. She did the same to him. They barely moved, half sitting, half reclining. Passion smoldered, creeping higher a degree at a time, toward the breaking point.

Alex swept both hands up her back to clutch her shoulders, his thumbs caressing the delicate hollows of her collarbone. Diana broke the kiss to boldly graze her teeth down the side of his throat. He groaned, the sound rumbling deep in his chest. Desperate hands cupped her face, tilting it so that she was looking up at him.

She melted at the blatant desire etched on his face. His beautiful mouth was still damp from their kisses, his jaw taut with control. She moved toward him at the same time he lowered his head. Their lips met halfway.

The tension kept so carefully in check exploded. Alex folded Diana into his arms, pressing her against him as if he would become a part of her. She touched places in him he had thought long dead. He wanted to fill himself with her essence, become one with her in every way possible. His body shook with the force of his emotions. "I need you," he whispered.

"Yes," she answered back. Greedy, she grabbed handfuls of his hair and tugged his head down for a hot, wet kiss. When she pulled back, her eyes were cloudy with longing.

"I don't want to hurt you," Alex said when he could form words. He rested his hands on her silk-covered hips and pulled her against his erection.

"Oh!" She was distracted from the strange hardness pressed against her when he slid his hands into the robe to cover her breasts with his palms. He kneaded the firm mounds and rained hungry kisses on her mouth, her ears, her throat. Gliding his palms upward, he pushed the robe off her shoulders and brought his mouth to hers again.

Diana curled her fingers into his hair and deepened the kiss with an innocent carnality that nearly brought him to his knees. He gripped a handful of the robe, her arms still in the sleeves. He tugged.

He swallowed, took a breath. "Diana." As she copied his movements and tongued his ear, he tugged the sash loose. The robe dangled off her elbows. "Take it off."

"Yes." She slipped her arms free and tossed the garment aside, then waited, shy and expectant. Candlelight gilded her fair skin with a golden glow. Reverently, he took in the sight of her beautiful breasts, her slender waist, her sweetly curved hips.

"Alex?" she whispered nervously, a becoming flush creeping into her cheeks.

Her beauty astounded him, but not just the physical. It was a light that shone from within her, the special spark that made her Diana. The passion that glowed in her face . . . for him.

He must have been staring, because she reached out to trail her fingers down his chest, over his navel, and beyond. "What about you?"

His control broke when her fingers grazed his straining erection. "Diana . . ."

"Yes?" She watched him with half-closed

eyes, wonder and sensuality curving her lips, as she touched him with unsubtle curiosity.

"God's teeth," he hissed. "You're making this impossible."

She popped open the buttons of his breeches one at a time. He raised an eyebrow at her deftness, and she giggled. "I wore breeches for two days, remember?"

"I do." He helped her peel them from his body. "I cursed them many a time."

As he tossed the garment to the floor, she looked down and gasped. He grinned at her expression, and she blushed. Silently, he took her hand and guided it to him.

Her face took on a speculative expression as she began to caress him. Her inexperienced touch aroused him more than the most practiced courtesan, and nearly brought him to climax. He managed to hold back. Taking her hand, he placed it on his shoulder, out of harm's way. He took her mouth in an openmouthed kiss that left them both breathless.

Her whimper of satisfaction dissolved into a moan as he slipped his hand between her legs. She arched against him, her fingers digging into the muscles of his shoulders. Groaning with the knowledge that she was indeed ready for him, he tumbled her onto her back, never breaking the contact. Lifting her hips, he entered her with one smooth motion. She made a small sound of pain as the proof of her virginity gave way. He paused, savoring that first, desperately sought contact. After a moment she moved her hips. He groaned and closed his eyes. She felt so good. He pulled her legs tightly around his waist and set an easy rhythm, reveling in the feel of her warm acceptance.

"Alex," Diana whispered, her head falling back. She said his name again and again, a litany of passion.

Each time he heard it, he wanted to drive her higher, make the climax better. He opened his eyes, saw her beautiful breasts inches from his face. He dipped his head down and caught one pebbled nipple in his mouth, sucking strongly.

"Oh, God," Diana gasped.

She convulsed around him, shuddering, calling his name. He was right behind her, her own release triggering his, falling over the edge in a powerful rush of pleasure.

They clung, drained, limbs heavy, with the realization that everything they had ever known had just changed forever.

Chapter 12

﹏⟡⟡﹏

Besosa loomed on the horizon, barely a shadow in the afternoon sun. Alex smiled with satisfaction from the quarterdeck. Home.

A familiar laugh made him turn his head. Down in the waist, Diana attempted to handle strong hemp ropes used for the sails. A lad with barely enough facial hair to shave showed her how to tie the various knots used to rig the ship. Each time she fumbled, she laughed, the lighthearted sound carrying across the deck like music. The lad watched her with a look of bedazzlement. Alex was sure that if he checked his own mirror, he would see a similar expression.

He smiled and stretched, turning his face up to the afternoon sun. He was as content as a cat sleeping before a fire, and had felt so ever since he had awakened early that morning. He was starting to believe that he had indeed been resurrected.

Until he met Diana, he hadn't realized how

submerged he had become in revenge. It was good to know he could still experience the softer feelings, that he was *not* becoming El Moreno as he had feared.

That he had a future beyond Marcus's death.

He leaned back against the rail and watched Diana. She had obviously not been exaggerating when she said she loved life at sea. He wondered what she would think when she discovered that she was to live the conventional life of a countess, and not the adventurous life of a pirate's mistress.

He had made love to her last night with the full knowledge that they would wed. Now that he had made the decision, he could see the logic in it. Diana was of good family, yet she wasn't a standard dull, meek miss. She was an unusual woman, passionate and loyal. With Diana as his countess, he knew his life would *never* be boring.

"Well, now. You're lookin' pleased with yourself."

Alex grinned at Birk as the physician climbed the ladder leading up to the deck. "I am."

Birk chuckled and took the last few rungs with ease. "At least there willna be a mutiny because o' your foul humor. I can lay my fears to rest."

Alex said nothing, his attention caught by the way the sun played on Diana's hair. She looked up and caught him watching her. A slow, sweet smile spread across her lips. Alex felt his body react immediately.

Birk laughed. "She's a fine woman, my friend. I'm pleased for you." He ruffled his shaggy hair with both hands and turned his face into the wind. "Aye, I slept fair well without your rummlin' and whummlin' on my floor. Now that the lassie kens your secrets, perhaps you'll keep *her* awake o' nights."

"She knows nothing."

"What?" Birk stared at him. "Are you daft, man? You canna take a woman like that to your bed and still keep secrets from her. She'll skin you alive when she finds out what you've hidden, as sure as I'm standin' here."

Alex grew solemn. "It's for her own good. I'll tell her, Birk. Just not until this masquerade is done."

"Bloody hell." Birk rubbed a hand over his face. "She willna ken it's for her own good, Alex. She'll think you dinna trust her." He shuddered. "Women always think that."

"It has to be this way." Alex watched Diana enchant Mister James with her smile as the men broke open a barrel of rum. "Thank God Marcus doesn't associate El Moreno with the Earl of Rothstone. It has kept my mother safe. And ignorance will serve to protect Diana as well. God forbid Marcus should get his hands on her again . . . but if he does, then the less she knows, the better. It could save her life, Birk."

"You're playin' with fire, man."

"I swear I will tell her the whole of it once

Marcus is in Morgan's hands. Until then, I'm going to leave her on Besosa so she will be safe." He grinned at Birk. "I hope you have suitable clothing to wear to my wedding, my friend."

"So you've come to your senses at last! It took you long enough." Birk clapped a hand on his shoulder. "Will you be married in Port Royal?"

"I rather fancy wedding Diana at home, on Besosa."

"Hmmm." Birk scratched his chin. "And were you thinkin' to invite Rosana as well?"

"Blast it all. I forgot about her." Alex frowned, considering the unpleasant notion of his hot-tempered Spanish mistress meeting up with his fiery bride-to-be. "I will deal with Rosana. Until then, you keep Diana out of sight."

"A wise move, Alex."

"I'll secure a room at the tavern for her, but I want you to stay with her, Birk."

"You're not bringin' her to stay with your mother?"

"I am indeed. However, I believe I should speak to her first." He smiled. "My mother should be prepared for Diana."

"If I had a bottle, I would salute your clear thinkin', man."

"Clear thinking my arse, Birk. I wish to survive to see my wedding night, is all."

The two men burst into laughter.

* * *

Diana dipped the cloth in the basin of water and dabbed at her neck and upper chest. It had been hot up on deck, and she had been sitting in the Caribbean sun for too long. She closed her eyes, enjoying the relief the cool water brought to her skin. Lifting her hair aside, she dipped the cloth in the basin again and ran it along the back of her neck.

Strong masculine fingers covered hers on the cloth and closed over her shoulder to steady her. She let out a soft gasp, then relaxed as lips she knew well brushed her nape, sending a shiver through her that hardened her nipples. She released the cloth to him and dropped her hand to her side as he continued to smooth it over her shoulder, his mouth following the damp trail of the cloth.

"Alex," she whispered, as he placed nibbling kisses along her collarbone.

"It had better not be anyone else," he murmured.

She inhaled sharply as familiar stirrings awakened in her body, bringing memories of the pleasures discovered the night before. "What are you doing?"

"You know what I'm doing." His breath swept over her throat as he nuzzled her neck.

She *did* know. She leaned back against him, very conscious of the bed only a few feet away. He dropped the cloth and slid his hands around her to cup her breasts.

"Isn't it early for this?" she breathed, her pulse racing.

He chuckled and rubbed the hardened nubs through the material of her gown. "You don't like it?"

"I didn't say that," she moaned. She pressed his hands hard against her, pleasure exploding low in her belly.

"I can see there are some ways in which you are still innocent, my sweet." Alex eased his hands away from her breasts with tortuous slowness and turned her around to face him. "One can make love before the sun sets, you know."

She blushed. He threw back his head and laughed, then hugged her tightly. "Don't laugh at me," she muttered into his shirt, her body still humming in reaction to his touch.

"I laugh with delight." He kissed the top of her head. "Unfortunately, there is no time to advance your education. We have arrived at Besosa."

"Your home."

"Yes. I think you will like it here."

"I'm sure I will." She nuzzled her face into his chest. "Though we will not be here for very long. You said it should only take a day or so to repair the ship."

"Yes." He pulled back and looked down at her, his dark eyes solemn. "But you will have plenty of time to come to love my home as I do, Diana. You will be staying here while I go find Marcus."

"What?" She pulled out of his arms. "You are leaving me behind?"

"Just until I capture Marcus."

"I will do no such thing!" Panic streaked through her. "I'm coming with you."

"I cannot allow that." He took her shoulders in his hands, but she stepped away from his touch.

"You cannot *allow* that?" Propping her hands on her hips, she glared at him even as her heart pounded with fear. "You have no right to order me about."

He clenched his jaw. "Oh, but I do. I am captain of this ship, and commander of all aboard . . . including you."

Her temper simmered like the fuse on a cannon, feeding on the frustrated desire of moments before. "And last night meant nothing to you?"

"Last night has nothing to do with this. I am trying to protect you, Diana."

"I am not a child who needs to be hidden away while you put yourself in danger." She tilted her chin. "If you go, then I go."

"Don't be ridiculous." He crossed his arms and glared at her with a commanding expression. "You asked me to help your father. I intend to do so. But I need to know that you are safe, or else I will not be able to do what must be done."

"I am safest with you," she retorted.

"Not while I am chasing Marcus. You will stay on Besosa. My decision is final."

Tears stung her eyes. She blinked them back.

"You cannot make me stay behind, Alex. Not unless it is by force."

"If that is how it needs to be." His expression remained unyielding.

"You would make me a prisoner? After last night?"

"Damn last night, woman! I will not risk your life!"

"But you will risk yours." She smiled bitterly. "I thought we had reached an understanding. I see I was wrong."

"Diana . . ." He took a step toward her, but she turned her back on him.

"You don't trust me, Alex. You treat me like a child."

"Bloody hell," he muttered. "Diana, I care about you. I am simply trying to keep you safe."

She cast him a baleful look over her shoulder. "You care about me so much that you leave me to worry while you risk your own neck. If you had any respect for me, Alex, you would allow me to make the choice myself."

"I'm sorry." The regret in his voice pierced her more than his toplofty commands had done. "I cannot do that. If I must bind you like a prisoner to see you safe, then so be it."

He turned and went to the door, then paused with his hand on the latch. "I have matters to see to ashore. Birk will be your guardian until I return."

"You mean my jailer," she corrected.

He sighed. "As you wish." He left the cabin,

closing the door very quietly behind him.

Diana stared after him. She could not believe that the tender lover of the night before had so easily become the autocratic captain with the rising of the sun. He said he left her behind for safety's sake. Yet she feared not for her own life, but for his.

She had experienced the terror that was Marcus. She had watched the two men duel, their skills evenly matched. She had even entered the fray when Scroggins sought to stab Alex in the back. If she stayed behind, who would be there for him if such a thing happened again?

It touched her heart that he was trying to protect her. But she had the horrible feeling that if he left her now, she would never see him alive again.

A splash reached her ears, then the sounds of voices and laughter. A rattle and thump made her frown in puzzlement. Suddenly she knew. The splash . . . a longboat? Voices, laughter . . . the rattling, thumping sound had to be the rope ladder tossed over the side. They must be going ashore.

Urgency seized her—she had to find Alex. She had to convince him to take her with him. Flinging open the door, she hurried to catch him.

The tiny island sat like a jewel in the crown of the Caribbean. Blue-shadowed mountains rose above green hills. White sandy beaches reflected the melon-colored hues of the setting sun. The water near the shore was so clear that a man could see straight to the bottom. Besosa. Home.

Alex inhaled the familiar scents of sea and hibiscus as the two crewmen steered the long-boat toward the sandy shore. The entire population of Besosa's only village cheered and called to him as he got out of the boat and helped the men drag it through the shallow surf and up onto the beach. It was always thus when El Moreno came back to the island. He was their hero, their provider. He supplemented their livelihoods with the spoils of his travels.

He smiled broadly and waved to the people gathered along the beach. They responded with a deafening cheer, and a rush of pleasure surged through him. These were his people—men and women who had lived under the protection of the Rawnsleys since his father had first purchased the island some thirty years ago.

Alex had been born on Besosa, and had spent his boyhood racing with William along the beaches and exploring the lush jungle. Each boy had been sent off to England at the age of seven for a formal education. William had learned of estates and tenants, and Alex had discovered the sea. He had rarely come back to the island after that, first joining His Majesty's navy and then sailing the world aboard his own ship.

He had only returned home after Marcus had murdered William.

The people of Besosa had no idea that El Moreno and the new Earl of Rothstone were the same man. It had been so long since anyone had seen him that no one recognized him as the sun-browned youth who had once pestered the villagers with his boyish pranks.

Many believed El Moreno to be a black sheep relative of the Rawnsleys. Others thought that El Moreno was enamored of *la patrona*, their lady, the Countess of Rothstone. The rumors flew and grew more outrageous every time he dropped anchor and went up to the great house to pay his respects.

Alex lifted his gaze to the stately manor on the hill. Though the distance was great, he thought he saw someone watching him from one of the windows. She knew he was home, he thought with a smile. She always knew.

A feminine shout made him jerk his head around. He had just enough time to catch the voluptuous young woman as she threw herself into his arms.

"*Querido*, you have returned to me at last." Her husky voice imbued the Spanish word for 'darling' with sensual promise. Ebony hair fell like hot silk over his hands clenched at her waist. Soft, rounded breasts pressed against his chest.

"Rosana." At a loss, Alex looked down into the hot brown eyes of the woman who had long been his lover.

She gave him a slow smile that once would have warmed his blood. Slyly, she insinuated one slender thigh between his legs. "So you remember me, Moreno."

He shifted so that she no longer pressed against his loins. "How could I forget?"

She frowned at his retreat and sinuously slid her arms around his neck. "To a man like you, I am just a woman." Her ruby lips pursed in a provocative pout.

"Never 'just' a woman, Rosana." With his hands on her waist, he managed to put a few inches between them. "I need to speak to you. Soon."

"Of course, *querido*." She eyed him like a starving woman at a feast. "Rosana is always here when you want her." Suddenly she pulled his head down to hers and kissed him intimately.

The crowd roared and the men laughed as Alex tried to free himself from her embrace. They had been lovers for months, and she knew exactly what to do to arouse him. Yet he felt nothing. Diana's sweet loving had spoiled him for anyone else.

He broke the kiss and saw confusion flicker across her face. "We have to talk," he repeated. "Meet me at the tavern in an hour."

"I will be there." She trailed a finger across his lips before sauntering away. Alex watched her, then shook his head, glad he had left Diana aboard ship. All hell would have broken loose if she had witnessed Rosana's antics.

* * *

From the deck of the *Vengeance*, Diana watched the couple embrace. Shaking from shock, she could not seem to take her eyes from the lovers. And lovers they were. Even she, in her relative innocence, recognized it.

McBride saw to the lowering of the boat that would take them to the island. Hearing the commotion, he cast a glance ashore and grinned. "It would seem Rosana hasn't forgotten the captain," he said to Birk.

Birk sent him a glare. "Hush up, you fool," he hissed. Turning to Diana, he took her hand in his. "Pay no mind to what you see, lassie. The wench is nothing to the captain."

"I would not agree, Mister Fraser." Squaring her shoulders, she tried to ignore the pain. "It would seem that I must reevaluate a few things. Obviously I was not as important to him as I thought."

"You're daft, woman. You mean more to him than you ken."

"No." She shook her head. "I should have expected this. Of course a man like Alex would have a mistress. It would be foolish to assume that there were no women in his life."

"He disna want Rosana," Birk insisted.

"I beg to differ, Mister Fraser." She held up a hand when Birk would have spoken again. "No. I believe I understand the situation quite well."

Birk muttered something under his breath, but Diana ignored him. She had thought that there was more to her and Alex's relationship than the physical. Obviously she had been wrong. Rather than cry about it as she longed to do, she pressed her lips together and maintained control. It had been naive of her to assume that one night had meant as much to him as it did to her. She would not make that mistake again. After all, it wasn't as if she loved the rogue . . .

Her thoughts halted as abruptly as if she had smacked into a stone wall. She did love him. By all the saints, Diana Covington, wealthy heiress and the pride of Port Royal, was in love with a pirate! The truth sparkled in her mind like a diamond, stunning her with its many hues and facets.

As she accepted the truth, strength flowed through her leaden limbs, revitalizing her. Yes, she loved him. She didn't know his full name or from whence he came, but she loved him. Even though he was a pirate, a wanted man, she loved him. She stood a little straighter and tilted her chin. Alex could kiss all the Spanish strumpets he wanted, but he was going to come to *her* bed that night.

She would see to it.

"I see that light in your eye, lass," Birk remarked. She merely smiled, and he shook his head. "A hot Spanish wench and a red-haired Scot fightin' over the same man. There's goin' to be a ruckus." He chuckled. "I wouldna want to be the captain. Then again, maybe I would."

Chapter 13

The sounds of the night masked the scrape of the shutters being forced open. Quietly, a man slipped through the window and paused, glancing about the moonlit room. He grinned as he spotted his quarry, then made his way to the ornate bed. Grabbing the mattress with both hands, he lifted it, dumping the occupant to the floor in a flurry of bedclothes.

"What the devil . . . !" Chilton spluttered and cursed, fighting his way free of the clinging sheets.

"You should not invoke the devil's name, Peter," the intruder said. He moved to the candle and lit it, then turned so the light played eerie shadows over his face. "Lest he appear."

"Marcus! Are you mad?" Chilton managed to get to his feet, then dug around in the pile of blankets until he found his nightcap. Plopping it on his nearly bald head, he looked back at the pirate, as if hoping he had imagined his presence. "What are you doing here at such an hour? Don't you realize you could be caught?"

"Only if you betray me, Peter." Marcus sat down in a nearby chair and withdrew a six-inch blade from its sheath. Examining the knife, he smiled and said, "And you would never do that, would you?"

Chilton swallowed hard. "Of course not. Never." He turned and scooped the blankets back onto the bed, then hurried to get beneath them, hiding his bare, bony legs from Marcus's penetrating gaze.

"I did not think so." Idly, Marcus began to clean his nails with the knife. "We have a problem that we need to discuss."

"What problem?" His gaze locked on the blade, Chilton clutched the bedclothes with white-knuckled fingers.

"El Moreno has interfered in our plans."

"El Moreno? What has he done now?"

"He had the temerity to attack my ship and make off with my lovely captive." Marcus held his hand out, fingers spread wide, to examine his manicure.

"You let him take her?" Chilton fisted his hand and pounded on the bed. "Everything is ruined now!"

"Let him?" Marcus repeated in a deadly voice. "*Let* him? I did not *let* him do anything! He damaged my ship—killed my men—clapped *me* in irons! And you say I *let* him?"

"Of course you did not let him," Chilton babbled, the color draining from his face. "You would never let such a thing happen. Ridiculous!"

"El Moreno is a bloody barnacle on my arse," Marcus sneered. "And the time has come to pry him loose."

"Indeed. Yes, I agree." Chilton tugged nervously at his nightshirt.

"I will get the wench back, and I will send El Moreno to hell on the point of my sword." The pirate grinned at the image. "I will make them both pay."

"Just . . . just remember not to kill Diana." Chilton cringed as Marcus turned his gaze on him. "She is to be my bride, you know."

"Ah, yes." Marcus turned the knife over and over in his hands and looked speculatively at Chilton. "I believe we must renegotiate, Peter."

"Re . . . renegotiate?"

"Indeed." Marcus tapped his chin with the flat of the blade. "I need to repair my ship. And there is a certain amount of revenge to be extracted. . . . Half ought to do nicely."

"Half?" Puzzled, Chilton frowned at Marcus. "Half of what?"

"The wench's dowry, of course." He pointed the knife at Chilton. "You do mean to wed her, correct?"

"Yes . . . I do . . . I just said that."

"Indeed. You will wed her, and we will divide her fortune between us. That should cover the cost of repairing my ship and replacing the men El Moreno killed." Marcus tossed the knife in the air and caught it again one-handed. "But there is the little matter of revenge, Peter. I must have it." He passed the knife from hand to hand. "Hmmm . . . I know. The wedding night."

"Wedding night? *My* wedding night?" Chilton swallowed hard. "You cannot mean—"

"*Droit de seigneur.*" Marcus smiled, pleased. "An excellent custom. I shall have half the riches as well as the bride's maidenhead." He chuckled and held the blade up to the candlelight. "I shall exact my vengeance on that sweet, fair skin."

"But . . . but she is *my* bride!" Chilton spluttered.

"You would deny me my revenge?" Marcus sat straight up and pinned Chilton with his stare. "A mere night's pleasure after all the trouble that red-haired witch has caused me?"

"I only meant—"

"You ungrateful bastard!" A flick of his wrist sent the knife streaking across the room. Chilton yelped as the weapon swept the nightcap from his head and pierced the wooden headboard with a thunk. The cap hung limply from the quivering blade.

Chilton turned frightened eyes to Marcus. The pirate rose and approached the bed. Yanking his knife from the headboard, he extended the weapon to Chilton, the nightcap still hanging from it.

"Next time," he said with a smile, "it will be your tongue."

Chilton snatched the cap from the blade and shrank into the bedclothes. Marcus laughed.

"Well, Peter? Do we have a bargain?"

"Yes, damn your eyes." Chilton plopped his cap on his head. "Though she will hate me for it."

Marcus shrugged. "Once she is your wife, she will have to obey you. 'Tis the law." He slid the knife back into its sheath. "As amusing as this is, I fear I must leave you, Peter. I shall notify you when I have the woman."

"See that you do." As Marcus moved toward the window, Chilton called after him, "And do not anticipate the vows. I must wed her first, or the dowry is lost."

Marcus paused, one foot on the windowsill. "Of course, Peter," he answered with a smile. "I would not dream of it."

"Very well, then." Chilton held the pirate's gaze for a long moment before looking away.

"Good night, Peter." Marcus slipped out the window. "Sweet dreams." His evil laugh echoed through the room long after he had left it.

Diana paced the tiny room above the Broken Lantern Tavern. Her gaze passed over the comfortable bed, sturdy washstand, ceramic water basin, and stubby candle. Apparently, Alex commanded the best accommodations available. Despite the cozy comfort of the room, however, she missed the intimacy of his cabin aboard the *Vengeance*.

She prowled the room, restless energy consuming her. She could not seem to stay still. Laughter echoed from below, combined with the sounds of men drinking and carousing. Occasionally, she heard a woman's playful shriek or a feminine peal of laughter. Obviously, the men were not celebrating alone.

Was Alex down there? She stopped pacing and frowned. Was he drinking with his men, his Spanish doxy in his arms? As the image came clearly to her, venomous feelings followed. She clenched her teeth as jealousy nipped at her. She despised herself for the emotion. She did not want to envy that black-haired whore—but she did.

She wanted to be the woman in Alex's arms. She was still not entirely comfortable with loving him, but she did not fool herself. She was indeed in love with the irritating man.

She admired his courage and his commanding presence. She reveled in his sharp wit and keen intelligence. His fierce temperament matched her own. No man had ever challenged her like he did. And most of all, he was a man with whom she could be free.

She had no need to hide her anger from him, as she did from her father or her other suitors. Every other man in Port Royal felt threatened when confronted with her temper and her stubbornness. Not Alex. His personality was powerful enough to complement hers. He seduced her with his sensuality and charmed her with his wit. His intelligence inspired her to think beyond the boundaries of her own world. Even as he tested her limits, his unapologetic strength comforted her and made her feel safe.

Last night she had fallen asleep thinking

they had merged in mind and soul as well as body. Even now she could feel the touch of his hands on her bare skin, the moist caress of his mouth on parts of her that had never seen the sun. She could hear his soft laughter at her flustered gasps, and she reveled in the fact that they did not always need words to communicate.

A loud crash followed by howls of laughter echoed up the stairs from the taproom, jolting her.

Here she stood reliving tender memories, while that scoundrel had abandoned her to make merry with his tawdry trollop. She had to speak to him. *Now*. She had to know what place she had in his life. Gathering her nerve, she marched to the door and flung it open.

Birk sat in the hall, his chair tipped back against the wall and a bottle in his hand. He paused in raising the whiskey to his lips. "Can I help you, lassie?"

"Aye, Mister Fraser." Hands on her hips, she tapped her foot. "I want to see Alex, and I want to see him now."

"Is that the way o' it?" Birk lowered the front legs of his chair to the floor.

Diana arched her brows. "It is. Now will you take me to him, or shall I search the taproom without you?"

Birk put down the bottle. "I ken you well enough to know that you'll do just that. I'd best go along to keep you out o' trouble."

*   *   *

"Must you go, Alejandro?" The Countess of Rothstone clung to her son's arm as he paused near the door to the walled garden. The full moon illuminated her tear-stained face.

"*Sí*, Mama." Alex squeezed her hands and pressed a kiss to her smooth forehead. It still amazed him that this beautiful woman with the ink-black hair and unlined skin had given birth to him some eight and twenty years ago. At two score and six, the countess had the youthful appearance of a woman ten years younger.

"I have missed you, *mi hijo*—my son." She smiled through the tears. "You were gone so long this time."

"I know." He brushed the moisture from her cheeks with the pads of his thumbs. "But I am very close. I had him, Mama. I will capture him again, and William's death will at last be avenged."

"And then you will come home? For good this time?"

"I hope so."

His mother reached up and cupped his face in her hands, her expression earnest. "You must come home, Alejandro. The estate needs your direction."

"I know, I know." He wrapped his arms around her and pulled her close, still reluctant to think about assuming the responsibilities of his title. All he had ever wanted was to sail the world freely, as he had done before his brother's murder. He was not a man to be tied to the land. Stepping back from the embrace, he met his mother's gaze.

He might not be tied to the land, but he was certainly bound to his family. And Miranda Rawnsley de Besosa, Countess of Rothstone, constituted all the family he had left. He would not disappoint her.

He squeezed her shoulders. "I promise that it shall all be over soon."

"Very well." She straightened and brushed the tears from her face. "I do not wish to waste our short time together with useless pleading. How long do you stay this time?"

"Only a day or two. Just long enough to lay in supplies and make some repairs to the *Vengeance*."

"So little time," she sighed.

"It is necessary." He grinned. "But this time you will not be alone when I leave."

"What do you mean by that?"

"I am leaving someone in your care. A young woman named Diana Covington."

"A young woman?" The countess's brows drew together in puzzlement. "Who is she? And why do you bring her here?"

"She is someone very special to me. She needs a safe place to stay while I go to hunt Marcus." He kissed her cheek. "I will tell you more on the morrow, when you meet her. For now I must take my leave. I will return in the morning."

"Be careful, Alejandro."

"I will." With one last tender touch to her

face, Alex slipped through the doorway in the wall, closing the iron gate behind him. He paused to listen to the soft rustle of his mother's skirts as she returned to the house, and the click of the door as she closed it behind her. He was alone in the silence of the night. Slowly, he began to pick his way along the narrow path that led back to the village.

The bright moonlight filtered through the trees, lighting the path in scattered patches. The briny breeze brushed through his hair and across his skin, soothing him like the touch of a lover. The distant lapping of the sea murmured to the night, like the whispers of a satisfied woman.

Diana.

Last night she had been warm and welcoming, her honest passion a balm to his tortured soul. Never had he met a woman who could touch the deepest parts of him like she could. There was more than passion between them, more than mutual liking and admiration. Yet as long as Marcus roamed free, he dared not give a name to this tender emotion that filled his heart.

He emerged from the trees to see the lights of the tavern before him. The flickering beam shining from the window of his room drew his attention and held it. He imagined Diana there, waiting for him. He quickened his step.

A shriek of feminine laughter emerged from the tavern, making him think of Rosana. She had not reacted well to his ending their relationship. He knew that her position had provided her with some sort of status, but he had not expected her fury to be so strong when he told her he no longer wanted her. It would be wise, he decided, to see that Rosana left the island. He would give her enough gold to start a new life somewhere else, so that she and Diana would never come into contact.

Diana had the heart of a warrior, but Rosana had the instincts of an adder. He had never before noticed the predatory side of his former mistress. Never noticed, or hadn't cared. He *cared* about Diana.

He smiled. Diana was strong and stubborn, yet also soft and feminine. Each emotion she felt exploded with vibrant life. She raged or sobbed or made love with all the energy and vitality she possessed. When she cared about someone, she stood by him with fierce loyalty.

She was the perfect mate for him.

She would probably throw things at him when they argued, and then scorch him with her passion when they made up. His body responded to the mental image of Diana beneath him, her legs wrapped around his waist as he . . .

He took a deep breath. The vision was entirely too clear. He reminded himself that there were still obstacles to overcome before he could plan a future with Diana. First he must capture Marcus. That duty came before all others.

A new thought occurred to him. He did not

feel duty-bound to wed Diana. He *chose* to make her his wife. Still, remembering that their sweet mating might bear fruit, he determined to marry her before he left the island. If he died by Marcus's hand, he wanted his child to have his name. He wanted *Diana* to have his name. She had entrusted her life and her innocence to a pirate, and he didn't want her to regret that decision.

And he would see to it that Henry Morgan validated their marriage, even though a Catholic ceremony would not normally be recognized by the Church of England. His wife and his child, were there one, would legally bear his name, no matter what happened. Morgan would see to it.

Enjoying a sense of peace he had not felt in a long time, he strode eagerly toward the tavern.

Diana stood on the bottom step of the staircase, her eyes wide at the sight before her. The taproom was crowded to bursting, the air smoky from dozens of pipes. In the center of the room a seaman beat out a steady rhythm on a small handmade drum, while another played the pipes. On top of the table beside them danced the woman who had greeted Alex so possessively on the shore.

Birk had called her Rosana.

The Spanish woman's black hair swirled around her like flowing satin, and her generous breasts swelled above her tightly laced black stomacher and white underdress. Her red hitched-up skirt revealed occasional glimpses of slender thighs as her lush body swayed in a blatantly sexual dance.

In response to the appreciative leers and cat-calls from the men, she danced faster, dipped lower, lifted her leg a bit higher. Diana stared, transfixed by the stark sensuality of the woman. Was this the kind of female Alex preferred? One who wore her sexuality as casually as another woman wore a cloak?

Behind her, Birk cleared his throat. "Ah, lassie, I see that Alex isna here. Perhaps we should wait for him in the room." He took her arm and turned back toward the stairs.

"No, I want to see this." Tugging loose of his grasp, she stepped out into the crowd. Birk cursed and followed her, glaring at any man who so much as looked at her.

She stopped near the table that served as Rosana's stage. Folding her arms over her chest, she studied the other woman.

Rosana stopped dancing when she noticed Diana. The sounds of the musicians faded to nothing. Rosana put her hands on her hips, raking her gaze over Diana with unconcealed scorn. The disappointed calls of the men quieted to a hush of anticipation as the two women silently appraised each other.

"So," Rosana spat. "You are the English whore."

A low murmur swept the room, broken by an occasional chuckle. Diana glanced at Birk as he opened his mouth to speak, silently warning him not to interfere. His face revealing his misgivings, the Scotsman pressed his lips together and said nothing. She turned her attention back to the dark-haired beauty and tilted her chin.

"I am English," she said. "And Scottish, too, since you ask. But I dare say that you would know more of whoring than I."

The crowd burst into laughter. Rosana's dark eyes flashed with fury. She sent a glare around the room before turning her attention back to Diana.

"Do you know who I am?" She tossed her head, sending black hair rippling over her shoulders. "I am Rosana. I am Moreno's woman."

"You *were* Moreno's woman," one of the barmaids called spitefully.

Diana raised her brows, wondering if she had encountered not a rival, but a woman scorned.

Rosana glared at the barmaid. "I am *still* Moreno's woman," she declared, then glared down at Diana in challenge.

Diana took in the woman's hitched-up skirts and overflowing bosom. "It looks to me like you are everyone's woman," she observed with amusement.

Laughter shook the walls of the tavern. Rosana's face reddened with rage. "So. Now you add to your crime with insults!"

"What crime?" Diana scoffed.

Rosana jumped down from the table. The

crowd obligingly moved out of the way. "You have tried to steal my man, *inglesa*."

"He was never yours. He merely rented you upon occasion."

The crowd snickered. Rosana glared them into silence before turning back to Diana. Her whole body trembled with wrath.

"You dare mock me? You, with your child's body and ugly red hair? My Moreno must have been desperate to have bedded such a creature." Rosana thrust her breasts forward. "*I* am more woman than most men can handle."

Diana rolled her eyes, growing tired of the conversation. "Mayhap 'tis why you seem to need more than one man."

"Whore! *Puta!*" Rosana clenched her hands into fists. "Moreno is mine, *inglesa*. See you remember that."

"See that *you* remember that El Moreno makes his own decisions." She gave the woman a pitying look. "I'm sorry he hurt you, but it is better if you just accept it." Diana turned away, determined to go back to her room and forget the entire unpleasant scene. She would wait for Alex to return. Then she would simply ask him what place she held in his life.

"It is you who must accept the truth," Rosana called after her. "Moreno has no need of an English whore when he can have Rosana."

Diana stopped, then turned to face the other woman, having reached the limit of her patience. "You keep coming back to the subject of whoring," she snapped. "I wonder why."

Titters of laughter came from the crowd. Rosana drew herself up, her lips compressing as her cheeks flamed. Diana shook her head, pitying the Spanish woman, then turned back toward the stairs.

"*Inglesa!*"

Diana ignored her and kept walking. Birk moved in front of her, clearing a path through the crowd.

"I am talking to you, *puta!*"

She had almost reached her destination when a low growl of fury sounded from behind her. She turned just as Rosana rushed up to her and shoved her. Hard.

"No one ignores Rosana!" the Spanish woman shrieked.

Diana stumbled backward into Birk, then righted herself. Before the Scotsman could interfere, she stepped up to Rosana and slapped the other woman across the face.

"There. Now I am not ignoring you," she retorted, her own temper flaring.

Rosana gasped and raised a hand to her reddening cheek. Stunned silence reigned in the taproom. Then, with a howl, she leaped at Diana.

The two women fell to the floor, clawing at clothing and yanking at hair. They crashed into tables and rolled over men's feet. Rosana wrestled Diana down and straddled her. With a triumphant smile, she pinned Diana's hands to the floor on either side of her head.

Diana turned her face and sank her teeth into Rosana's wrist. With a cry of pain, Rosana released Diana to cradle her own injured arm. "You bit me!"

"Aye." Diana shoved Rosana off her, sending the other woman tumbling into a nearby table. She rose to her feet and watched as an onlooker helped Rosana stand.

The dark-haired woman shook off the seaman's helping hands. Boisterous laughter echoed through the tavern, making her stiffen. She pushed her hair out of her face and glared at Diana with pure hatred.

"Today, *inglesa*, you die." She jerked up her skirt and yanked a slender dagger from the sheath strapped to her thigh.

Light flashed off the blade as Rosana lunged. Diana heard Birk cry out in alarm, but she kept her eyes on the weapon. As Rosana slashed at her face, Diana jumped back and avoided the blade. Rosana stabbed out again. Diana fell back another step. Her thigh bumped against a table.

Rosana came at her once more. Diana whirled out of the way, grabbing a bottle from the table as she did so. She came around swinging.

"Lassie!" Birk cried.

Horrified, yet unable to stop, Diana watched the bottle crash against the physician's skull, shattering on impact. Birk gave a startled grunt and crumpled to the floor.

"Birk!" Still holding the jagged neck of the

bottle, she crouched beside his inert form. She held a hand beneath his nose to see if he still breathed.

"Watch out!"

Diana whirled at the warning, but not quickly enough to avoid Rosana's blade. The blow that had been meant for her throat slashed her upper arm instead. Rosana lunged for her again, and Diana dove out of her crouch and tackled the Spanish woman around the legs, sending her crashing to the floor.

Diana scrambled to her feet, bottleneck at the ready. Rosana regained her own footing and took up a fighter's crouch, her blade gleaming in the candlelight. In the crowd, whispered wagers were placed. From the corner of her eye, Diana noticed that one of the barmaids tended to Birk.

"*Inglesa*," Rosana snarled.

"Trollop," Diana returned.

The two women circled each other, holding back at first, jabbing and darting to feel out the other's weaknesses. Little by little the jabs grew swifter, the slashes more serious. They stalked each other, both waiting for the perfect opening.

"*Puta*," Rosana hissed. She jabbed upward. "I will fix your face so Moreno will never look at you again."

"You can try." Panting, Diana ducked out of the knife's way and slashed with the broken bottle.

Rosana dodged and then leaped forward to

slice the air near Diana's stomach. The woman's eyes narrowed and Diana whirled out of the way just as the other woman swung wildly. Off balance at the unexpected move, Rosana stumbled. Diana grabbed her skirt and jerked her around, then grabbed Rosana's wrist. She twisted it, forcing the other woman to drop the weapon, then shoved her.

As Rosana stumbled backward, Diana grabbed the knife from the floor and tossed aside the broken bottle. Shrieking with rage at the sight of her weapon in Diana's hand, Rosana threw herself at Diana with the obvious intent of knocking her down.

Diana sidestepped the move, and as Rosana's momentum sent the other woman crashing to the floor, she closed in, straddling Rosana's back. Grabbing a handful of ebony hair, she yanked the other woman's head back and pressed the dagger to her throat.

"Do you surrender?" The soft words sounded unusually loud in the silence of the room. Rosana nodded as much as she was able. Diana relaxed her grip, but not her guard.

"What the devil is going on here?"

Diana jerked her gaze in the direction of that familiar, authoritative voice and saw Alex standing in the doorway of the tavern. Hands on his hips, he glared and awaited an answer.

Chapter 14

Alex stared at the tableau of Diana holding a blade to Rosana's throat. Pride surged hard and fast ahead of the many emotions that inundated him. He had no doubt that Rosana had incited the altercation—but she had not expected Diana to finish it, he thought with a quick flash of amusement,.

Still, a man did not want his intended bride engaging in tavern brawls. Especially not with a woman of loose morals who had once been his mistress! And what the hell was Diana doing in the taproom anyway? He had left her upstairs in his room, under guard, protected. He had left orders that she was to stay there until he himself came to fetch her. Someone would suffer his wrath for this.

"I said, what the devil is going on here?" he repeated darkly.

Rosana, whose face had been a mask of thwarted fury only moments before, assumed a frightened expression.

"Oh, Moreno," she sobbed. "She is trying to kill me!"

Alex merely raised an eyebrow, more than familiar with Rosana's machinations. "Release her, Diana."

Diana gave him an arch look, but removed the blade from the other woman's throat and released the grip on her hair. Rosana's head hit the floor with a thump. Diana rose from her position on Rosana's spine and took a step back. Rosana leaped to her feet and ran to Alex.

"Oh, *gracias*, Moreno!" The Spanish woman threw her arms around Alex and lay her head on his chest. "She is *loca*, a madwoman! She was jealous and tried to kill me."

"Would anyone care to tell me what just occurred here?" he asked, ignoring Rosana. He looked around the room. No one would meet his gaze. A groan claimed his attention as Birk stumbled toward him, holding his head as if it might fall off at any moment. The trickle of blood at his temple alerted Alex to the fact that injury, not drunkenness, caused his friend's unsteadiness.

"Birk! What happened to you?" Pushing Rosana away, he went to his friend and steadied him with a hand on his shoulder.

"The lassie near killed me with a bottle o' whiskey." Birk gave a faint imitation of his usual mischievous grin. "I was plannin' on doin' that myself, you ken."

"I understand." Alex glared at his former mistress. "I do not take kindly to those who wound my men."

"It wasna that one, Captain." With pride in

his voice, Birk indicated Diana. "It was the other. The *Scottish* lassie."

"Indeed." Alex looked at Diana, who sat on a bench with her arms folded. He studied her profile until she turned her head to face him. Their eyes met in a moment of silent communication. " 'Twould seem you are of a murderous bent this night, my sweet."

"Only through error or provocation, Captain."

Though tempted to smile at her spirited answer, he managed to keep his expression solemn. "Tell me what happened here."

She shrugged. "Of the one," she said, indicating Birk, " 'twas a matter of his hard head appearing where it did not belong. Of the other, 'twas a matter of defending myself."

"She lies!" Rosana cried. "*She* tried to kill *me*!" She grabbed Alex's arm. "She is jealous of me, Moreno. When she found out that I am your woman, she came down here and attacked me."

"You lie!" Birk snarled, his tone so ferocious that Rosana flinched. "It was *you* that was jealous, wench!"

"Birk." Alex gave the physician a quelling look, then gently peeled Rosana's fingers from his arm. "Our association is at an end, Rosana," he said quietly. "I thought we settled this."

"I cannot believe that you leave me for *her*," Rosana wailed. "She insulted me—attacked me—tried to kill me!"

"It was *you* that started the insults, you jealous wretch," Birk growled. "And *you* were the one to draw first blood!"

"First blood?" Alex looked at Diana, a cold feeling settling in the pit of his stomach. "You are wounded?"

" 'Tis naught but a small cut."

With a grim expression, he pulled her from the bench, turning her so that he could see her torn sleeve and the jagged slice that marred her upper arm.

"Were you hiding this from me?"

" 'Tis nothing. Mister Fraser can see to it." She dismissed the wound with a shrug.

"Mister Fraser has done quite enough for one evening," he snapped, suddenly remembering who had been guarding Diana's door. "And as for you, Rosana . . ." He turned to face his former mistress, keeping a proprietary hand on Diana's arm. "You will explain your actions."

"She tried to kill me!" Rosana looked around the room in a plea for support, but no one stepped forward to lend credence to her words. She stood alone in her lie. "So," she snarled, her features contorting with fury. "This is how much our time together has meant to you. You would toss me aside for this skinny she-dog!"

"I treated you with respect, Rosana." He gave her a contemptuous look. "Obviously more than you deserved."

Rosana stiffened, inhaling sharply. She glanced from him to Diana, her dark eyes a mirror of seething rage. "You will see," she spat, pointing at Diana. "You hold Moreno in your arms now, but soon he will leave you alone in your cold bed while he visits his rich *puta* on the hill! Then you will be alone . . . as I am."

Alex clenched his jaw and reminded himself that Rosana had no idea she had just insulted his mother. "Rosana," he warned.

"Do not deny it, Moreno," the Spanish woman hissed. "The whole island knows that she is your true love, that someday you will return with a ship full of gold and marry her." She sent Diana a hard look. "Until then, the rest of us are just bodies to warm your bed."

"Enough. I think it is best if you leave the island. Mister McBride will see to it." He gestured, and McBride stepped from the crowd.

Rosana paled. She sent a pleading glance around the room, but no one would look at her. Eyes shining with tears, she straightened her spine, tossed her black mane, and swept toward the door. She paused in the doorway and looked back at Diana.

"Beware, *inglesa*. Do not give your heart to him. His is already given." She turned her back and flounced out of the tavern.

Alex gave a brief nod at the door, and McBride hurried after her.

Birk's voice shattered the quiet left by Rosana's exit. "Would you be needin' me to tend the lassie? I can fetch my tools."

"Nay, Birk. I shall tend her myself." Alex

gave him an angry look. "See to your own wound, my friend. Then you can present yourself to me tomorrow morning and explain why you disobeyed my orders."

"Aye, Captain," Birk sighed.

Alex swept Diana into his arms and resisted the impulse to crush her to him. He could have lost her. Tonight's incident only reinforced his decision to leave her behind while he went after Marcus. With Rosana gone, she would be safe.

Holding her close, he carried her out of the tavern and into the night.

The dark warm silence enveloped them as if they had stepped into another world. The sounds of the tavern faded, drowned out by the crunch of Alex's footfalls as he picked his way along a narrow path through the tropical vegetation.

"Where are you taking me?" Diana asked.

"Hush." Her heart stopped at the tender smile he gave her, then sped up again at his intimate whisper. "I'm taking you to a secret place."

She laid her head against his shoulder and enjoyed the way his muscles flexed beneath her cheek. His heart pounded against the hand she rested upon his chest. She knew he was displeased by what had happened at the tavern and did not look forward to whatever scolding awaited. But his gentle care pleased her.

Perhaps now he would see that she could

take care of herself, she thought, nuzzling her face into his shirt. She had defended herself against Rosana and won. Maybe now that she had proven herself before the entire crew, he would reconsider his decision to leave her here.

The path abruptly opened into a clearing. Diana stared, her mouth falling open in delight. Vegetation surrounded the clearing on three sides, crowding up against a craggy hill that rose high above their heads. From somewhere atop the rocky formation a stream of water snaked down to empty into a quiet pool at the hill's base. Moonlight shimmered off the rippling surface of the water.

"What do you think?" His quiet tone blended with the trill of insects calling to their mates and the soothing splash of the water.

" 'Tis beautiful."

"I knew you would like it."

As he walked forward, his footsteps grew muffled by the softer ground near the pool. Diana looked around with awe. It was an enchanted place, the air heavy with the scent of hibiscus, the trickling sound of the water blending with the whisper of the breeze through the trees to create nature's music. The world beyond the clearing seemed far away.

Alex stopped at a boulder near the edge of the water. He released Diana, guiding her so that she slid down along his body. She was breathless by the time he stepped away from her, her pulse thrumming even from that brief contact.

"Sit down." She sat on the boulder, and he caressed her cheek with his fingers before turning away.

Her heart tripped into double time as he stripped off his shirt. Moonlight played off the sculpted sinew of his chest and arms as he ripped two strips of material off the bottom of the garment.

"What are you doing?"

"Making a bandage." He smiled. "Never worry, my sweet. I have other shirts."

She watched him as he turned away from her, his breeches pulling tautly across his trim backside as he crouched beside the pool. He reached down to soak a strip of cloth in water, and the motion made the muscles of his back ripple in a most enticing way. Her palms itched to stroke him. Then he rose and came to kneel before her, his head almost at a level with her own, and she clenched her hands into fists.

"I need to see that wound."

Still absorbed in the flush of awakening desire, she presented her arm. He shook his head. "No, the sleeve is in the way." Meeting her gaze, he gave her a lusty grin. "You will have to remove your gown."

A quiver vibrated along her spine. Danger blended with the obvious desire in his eyes, exciting her. She knew he would never hurt her. But there was something thrilling about the way his passion seemed barely under control.

"Diana," he said softly. "Take it off."

Without a word, she kept her eyes on his and reached behind her to fumble for the laces. After a few moments with no progress, he chuckled and reached around her.

"Allow me." His fingers brushed hers. She dropped her hands to her thighs, bunching her skirt in her fists as the familiar hunger slowly grew. She could feel the tug from his hands plucking at the laces. The bodice loosened. He tugged at it until her upper body remained clad in nothing more than the smocklike chemise. For a moment he just looked at her. She followed his gaze and realized that the shadowy impression of her nipples could be seen through the thin white material. She started to raise her hands to cover herself, but then he turned his attention to her wound. After a moment's hesitation, she dropped her hands to her lap again.

He rolled up the elbow-length sleeve of the chemise until the wound was exposed. Dabbing at it with the damp scrap of cloth, he said, " 'Tis not a deep cut. Your gown seems to have taken the brunt of it."

She took a shaky breath. He curled the fingers of one hand around her bare arm as he cleaned the slash with the other. His touch made her tremble.

"Better to have taken a death blow," she quipped, trying to control the craving flowing through her veins. " 'Tis the only gown I have, and not even one petticoat to speak of."

"I would not mourn the lack." He used the other scrap of cloth as a makeshift bandage and tied it around her arm. Then he looked up at her. The hunger in his dark gaze made her heart skip a beat. He smoothed one hand along her thigh. "I do not miss those many layers between me and your soft skin."

"Alex." Even she heard the undisguised longing in her voice.

He took her hand and stood, pulling her to her feet all in one fluid movement. "Come, let us bathe."

"Together?"

Her scandalized gasp made him laugh. "Aye, my sweet. Together."

She blushed at the teasing note in his voice. Then she squealed as he expertly stripped the gown from her, letting it crumple to the ground in a pool of saffron silk. He overrode her exclamations of modesty and pulled the chemise over her head, then crouched down to tug the slippers from her feet, leaving her naked before him.

"You are so beautiful," he whispered, looking up at her. Without rising to his feet, he reached out and caressed her stomach. "Your skin is glorious."

"So are you." She touched his shoulder, his hair. "You are the most beautiful man I have ever seen."

He rose, gliding his hands all the way up her

body to cup her face. Something inside her loosened and yielded to the mastery in his touch.

" 'Tis not just your fair looks of which I speak." He tugged the ribbon from her hair. " 'Tis your courage. Your spirit. Your excellent fighting skills."

She gave a breathless laugh as he lifted a lock of her hair to his lips. "You may thank my father for the last. 'Twas he who decided a young woman living so close to Port Royal needed to know how to defend herself. Truth be told, the knife is the only weapon I wield well."

"Never forget your tongue," he teased, twining her hair slowly and surely around his finger. "It is indeed deadly."

"To other men, but not to you." Her newly awakened needs clamored for attention, making her bold. She pressed herself against him. "I understand that you, too, wield your weapon well."

"Indeed." He wrapped his arms around her and lowered his head. "Come here, wench, and I will demonstrate."

Even as her blood simmered, some demon within her made her slip from his grasp just when his lips would have met hers. "Alas, kind sir, I cannot. My captain has ordered me to bathe."

"Mayhap your captain has other orders for you as well." His heated gaze followed her movements as she slowly waded into the pool.

Expecting the water to be cold, she gave a yelp of surprise that made Alex grin.

" 'Tis warm!" she exclaimed.

"Aye, this pool is always warm. Go to the center."

She did so, then squealed, "Bubbles!"

"Indeed. The pool is fed from an underground source, and the water bubbles up through cracks in the rock."

She laughed with delight, holding her hands out so the bubbles tickled her palms.

"You look like a water nymph," he said huskily.

She slanted her gaze to his, hearing the rumble of desire behind the words. A quick glance confirmed that he was heavily aroused. Heat seared her cheeks, and she looked into his eyes once more. She had never known that a man's eyes could look like that, hungry and dark with need.

Suddenly she was very conscious of the fact that he was dressed and she was not. She shivered, though not from cold. Her nipples hardened and her flesh rippled with reaction under his blatantly sexual regard. She crossed her arms over her breasts.

"No." His voice came to her across the water, quiet yet commanding. Something feminine inside her responded to that tone of voice, and she realized that he wanted to see her. She slowly lowered her arms to her sides.

"That's right. Let me look at you." He studied her, taking in every curve of her body, every shade of her skin, every involuntary ripple of muscle. "Stand straight, and toss back your hair."

She obeyed him, compelled by the quiet authority in his voice. His gaze slid over her like hot wax, and she stood proudly, aware that her breasts thrust forward for his inspection.

He made a sound of approval. "Lift your hands and cup your breasts."

Her eyes widened. "What?"

"You heard me. Do it, my beautiful water sprite. Now."

Slowly she obeyed, lifting her hands and cupping her breasts. Her eyes drifted closed, and her blush deepened. Her pose made her seem as if she were offering herself to him, like a sacrifice to a pagan god. The idea thrilled rather than alarmed her.

He gave a low purr of encouragement. "Yes, like that. You have no idea how arousing you look, my sweet."

Her breath panted between parted lips as she kept her eyes closed and waited for further instructions. There was a rustling sound, then a quiet splash. She opened her eyes just as Alex reached out to cover her hands with his.

Her blood thundered in her ears. The things he had told her to do seemed so forbidden, so exciting, and she couldn't imagine what was next.

He pressed her hands against her breasts, plumping the soft globes, pushing them together, gently pinching and rolling the nipples.

Scandalous. Simply, incredibly scandalous. It was one thing for him to caress her, but for him to guide her hands and have her do it to herself . . . A knot of hunger tightened in her loins, making her press her legs together.

A low growl emerged from his throat.

She glanced up, lost to the sweeping emotions that simmered through her. "Alex?" she whispered uncertainly.

"Spread your legs," he said quietly.

Her breath caught. She couldn't move.

He gave her a tender smile and reached down himself, slipping a hand between her thighs to cup her feminine mound. "Spread your legs, my sweet. Trust me, you'll like it."

She shifted, opening her legs. He took her hips in his hands and tugged her forward a step.

"Oh!" She started to move away, but he held her still. "Alex, this is . . . oh, my goodness!" The bubbles rippling up from the floor of the pool vibrated delicately along her inner thighs and over her feminine folds. The sensation was incredibly erotic.

"Do you like that?" he murmured. He placed her hands firmly on his shoulders, then cupped her breasts again, rubbing the nipples with his thumbs.

"Alex . . ." It was all she could manage. Her knees weakened, and she clung to him, lost in a haze of new and tingling sensation.

"You look so beautiful," he murmured, lifting a hand to her face. "Your eyes are so wide,

I can see everything you're feeling. It makes me hot." He pressed a gentle, lingering kiss to her parted lips.

Her entire body felt flushed with warmth. The tickling caress of the bubbles, and the tender touch of this man who knew her body so well, bathed her in a carnal hunger that she had never felt before.

"Alex." It was all she could say, all she wanted to say. She arched into him, craving more, needing everything.

"Easy, my sweet." His hands slid over her bottom and pulled her tightly against him, sealing his erection tightly against her belly. At the feel of his shaft, hard and hot between them, she purred in the back of her throat and rubbed against him, guided by primitive instincts that she barely understood. As she spread openmouthed kisses over his chest, he let out a low groan.

"I meant this to be slow," he whispered harshly. His finger traced the indentation between her buttocks, spiking her arousal higher.

"Not slow," she insisted, reaching between them to take his hardness in her hand. She explored him with fascination, alternately squeezing him and stroking him with an urgency that was contagious.

"Dear God, woman." He closed his eyes, his fingers spasming on her bottom as he nipped at her neck and shoulder. "I want to be inside you."

"Yes," she gasped.

"You feel so good when I'm inside you," he muttered. "So hot and tight." He lifted her off her feet with his hands on her bottom. "Put your legs around me," he urged.

She eagerly complied, his words wildly arousing her. As she curled her legs around his lean waist, he held her with one hand on her bottom and dipped the other between her thighs. He stroked the flesh that had been rendered so intensely sensitive by the bubbles, making her whimper and clench the muscles of her womb. A rumble of masculine satisfaction escaped his throat. Then he took his hand away and guided himself into her.

She moaned at the sweet invasion. She could feel herself stretching around him, and gloried in the feeling of being *taken*. He sheltered her with his strength, holding her steady with both hands on her bottom. His muscles quivered, and perspiration misted his skin. His shaft touched her womb, and she realized that she was completely filled by him. She tightened her legs around his waist, squeezing him with her inner muscles. He groaned and opened his eyes.

For a moment they stared at each other, savoring the exquisite sensation of being one.

As if he were content to hold still inside her forever, he dipped his head to place a soft kiss on her lips. The kisses continued, as gentle as the touch of a flower petal, at the corners of her mouth, on her jaw, beneath her ear.

Her head spun as he introduced her to a new

kind of loving. Their first encounter had been passionate and urgent. Now he took his time. Tasting her. Absorbing her. Learning her.

He nibbled along her throat to her collarbone. His gentle handling was lighter than the breeze blowing through the trees, yet as potent as a bolt of lightning. He murmured sweet words against her skin, his lips tenderly exploring the resilience of her flesh. Her body had no secrets from him. There were no places he did not touch, taste, or tease. The contrast of the chastity of his kisses with his erection deep inside her drove her mad.

She slid her hands over his wet flesh, learning what pleased him. Copying his movements, she brought forth groans of pleasure from him.

"I love you," she whispered against his skin.

He murmured her name and pulled her closer.

Her body pulsed as his hands and mouth coaxed her to the peak of desire. His caresses seduced her with heartbreaking tenderness and devastating experience. She arched her back as he took her beaded nipple into his mouth and suckled.

Moaning and trembling with reaction, she begged, "Please."

He shifted his stance, moving within her and making her gasp. The bubbles brushed against her bottom, and she realized that he must have angled her that way for just that reason. Her skin prickled with sensitivity. Every touch seemed magnified a hundred times.

"Please," she whispered again.

"I will please you," he murmured. He slid one hand between them and stroked her where their bodies joined.

She stiffened, her inner muscles clenching tightly around him as the climax ripped through her, the slow river of passion suddenly raging. Bent to its will, she rode the rapids toward the falls and slipped over, rushing down a waterfall of pleasure so intense that she must have dreamed it. She hit the bottom with a splash that stole the breath from her lungs. Her limbs like water, she clung to him and waited for her tilting world to right itself again.

When her tremors ceased, Alex pulled out of her and slowly carried her to shore. He seated himself on the boulder and settled her in his lap.

"Are you all right?" He stroked the hair back from her face.

"Aye." She took a shuddering breath. "But what about you? You didn't . . . you still appear quite . . . ready."

"I am, but I didn't want us to drown." With a sensual smile, he lifted her and arranged her thighs on either side of his. "Tell me, milady. Do you ride?"

"On occasion." She balanced herself with her hands on his shoulders.

"My sweet," he said with a kiss to her lips, "you ride tonight." He lowered her slowly onto his straining shaft.

She moaned with delight as he filled her once more. Closing her eyes, she shifted her hips, shuddering at the feel of him inside her ultra-sensitive channel.

He cupped her hips in his hands and began to slide her up and down with powerful, un-hurried movements. She picked up the rhythm, using her inner muscles to caress him. His groans of pleasure spurred her on. Her nails scored his shoulders as she shifted to find a better seat and tightened her legs around his flanks. Her hair whipped around them, and fi-nally she surged with him over the edge into a storm of potent pleasure.

Much later Alex led Diana back to his room at the tavern. The candles were already lit and the bed neatly made. Alex latched the door be-hind him.

She glanced toward the window, where she could see the full moon shining in the dark night sky. Regret squeezed her heart as she thought of their moonlit paradise by the pool. She sighed, not wanting the magic to end.

Alex snuffed a candle at the far side of the room, leaving the one beside the bed still lit. "What troubles you, Diana?"

"I did not want to leave the pool." She gave him a sad smile. " 'Twas such a beautiful place."

"It was indeed." He took her in his arms, pressing a kiss to her forehead. Then he grinned, his eyes taking on a wicked gleam.

"Should you ever need assistance while bathing again, I offer my services."

"Why, thank you, kind sir." She traced a finger over his heart. "I will be sure to summon you when your 'services' are needed."

"Mouthy wench." He grinned and swatted her bottom, then turned to pull back the coverlet from the bed.

"Wench? Is that all I am, just another woman warming your bed?" She said the words teasingly, though part of her was serious.

He paused and looked at her. "Is this about Rosana?" he asked quietly.

She shrugged. "I simply want to know my place in your life."

"I ended my association with Rosana as soon as we arrived."

"All right." She longed to ask him if there were any other women, but decided to content herself with what he had revealed thus far. "How long will the repairs to the ship take?"

"Two days, perhaps three to lay in stores." He sat on the edge of the bed and started to take off his boots.

"I want to go with you."

He dropped a boot to the floor with a thud, then stared at her. "We discussed this. You are *not* going."

"We did not 'discuss' this, Captain. *You* issued an order."

He removed his other boot. "Indeed I did. You will stay here, where it is safe."

"Have I not proven my worth?" She

propped her hands on her hips. "I am not help-less."

"I said no."

"But—"

"No!" he shouted. "Bloody hell, woman, are you deaf?"

She stiffened her spine. "I am not. Neither, I suspect, are the people in the taproom."

"You are not going," he said in a slow, deliberate tone. "My decision is final."

"Why?"

"*I want you safe!*" He leaped to his feet and threw one boot across the room. It hit the wall and fell to the floor. They both stared at it. Then they looked at each other. "Diana," he said almost pleadingly, "I need to know that you are safe."

"I am safe with you," she answered quietly. "I can defend myself. Why won't you relent? Let me come with you."

"Because Marcus is a murderer, that's why." He sat on the bed again and stripped off his stockings. "I don't want you within ten leagues of him."

She heard something in his voice, something that sounded like fear. His reaction seemed too extreme for a mere rivalry between two pirates. "Alex, why do you hate Marcus so? It is more than competition, isn't it?"

He paused in the act of removing his shirt, then pulled the garment over his head. Folding it with precise care, he laid it on the floor beside the bed.

"Alex?"

He looked at her. For a moment she saw a terrible pain in his eyes. Then he masked it. Very quietly, he said, "He murdered someone I loved."

"A woman?" She held her breath as she awaited the answer.

"No, my brother." He stood and unbuttoned his breeches.

"Oh, Alex, I am so sorry." She wanted to go to him, but something about the set of his shoulders warned her not to.

" 'Tis done." He paused, breeches unfastened, and put his hands on his hips. "But now you see why I cannot allow you near Marcus. If I am to do what I must, I have to know that you are safe, Diana."

"But—"

"I no longer wish to speak of this." He stripped off the breeches and placed them neatly with the rest of his clothing. "I suggest you ready yourself for bed."

She longed to assuage his pain. Ignoring his naked body, she put her hands on her hips and raised her chin. "I would do that, Captain," she replied in a saucy tone, "had I any nightclothes. What do you suggest I wear?"

He slipped beneath the covers and settled himself against the pillows, hands folded behind his head. The haunted look left his eyes, replaced by a wicked gleam. "What you always wear to bed with me, my sweet. Nothing."

"Alex!"

He gave her a lusty grin. "Come, milady. Your stallion awaits."

"You . . . you . . ." Her words stumbled to a halt, her cheeks reddening.

"What was that you were saying?" He threw back the bedclothes to reveal his readiness for her. "You—rogue? You rake? You scoundrel?"

She tore her eyes away from his naked glory and met his gaze squarely. "Aye, all of those!"

"Indeed?" He leered and patted the bed next to him. "Come lie with me, my lovely, and I shall try to live up to your expectations."

"Perhaps I am tired." She feigned a yawn, all the while delighting in the excitement bubbling through her veins. He looked so dangerous, and so desirable, his bronzed, muscular body laid out against the snowy linens like a banquet for her to savor. She wanted nothing more than to feast on him, but she held back and let the anticipation grow.

"Come to me, Diana." He paused. "Or shall I come and fetch you?"

He *would* come fetch her, she thought with a little thrill. With trembling fingers, she managed to unlace her gown and step out of it. She avoided looking at him as she slipped off her chemise and discarded her slippers. Finally she approached the bed.

He closed strong, sun-browned hands around her waist and pulled her down on top of him.

"Alex!" Wriggling free, she scooted to her side of the bed.

"Aye, my love?"

She froze. Love? Had he really called her that? She chanced a glance at him. He looked no different, certainly not like a man who had just made a declaration. Mayhap it had been a slip of the tongue. A meaningless endearment.

But as she gave herself up to his embrace, she couldn't help but wish that his tongue would slip again. And mean it.

Chapter 15

Alex blinked against the glare of the morning sun. He started to lift his arm to shade his eyes, but something warm and heavy pinned the limb to the bed. Memory rushed back as he looked at Diana curled against his side, her coppery curls spilling over his chest. With a nostalgic smile, he fingered one of the silky locks and considered the events of the night before.

How could he have known that he would ever feel like this? Tenderness engulfed him as she shifted in her sleep, cuddling closer to him. She was so soft, so delicate, and yet that slender body housed a fiery temperament and a bottomless well of emotion that amazed him. He had never felt this way before.

Not even about Bianca.

He tried to recall Bianca's face, and found he couldn't. She had been built much like Diana, but there the similarity between the two women ended. Bianca had thought him huge and terrifying, a rutting beast. She had hardly spoken to him above a whisper, and almost never unless he spoke to her first. She had certainly never kicked him in the shin or brazenly offered herself to him. He realized with sudden hindsight that he and Bianca had been ill-suited.

A small amount of the guilt he had carried for so long shifted. They had been two completely different people, he mused, idly stroking a hand over Diana's slim hip. He had always been a man of strong passions. Bianca had intended to enter a convent when her father signed the betrothal agreement.

This fact took on greater meaning as he considered it from a new perspective. Bianca had not been prepared for marriage, much less the marriage bed. She had been completely incapable of dealing with his strong sexual appetites. One night her fear had caused her to flee from him, and she had fallen down the stairs and broken her neck. He stared up at the ceiling and let out a slow breath. Bianca should have been allowed to give herself to the church. She had not been meant to be any man's wife.

Mayhap her death had not entirely been his fault.

"Good morning."

Diana's soft voice broke into his thoughts, dispelling the ghosts of the past. He looked down into her face and stroked a thumb over her lips. "Good morning, *amada*." *Beloved*, he echoed in his mind. He gazed at her so long that she flushed.

"Alex, cease your staring." She pulled the covers to her chin.

"Very well." He yanked the bedclothes from her hands and pulled her atop him. Her soft curves molded to his body and aroused him all over again. He took her mouth in a long, thorough kiss.

She was breathless when he finally released her.

" 'Tis indeed a pleasant morning," he said. Then he slapped her bare buttocks. "Up with you, wench! We have much to do today."

" 'Twas not I who started things," she muttered, rubbing her abused posterior.

He laughed at her disgruntled tone and kissed her lips. "Fetch your clothes, my sweet." He tumbled her from atop him and rose from the bed.

Diana stretched out on the mattress and surreptitiously eyed his naked body. Memories of their passion swept through her mind, and her cheeks heated as she remembered her own abandon. She was still not quite comfortable with this new aspect of her personality. She tore her gaze away and glanced out the window. The sun shone brightly in a clear, blue sky.

" 'Tis a beautiful morning," she said.

"Indeed. A fine morning." Whistling, Alex did up the buttons of his breeches. "Come, you lazy wench. We have no time to lie abed all day."

She sat up, pushing her hair out of her face. "And why is that?"

"We are going visiting this morning."

"Who are we going to see?" She slid from the bed, very self-conscious of her nudity.

Grinning, he pulled on his shirt. "We are going to call on the countess. I always visit her when I am here."

"Oh." She bent and picked up the damaged yellow silk she had worn the day before. She had no wish to meet this mysterious countess, though she should probably be flattered that he deigned to introduce her. Fingering the torn and bloody sleeve, she said, "This seems the worse for wear."

He frowned as he tucked the edges of a fresh black shirt into the waist of his breeches. "I suppose I shall have to find something. I can't introduce you to M—the countess in blood-stained clothing."

"I suppose not," she echoed in a thin voice. She had noticed his slip of the tongue. What had he been about to call the countess? Obviously, he did not normally use her title. Perhaps they were on such intimate terms that she allowed him to use her given name.

Rosana's accusations came back to her. *The whole island knows that she is your true love, that someday you will return with a ship full of gold and marry her. Until then, the rest of us are just bodies to warm your bed.*

She looked out the window again, her heart heavy. If Rosana was to be believed, then Diana was about to meet the woman who held the key to Alex's heart. Was the countess truly the woman Alex loved, or was this merely another figment of Rosana's jealousy?

She would soon find out.

An hour later, Alex escorted her to the door of the huge manor house.

"Are you certain I am presentable?" Diana asked for the third time.

"You look beautiful." Alex gave her an approving look.

Diana glanced down at the outfit he had bought for her: a dark brown skirt and a new chemise, with a stomacher that was more laces than material. It was a more provocative outfit than she was used to wearing, but it was the standard costume for the women of the island. She had tied her hair back with ribbons, in an attempt to attain a modest effect that was absent from most of the village wenches.

"I feel strange in these clothes, though I admit they are cooler than what I would normally wear."

"Indeed they are." After rapping the heavy brass knocker against the door, he raised her hand to his lips and teased her knuckles with his tongue. "They are also easier to get off you."

"Alex, stop." She snatched her hand away, her body warming at the lusty look in his eyes.

"But, darling, I thought you enjoyed my kisses," he teased.

"I am sure she does."

Both of them turned at the sound of the voice. While they had been talking, the door had been opened by a woman of such beauty that Diana felt a pang of envy. Though she didn't want to believe Rosana's words, she could easily see how Alex might love this woman.

She was older than Diana had expected. Strands of silver shot through her luxurious midnight-black hair, but few lines marred her porcelain-like skin. Clad in black satin, she possessed the rounded curves and trim waist of a much younger woman.

Alex smiled. "What are you doing opening your own door?" he teased with a tender note in his voice. "Do you not have servants for that very purpose?"

"I do." Her dark gaze settled on him with distinct disapproval. "But I wanted to greet you myself, Alejandro. We have much to discuss."

Diana wondered at her tone. Was she displeased that Alex had brought another woman to her home? And why did the countess wear black in this heat? Was she in mourning, and if so, for whom? Her husband, perhaps? Was it only the mourning period that kept the countess and Alex apart?

"Indeed, we have much to talk about," Alex said, apparently undisturbed by the countess's tone. He pulled Diana forward. "Diana, I am pleased to present to you Lady Miranda Rawnsley de Besosa, Countess of Rothstone. My lady, may I present Mistress Diana Covington of Jamaica?"

"I am most pleased to have you in my home," Lady Rothstone said. "Please come in."

"Thank you," Diana murmured, stepping reluctantly through the door. *Miranda*, she thought, recalling Alex's slip of the tongue back at the tavern. *He must have been about to say Miranda, but he caught himself. Was Rosana right? Does he love her? And if so, what part do I hold in his life?*

She resolved to watch the two closely to gauge their relationship for herself.

Alex frowned as he followed Diana into the house. He could tell that something was bothering her, and he made a note to ask her about it later.

"I was just breaking my fast when you arrived," the countess said. "I hope you will both join me."

The pointed look Lady Rothstone sent Alex made the words not a request, but a command.

"We would be honored," he responded obediently.

"Excellent." Giving them a regal nod, the countess led them through the house into an ornate dining room. Alex allowed both his mother and Diana to precede him into the room; then he followed. He stopped dead in the doorway.

"Good mornin' to you, Captain." His mouth full of food, Birk saluted them with a piece of bread. "And to you as well, lassie."

Alex shot his mother a look of outraged anger as she seated herself at the head of the table, beside Birk. "What the devil is this?"

"Breakfast," Birk answered. He turned to the countess. "More chocolate, milady?" At her nod, he poured hot cocoa into her cup.

"How long has this been going on?" Forgetting Diana's presence, Alex placed his hands flat on the table across from Birk and leaned forward. His entire body vibrated with the urge to smash his fist into his best friend's face.

"Breakfast? Since the dawn o' time, my friend." Birk sipped at his glass of Madeira and grinned. "Set yourself down, Alex. Have a bite to eat."

"My stomach turns at the thought," Alex sneered. "Tell me, Birk, how long have you been here? Since last night, perhaps?"

"Alejandro!"

He ignored his mother's shocked exclamation and focused on the man he considered his best friend. He of all people knew of Birk's prowess in charming the fairer sex. He had thought, however, that his mother at least would be safe from Birk's wenching ways!

Understanding dawned on Birk's face. Slowly he stood, holding Alex's gaze with his own. "You're not thinkin' that the countess and I—"

"What would you think, Birk? 'Tis quite a

cozy scene." He gestured around him. "A beautiful, wealthy widow. A lavish breakfast. You here, at an hour so early that even I hesitated to call." He rested one hand on the hilt of his dagger. "Tell me I am wrong."

"You are wrong."

The words came not from Birk, but from the countess. Alex glanced at her. She stood proudly, her chin lifted.

"Be seated, madame. This is a matter best handled between men."

"I will not be seated! You forget to whom you are speaking, Alejandro."

"My lady—" the Scotsman started.

"Silence, Birk. This is between Alejandro and myself." She glared at Alex, making him feel as if he were a babe all over again. "How dare you enter this house and start flinging accusations! Even if Birk *had* been here since last night, even if we *were* lovers, it would not be your concern."

"The hell it would not!"

Lady Rothstone closed her hand around the heavy gold crucifix she wore around her neck. "You dare speak such blasphemy in this house?"

Alex flushed. His mother was a devout Catholic and did not tolerate the slightest profanity to be uttered in her presence. "I apologize," he said with true contrition. "But what am I to think?"

"Alex, were the countess to look at me in such a manner, you ken I would be truly flattered. But I wouldna betray you like that."

Alex extended his hand and gave his friend a wry smile. "I know that, Birk, and I apologize."

"Dinna apologize to me." Birk laughed, seating himself again. "It's a compliment that you thought me handsome enough to catch the lady's eye."

Alex went over to his mother and took her hands in both of his. He kissed her fingers, then her cheek. "Forgive me," he murmured. "I have a terrible temper, as you well know."

"I know." She lifted a hand to stroke his face.

He closed his eyes against her gentle touch. "I promise to control myself from now on."

Her caress turned to a light slap, enough to admonish but not sting. "See that you do, Alejandro *mio*."

The two exchanged smiles of understanding.

"Pardon me."

Alex turned at the sound of Diana's voice, suddenly realizing he had forgotten her presence. "Yes, Diana?"

"I do not feel well, Alex. Perhaps it would be best if I went back to the tavern."

"Nonsense," the countess said before Alex could answer. "You will not be going back to that nasty place. You are going to stay here with me. Has Alejandro not told you?"

Diana slanted a look at Alex. "It must have slipped his mind."

"Diana—" Alex began.

"But you do look pale," Lady Rothstone interrupted. "I shall have someone show you to your room. A little rest may help."

"Thank you," Diana murmured.

The countess picked up a small silver bell from the table and rang it. Moments later, a young, pretty Spanish girl entered the room.

"Maria, please show this lady to the corner bedroom."

Maria bobbed a curtsy and glanced at Diana. "This way, *señorita*."

Diana nodded and followed the maid. She paused in the doorway and cast Alex an enigmatic look before she left the room.

Alex frowned as he watched her leave. He didn't doubt her fatigue after the events of last night, but why had she looked at him with such pain in her eyes?

"Och, the poor lassie."

He looked at Birk. "She's just tired."

Birk shook his head. "Alex, you're the blindest man I ever kent. The lass cares for you, and she thinks you're in love with the countess."

"*What?*" Astounded, Alex demanded, "Why would she think that?"

"Because o' what Rosana said last evenin' in the tavern. You've heard the rumors, my friend. Most o' the island thinks you're havin' an affair with Lady Rothstone."

"Blast it!" Remembering his manners, he glanced at his mother. "My apologies, Mama."

Graciously ignoring his profanity, she said, "You must go talk to her, Alejandro."

"Aye, man. Go after her." Birk toasted him with his Madeira.

Alex wasted no time in following their advice. However, he had barely reached the door before his mother's voice stopped him.

"Alejandro." She paused until he met her gaze. "When you return, we will have words on the subject of ladies. Specifically, well-born ladies who duel with trollops in taverns."

He nodded and left the room, not wanting to contemplate just what those words might be.

Diana dismissed the servant and looked around the ornately decorated bedroom. Some might have considered the airy room with its rich decor the very pinnacle of luxury. But to her it was another prison.

She spared a glance at the huge bed with its blue velvet hangings. It was the fashion for the wealthy to measure their affluence by the extravagance of their beds. Though this bed was very large, it was tastefully decorated with blue velvet and gold trim. Diana's educated eye picked out the high quality of the materials. Obviously the countess was a woman of means who preferred simplicity.

Diana sighed. She wasn't sure what to make of Lady Rothstone, other than the fact that Alex apparently loved her.

She turned her back on the bed and walked to the slatted wooden doors opening out to the terrace. She had no interest in a bedroom that she would occupy alone. Opening the doors, she stepped out to a breathtaking view of Besosa. But she didn't see the cerulean sea or the bone-white sand. Instead all she could see was Alex . . . and the countess.

Her mind swam with images of Alex kissing Lady Rothstone's fingers. Embracing her. The tender note in his voice when he spoke to her. Pain squeezed her heart. Indeed, it seemed as if Rosana's words had been more than the ramblings of a woman scorned.

The bond between Alex and the countess obviously ran very deep.

She let out a heavy breath and moved to the stone balustrade of the balcony, staring up at the cloudless blue sky. She wanted to have such a bond with him. She had thought they'd begun to develop that sort of understanding. But his relationship with the countess appeared stronger and more intimate than the fragile affinity growing between Alex and herself.

She could see why he loved her. Lady Rothstone was beautiful and gracious, and evidently cared for him a great deal. Diana felt like an awkward young girl beside the countess's confident maturity. Yet she longed to be the woman to capture Alex's heart.

Why couldn't she be?

She frowned as she noticed that she was methodically shredding one of the brilliant blossoms she had unconsciously plucked from the vines that crept over the balustrade. The tattered petals limply tumbled across the stone in the breeze, a silent chastisement for such destruction. She had wrecked the fragile bloom with all the petulance of a little girl who smashed her favorite toy out of rage.

She had to stop this kind of behavior immediately. Alex was a strong man who needed an equally strong, mature, and capable woman by his side. Why, then, was she sulking like a child? And regarding a perfectly cordial woman as a rival? She was letting rumor and her own uncertainty create doubts in her mind. What she should do was have faith in Alex.

A footstep sounded behind her. She glanced over her shoulder just as Alex stepped out onto the terrace. Their gazes held for a long moment, then she held out her hand to him.

"Diana." He came to her and took her hand. His warm touch ignited her nerve endings as always, and the glide of his sea-roughened fingers brought sweet pleasure as they tangled with hers. Taking his arms, she folded them firmly around her waist, then leaned back against his broad chest with a contented sigh, still feeling enough shame over her childish doubts that she didn't want to face him just yet.

"Diana," he said again. "What troubles you, *amada*?"

"I am not troubled." She turned her head and rubbed her cheek against his chest. "Not anymore."

He kissed her temple, then turned her around to look at him. Tilting her face up, he asked, "Would you care to explain what just happened in the dining room?"

"Not exactly." She tried to step away from him, but he held her firmly. She raised pleading eyes to his, her face burning with chagrin. "Please don't ask me, Alex. Just let it lie."

"Nay, I cannot." He pressed a kiss to her lips. "I see that something has made you uncomfortable, and I would like to know what it is."

"It's silly. And petty. And I'm ashamed to speak of it." She rested her forehead against his chest, taking comfort from his embrace.

"Diana." He stroked her hair. "Talk to me."

She sighed. It was clear to her that he would be as relentless in this matter as he was in his pursuit of Marcus. "It's Lady Rothstone," she admitted in a whisper. "I thought that you . . . then I realized that it probably wasn't the way it looked . . . but I am so confused," she concluded.

Alex sighed. He looked pensive for a long moment, as if wrestling with a weighty decision. Finally, he spoke.

"Lady Rothstone is not now, nor ever has been, my lover."

Her heart flooded with relief. "I wasn't sure at first. Rosana said—"

"Rosana repeated one of the many rumors started by the people of Besosa. She was jealous because I could not love her."

"But do you love Lady Rothstone?" She stepped out of his arms, and this time he let her go. "Forgive me for asking, Alex, but I need to know, as much as it shames me. You kissed her. Embraced her. I heard how you speak to her. You treat her as someone very special."

"She is very special. Diana, I have known the countess all my life." He took her hand. "She held me in her arms when I was but an infant. Of course I love her, but more like an aunt or a mother. Not in the way you were thinking."

"I wasn't sure what to think after what happened at the breakfast table. You acted more like a jealous suitor than a nephew, Alex."

"She is not my lover, Diana." He coaxed her back into his embrace. "You are."

"I believe you, Alex."

He sighed. "The countess is in just as much danger from Marcus as you are." As she rested her head against his chest, he caressed her nape. "She is isolated from society, and I am protective of her. My quest is her quest."

"Your quest . . . ?" Diana paused as a new idea took shape. It was true; she had seen no sign of passion between Alex and Lady Rothstone. No sexual intimations whatsoever. Nothing like the attraction that sizzled between *them*. "She loved your brother, didn't she, Alex?"

His fingers stilled, then continued stroking. "She did."

"So she, too, wants to see Marcus hang."

"Aye, that she does."

"And what is that name she calls you?"

Alex laughed. "You could give the Inquisitors lessons in interrogation, my sweet."

She gave his shoulder a playful swipe. "Answer the question. What does that name mean?"

"Alejandro? 'Tis merely Spanish for Alexander."

"Oh." The more she thought about it, the more foolish she felt. Compared to the sophisticated Lady Rothstone, Diana appeared an immature young girl, given to fits of temper. She made a silent vow to change that part of her. Alex needed a woman at his side, not a petulant child.

"Diana, trust me." He stroked her hair.

"I do trust you."

"Good." He looked down at her and smiled. "You must rest. Lady Rothstone is right; you do look pale."

"I am tired."

"Then sleep." He traced a finger over her parted lips. "For you will not get much rest tonight."

Her cheeks warmed, and her pulse fluttered. She shoved him playfully. "Out with you. I cannot sleep with you here."

He took her hand and pressed a kiss to the palm. "Indeed, when I return, you will not sleep at all," he promised. With a wicked grin, he turned away.

Heart pounding, she watched him go, tingling at the knowledge that she would not be alone in that magnificent bed that night.

*   *   *

Alex stopped just inside the door to the dining room. He glanced at Birk's empty chair before looking at his mother, who still sat at the table.

"Where is your suitor, Mama?" he teased. "Has that fickle Scot's head already been turned by another pretty smile?"

Lady Rothstone raised her head, a flush spreading across the aristocratic cheekbones she had passed on to her son. "Birk has taken his leave, Alejandro, but not before informing me of last night's events."

"I had gathered as much." He sat down at the table and helped himself to a piece of bread, trying to delay the inevitable.

His mother's fingers tightened around the knife she was using to peel a piece of fruit. "He told me all about that deplorable knife fight. Really, Alejandro! What sort of woman is this that you have brought into my home?"

"She is a lady, Mama."

"Birk has said that. But what lady of breeding engages in tavern brawls?"

A smile tugged at his lips. "Diana is an original, Mama."

"I do not yet know her, but she holds herself well." She pointed the knife at him. "So I blame *you*, Alejandro. What possessed you to bring an impressionable girl of good family to a tavern?"

He resisted the urge to squirm in his chair. He recognized that tone of voice from being taken to task for childhood pranks. "She was not there for long, Mama."

"Long enough!" His mother put down her utensils. "Had you brought her straight to me, she would not have been forced to defend herself against that doxy. Imagine, a young woman of her class forced to fight for her life in such surroundings! I am very disappointed in you, Alejandro."

He swallowed a mouthful of bread. "But she won the battle," he pointed out.

"No matter. It should never have occurred." She lifted her cup of cocoa to her lips and sipped. "And would you care to explain why you have brought her here? Why is she not home in the bosom of her family? Not that I question your decisions, Alejandro. After all, this is your house. But I am curious."

Alex poured himself a cup of coffee from the pot on the table, since his mother had dismissed the servants in favor of privacy. He raised the cup and paused before drinking, inhaling the pungent scent of the steaming black liquid.

"You must wish me happy, Mama. Diana is to be my bride."

"Alejandro!" She put down her own cup with an audible click, her face reflecting her stunned joy. "Why did you not tell me sooner?"

"Because Diana does not yet know." He selected a tart from the tray in front of him. "How could I ask her to wed a pirate?"

"But you are not a pirate! You are the Earl of Rothstone. She should fall to her knees and thank *Dios* for such an opportunity!"

Grinning, he took a bite of the tart. Fresh berries exploded in his mouth. "I am gratified you think so highly of me, Mama, but you must remember that Diana knows nothing of my title. To her I am only El Moreno. And until Marcus is captured, I must remain so."

"Marcus," she spat. "I shall be thankful the day he is no longer alive."

"I, too." He finished the tart and picked up a napkin to wipe the stickiness from his fingers. "Mama, it is imperative that Diana not know who I am. I have told her that you are an old family friend who has known me since I was born."

"Which is partly the truth." She sipped her chocolate. "But why the masquerade? Surely she is safe here on Besosa. Surely you can reveal yourself now."

"I dare not." He met her gaze and held it. "This 'masquerade,' as you put it, has protected you thus far. Marcus has never associated Lady Rothstone with El Moreno. I shudder to think what might happen if he did."

"But here on Besosa . . . Marcus never comes here, *hijo*. Surely you can tell her the truth while she is safe in your own home."

"No, the less she knows, the better. He has abducted her once. I cannot take the chance of him doing so again."

"He abducted her?" She clutched her crucifix. "The poor child! Is that how she came to be with you?"

"Yes, I rescued her from his ship—though by the time I got to her, she had already escaped from him." He chuckled. "She is quite resourceful."

"She must be, to have escaped such a villain."

"Indeed." He grew serious once more. "But Marcus is relentless. If he captures her again, her ignorance may save her life. And yours."

"I see." She paused. "Did he . . . harm her, Alejandro? Is that why you wish to wed her?"

"No, he did not harm her, though he certainly tried. I arrived just in time." He stood and took a last swallow of his coffee. "And I mean to wed her because I cannot live without her. I plan to speak to Father Felipe today. We will be married before I leave."

The countess shook her head. "That will be impossible, Alejandro," she said. "Father Felipe left a few days ago to help with an epidemic of fever on another island. It could be weeks before he returns."

"Blast it!" He let out an exasperated breath. "I had hoped to give her my name before I left. Just in case . . ."

"You will not speak of such things." Her face pale, the countess began peeling her fruit once more. "You will return to claim your bride, *hijo*. I insist."

"Of course, Mama. I would not dare disobey

you." He dropped a kiss on her cheek. "Now I have to take my leave. I must see to the careening of the *Vengeance*. But I shall return for the evening meal."

"Very well." She took his hand and squeezed it. "I shall take the opportunity to get to know my new daughter."

He grinned. "I think she will surprise you, Mama. She is different from any woman I have ever known."

"I certainly hope so, given the unsuitable women you usually prefer."

"Mama!" To his consternation, he felt his cheeks flush.

Lady Rothstone laughed. "Do you think me so innocent, Alejandro? How do you think you came to be born?"

His ears burned as his face grew hotter. "I choose not to think of that at all."

He kissed her hand and exited the room before she could comment.

Chapter 16

∽⧵◯◯⧸∾

Something strange was going on.

Diana paced her room, her silk and lace night rail billowing about her. The nightclothes had been provided by the countess, as had the other garments Diana had worn for the past two days. The clothes Alex had bought her had disappeared, and she regretted that they had been taken without her permission. She had enjoyed wearing his gift, although the clothing the countess had lent her fit fairly well.

Diana sighed as she thought of the countess. Something odd was going on. The woman appeared to be generous and kind, determined to see that even Diana's smallest needs were met. She was the soul of courtesy—and apparently determined to keep Alex and Diana apart.

Oh, she was discreet about it. But it was amazing how often she would appear just as Alex made some romantic overture. How she would need him for some small task right that moment.

Sometimes when Alex wanted to speak privately with Diana, the countess would ignore all hints to leave the room, forcing him to either forget what he wanted to say or to whisper it.

She seemed determined to ensure that Alex and Diana had no private moments together. Alex said that Lady Rothstone had loved his brother, and Diana believed him. But the countess's behavior was most confusing.

A breeze blew through the chamber from the open terrace doors, making the candles flicker. The briny scent of the ocean filled the room, reminding her of those last blissful days aboard Alex's ship. She glanced outside. The full moon hung like a silver coin against the black velvet of the night sky, beckoning her. She drifted out to the terrace and stared up at the stars.

"Alex," she whispered into the night. "Where are you?"

"Right here, my sweet."

She whirled at the sound of his voice. He sat on the stone balustrade in a darkened corner of the terrace. A grappling iron and a coil of rope lay at his feet.

"What are you doing here?"

"I came to see you."

"But how did you get here?" He held up a rope with a grappling iron attached. "You didn't . . ."

"Indeed I did."

"You climbed up the side of the house? Using that? You could have been killed!"

He laughed. "Hardly, love. You forget, I climb masts higher than this wall every day."

There it was again—that word. *Love.* Her heart clenched painfully as she wondered if he meant it, or if it was just a casual endearment to him. She almost asked him, but a knock on her bedroom door forestalled the question. Lady Rothstone's muffled voice carried out to the terrace.

"Diana, are you there?"

"How does she do it?" Diana mumbled.

"Answer the door," Alex said. "I'll still be here when you return."

Muttering under her breath, Diana went back into her room and opened the door to yet another intrusion.

"I'm so sorry to disturb you, my dear," Lady Rothstone said with a sweet smile. "I just wanted to be sure you had everything you needed."

"Oh, yes," Diana responded. "I have just what I need. Thank you for asking."

"I want you to be comfortable here." The countess glanced past her at the terrace doors and frowned. "You really should not leave the doors open at night. All manner of nasty creatures can wander into your room."

"I enjoy the night air."

"Nonetheless, I would not wish any harm to befall you." She slipped past Diana and headed straight for the terrace.

"Lady Rothstone, wait." Diana attempted to stop her, but the countess was already standing out on the terrace. She looked around and seemed to find everything to her satisfaction.

"Well, 'tis a beautiful night, isn't it?" she said as she came back into the room. "Just don't leave the doors open all night, my dear. You don't want a snake slithering into your bed."

"Certainly not." Bemused, Diana watched her hostess cross the room to the door.

"Sleep well, Diana." With a placid smile, Lady Rothstone left the room, closing the door behind her.

Diana rushed out onto the terrace. She looked to the corner where Alex had been sitting. No one was there.

"Alex?"

"Stand back," came the muffled reply. She heard a scraping noise, and moonlight flashed off a metal object that flew over the balustrade to hook there firmly.

She rushed over and looked down. As she watched, Alex took hold of the rope and began to pull himself up.

"What in heaven are you doing down there?"

"Hanging," came the grunted reply. One hand appeared, followed by Alex's head and shoulders.

She grabbed two handfuls of his shirt and tugged just as he shoved himself over. The two of them fell in a tangled heap.

"God's bones, Diana! Are you hurt?" He quickly rose and extended his hand.

"I'm fine." She allowed him to pull her to her feet. "I cannot say the same for this nightdress, however." She sighed at the tear in the shoulder of the fragile silk garment. "How shall I explain this to Lady Rothstone?"

Alex fingered a dangling piece of lace. "You could tell her you were overcome with lust, and the gown tore while you were ravishing me."

She widened her eyes. "Should I tell her that, she might take to sleeping in my room, or something even more drastic to prevent us from having any time together!"

He stared at her for a moment before he burst out laughing.

"Don't laugh." She hit him in the chest with her fist. "She has been plotting to keep us apart, though I have no idea why. We haven't had more than a few moments alone together in the past two days!"

"Aye, 'tis true." Trying to stifle his chuckles, he took her shoulders and rested his forehead against hers. "My sweet, do you not realize what she has been doing? She has become your duenna."

"What are you talking about?"

" 'Tis the way of the Spanish. In Spain an unmarried young woman of good family is never left alone at any time, especially with a man. Lady Rothstone respects you. She knows you are a lady and sees chaperoning you as her duty."

She stared at him. "Are you certain?"

"Quite certain. She has merely been treating you as befits your station. She was trying to protect your virtue, my sweet."

"Ha!" Playing with the lacing of his shirt, she slanted him a seductive look. "Unfortunately, my virtue has already been stolen by a charming, dark-eyed scoundrel."

"Scoundrel, eh? I suppose your seductive wiles had naught to do with it."

"Never. I was an innocent victim."

"Poor child." He pulled her close against him. "Ravished, were you?"

"Aye." She stared at the masculine mouth poised above hers, longing to taste his kiss. "And I have not even told you the worst part."

He slid her nightgown off one shoulder and pressed his lips there. "And what is that?"

She brought her lips close to his ear. "I want to be ravished again, but there are no charming scoundrels about."

"Well, then," he murmured, scooping her into his arms, "I suppose I will have to do the deed."

Her whisper of assent drifted away on the breeze as he carried her to the bed.

Much later, Alex stroked a hand over Diana's naked hip and murmured, "I must leave in the morning."

"What?" She lifted her head from his chest and looked at him with distress in her gray eyes. "You still intend to leave me behind?"

"Only for a short while, my sweet." He

smoothed a lock of hair back from her face, marveling yet again at her beauty. "Marcus awaits, and I must leave with the tide."

"Take me with you."

"I cannot."

"But why? I will be safe with you. And perhaps I can help."

He closed his eyes and sighed, then rolled away from her and sat on the edge of the bed. The covers rustled as she sat up as well.

"Talk to me, Alex. There is something more to this than fear for my safety. You know I can take care of myself."

"Bloody hell, woman!" He rose from the bed and turned to face her. "There are reasons why I will not allow you to accompany me."

"And there are reasons why I insist on coming with you."

"No."

She bit her lip. "Tell me the truth, Alex. Tell me the real reason, and I will not ask you again."

The plea in her eyes tugged at his heart. He raked a hand though his hair and stared at the floor for a long moment. Finally he said, "I was married once."

Her mouth fell open. "You were married? You are not any longer?"

"She died."

"Oh." She plucked at the coverlet, obviously curious yet not voicing the questions he knew she must have.

"It was a long time ago." He came to sit beside her on the bed and took her hand. "I don't want to lose you as I lost her."

"Alex." She took a deep breath and stared at their entwined hands. "I care for you. And I am so afraid you will be killed, and I will never see you again."

"I care for you as well." He kissed her fingers. She was already so precious to him. The possibility of Marcus getting his hands on her again was unthinkable. "I will conduct this business all the quicker, knowing you await me here."

"I have been afraid to ask how I fit into your life," she said.

"Diana, I have every intention of building a future with you."

"I needed to hear that," she whispered.

"Trust me, *amada*."

"You have called me that before," she said. He felt her pulse speed up as he brushed his lips over her wrist. "What does it mean?"

"It is Spanish. It means 'beloved.' "

"Beloved." Her voice trembled. "I like that."

"*Amada*," he whispered in her ear, then bent his head to nuzzle her neck. Apparently she had accepted his decision to go after Marcus alone. And he felt better for telling her about Bianca. Now he wanted to make love to her until dawn parted them.

"Alex?"

"Hmmm?" He tangled his fingers in her hair and gently pulled her head back so he could nip at the sweet skin of her throat.

"I know you are Spanish," she said. "But how is it that you speak English with no accent?"

"My father was English," he murmured, distracted by the pulse at the base of her neck.

"What!" She jerked from his embrace. "You are half English?"

"Blast it," he muttered. He had inadvertently given her a key to the mystery of El Moreno. How long would it take her to associate him with the Rawnsleys?

"Alex?"

"Aye, my sweet. Half English, but still a passionate Spaniard." He stretched out over her, pressing her back into the pillows. "Let me show you."

She gave a little gasp as he settled on top of her, his hardening shaft pressing against the juncture of her thighs. He took her hands in his and pinned them to either side of her head, then dipped down to nibble at her mouth. The instant she tried to deepen the kiss, he pulled back.

She lifted her hips, pressing her softness against his erection. He gave a groan of pleasure. Such sweet torture, he could hardly stand it.

His heart ached at the thought of leaving her behind. As he continued to tease her mouth with whisperlike kisses, he imbued each caress with the longing that haunted him. Nipping at her eager mouth, barely stroking his tongue over her lower lip before pulling away—with each touch, he told her how he would miss her. How he wanted her with him, always. How desperately he needed her.

She undulated beneath him, moaning his name. He could listen to that sound forever. Stretching her arms high above her head, he flicked his tongue over one pouting nipple. She arched her back with a long, low sound of need. Her legs moved restlessly.

"Easy, love," he murmured. Nudging her legs apart with his knee, he shifted until he lay between her fully spread thighs. As he lowered his head to her other breast, he slowly slipped into her welcoming body, her hot, damp passage grasping at his shaft and pulling him deeper.

She made that whimpering sound in the back of her throat that made him wild, and it was all he could do not to take her hard and fast. But he wanted to linger. To savor. To commit to memory every touch and taste and scent of her. So he forced himself to move slowly within her tight sheath, to keep his kisses gentle and soft as he fed on her mouth. She shuddered beneath him, her body slick with perspiration as she tried to deepen the kisses and quicken the rhythm of their joined bodies. She tried to free her hands, but he wouldn't let her go. She moaned and begged and moved against him until he thought he'd go mad. But somehow he maintained the excruciatingly slow pace.

He didn't know if he'd return from his mission, and he intended this to be a night they would both remember forever.

He nuzzled the frantic pulse beating in her neck, then pressed his teeth gently against the tender flesh of her shoulder. She shuddered; then, with a feminine growl of need, she wrapped her long legs around his waist and lifted her hips, driving him deeply into her. He closed his eyes in bliss as her sensitive flesh rippled around him. Her breath caught. He knew she was close, and he didn't have the heart or the will to make either of them wait any longer. Taking her hips in his hands, he began to move with strong, possessive strokes. A moan slipped past her parted lips. Her eyelids slowly lifted, and he held her gaze as she shattered in his arms, convulsing and crying his name.

A moment later he followed her over the edge, a prisoner to the same desperate desire that made him both love her and leave her. For only a love like theirs, one of unrelenting power that gripped the soul, could force him to leave her with the dawn's light.

But leave he would, and nothing could change what had to be.

The tremors still shook her, and he gathered her close, still joined with her. He tangled his fingers in her hair and buried his face in her neck as he fought back the unmanly tears that stung his eyes.

"I will return for you, *amada*—my greatest love," he whispered. "I promise."

*   *   *

The tide would soon be in.

Alex stood on the deck of the *Vengeance* and watched his crew lay in supplies. Cask after cask of rum came aboard, as well as sacks of flour, salted meats, and fresh fruit. They would eat well—but it would be a long, lonely voyage.

"Captain?"

He scowled at the interruption. "What is it, Mister McBride?"

The Irishman showed no concern over Alex's irate tone. " 'Tis Mister Fraser, Captain. He isn't aboard, and no one knows where he is."

"Blast that randy Scot!" Slamming his hands down on the rail, he barked, "Send out a few men and roust the bawdy houses. If I know Mister Fraser, he is sleeping off the night's pleasure in some wench's bed."

"I'll do that, sir." McBride hurried off.

Alex watched him go, already regretting his caustic tone. Aside from Birk, McBride was the only one aboard who knew the true identity of El Moreno. He was also one of the most loyal members of the crew, since Alex had saved him from being flogged to death when they had both served in His Majesty's navy. Of course, Alex's service had been voluntary, whereas McBride's had not.

McBride was a good man, who had not deserved to be spoken to so sharply.

He looked up at the shadow that was Rothstone Manor and thought of Diana, asleep in her bed, her body still flushed from his touch. The image heated his blood, raising memories of the night's erotic adventures. He clenched his hands with the need to touch her.

"Sleep well, my love," he whispered. Turning on his heel, he went below.

Diana peered out from behind a rum barrel and watched as two crewmen transported more casks on board the *Vengeance*. Soon she would have her chance.

She glanced at the barrel beside her. The rum was almost drained from it now. The gush of fluid that had poured out of the cask after she had pulled its plug had now trickled to a tiny stream. In a few more seconds the cask would be nearly empty.

Footsteps crunched on the beach, and she ducked. A seaman passed by without so much as glancing at her hiding place. When he was gone, she peered out again. No one was about. Only the merest trickle leaked out of the barrel now, so she pushed the plug back into the hole. Then she looked around again.

The beach was deserted. It was time.

Using a knife she had stolen from the kitchens of Rothstone Manor, she pried the top off the barrel and looked in. A couple inches of rum remained at the bottom. Wrinkling her nose at the smell, she lifted her skirts and climbed in anyway.

She made a sound of disgust as her slippers quickly became soaked. But she was determined to go with Alex, and this was the only way she could think of to get aboard without being seen. Pulling her dark cloak closer with one hand, she sank down into the barrel and slid the lid closed with the other.

She had chosen one of the last casks to be loaded, so she wouldn't end up in the back of the hold with the other barrels piled atop hers. She needed to be able to escape her pungent prison as soon as the ship set sail.

She shifted and tried to get comfortable. Trying to ignore the strong odor of rum-soaked wood, she settled down to wait.

From a few yards down the beach, Birk watched Diana climb into the barrel. He shook his head in disbelief. "What the devil does she think she's about?" he muttered.

His first instinct was to stop her, but then he reconsidered. Alex tended to go mad when confronted with Marcus. Perhaps with Diana by his side, he would have a care for himself.

He saw the boatswain, Mister James, help young, bare-faced Thomas Carver drag the longboat through the shallow surf and up onto the sand. Laughing and joking, they made their way toward the last few barrels that sat at the water's edge. Carver laid his hand atop the one containing Diana. Birk swore and started forward.

"Good evenin' to you, mates!" he called.

"Where you been?" Mister James called. "De

captain's in a temper cuz he couldn't find you."

Birk grinned and leaned his hip against the barrel containing Diana, preventing Carver from lifting it. "As handsome as the captain is, he canna hold a candle to the bonnie lassie who shared her bed with me last night."

"You have the devil's luck with women, Mister Fraser," young Carver said, his eyes wide with admiration. "How do you do it?"

" 'Tis the Fraser charm. I'm cursed with it."

"Cursed, my arse," Mister James grumbled. The huge black man hefted a nearby cask and turned toward the longboat.

"He's jealous," Birk confided, loud enough for James to hear.

"Kiss my blindcheeks, little man," James called back, tipping the cask into the boat.

"I'm thinkin' that's your problem, man! You've no lassie to do that for you!"

James responded with an anatomically impossible suggestion that turned Carver's fair complexion beet red. Birk laughed and slapped the young man's bony shoulder.

"When you've grown a bit more, young Thomas, I'll teach you the Scot's way o' wooin' a lassie."

Carver swallowed and nodded.

Birk slid off the barrel. "Would you care for an extra pair o' hands, lad? I've a mind to get back in the captain's good graces. The sooner these casks are stowed, the sooner we set sail."

" 'Tis all the same to me," Carver answered.

"That's the spirit!" Birk slapped his hand down on the top of Diana's barrel, locking the lid into place. "I'll take this one."

James came back, gave Birk a look, and hefted another barrel. "You goin' to work or talk?" he asked Carver.

The boy grabbed a barrel. "Work," he answered, his puny muscles straining beneath the weight of the cask.

Birk hefted Diana's barrel. "God's teeth, lad! What have you got in here? Rocks? It's bloody heavy!"

Already halfway to the longboat, James turned. His stark white smile contrasted with the early morning dark and his own dark skin. "You just not used to dis kind of work," he said.

"Never you mind about that," Birk said, balancing the barrel on his shoulder. "Just lead the way."

With one cask balanced on his shoulder and another tucked under his arm, James continued to the longboat. Birk and Carver trailed behind with the last of the stores.

"I suppose these will be goin' in the hold," Birk said to the younger man, knowing Diana could overhear every word. "Och, I dinna like goin' down there. Too many rats for my way o' thinkin'."

He continued in a similar vein as he tipped the cask into the boat, then rested his hand upon it. "Aye, the hold is a nasty place. As dark as hell, and the smell is worse."

His companions said nothing. Together the three men pushed the boat into the water, then hopped inside. Birk made sure to sit beside Diana's barrel. As the two seaman rowed out to the *Vengeance,* he sang a rowdy Scottish ditty and thumped his hand on the barrel in rhythm with it.

He hoped the pounding gave the troublesome lassie a devil of a headache.

When they reached the ship, Birk scrambled aboard and helped bring the casks up on deck. He set the one containing Diana aside and kept a careful eye on it until all the stores were aboard. When a burly crewman moved to take Diana's barrel below, Birk stopped him.

"Nah, man," he said, hefting the cask himself. "I'm takin' this rum to the captain's cabin." He turned and walked straight into Mister James.

"I will take that," the boatswain said.

"You will not." Birk refused to relinquish his prize. The bigger man scowled.

"You don' fool me. You want dat keg for youself. Not for de captain."

Birk let his mouth fall open and his eyes bulge with feigned shock. "The devil I do! I wouldna do a thing like that. Sure as the devil's in hell, it's a gift for the captain."

James eyed him with suspicion. "I don' trust you." He tried to grab the barrel, but Birk whirled out of the way, almost losing his balance from the weight he hauled.

"Is that any way to be talkin' about the man

who took the splinter out o' your leg durin' the last battle?'' Birk edged in the direction of the captain's cabin. James shadowed his every step. ''As long as my hand, it was, and the very devil to get out.''

''Leave da cask here.'' James blocked his way just when he would have reached the hatch.

''You're in my path, James.''

The huge boatswain folded his arms across his chest in answer.

''Well, if that's the way o' it . . .'' Birk put the barrel down in a shadowy corner near the hatch where it would remain safely out of the way. Then he spun around and punched Mister James in the jaw. The bigger man grinned, unfazed by the blow, and balled his own fist.

The brawl drew everyone's attention. Men called out wagers as Birk and James went at it. In the midst of the fight, Birk saw Diana climb out of the barrel and slip down the hatch. With the sun not yet risen, no one else noticed her.

Then Birk saw stars as his opponent landed a blow that sent him sprawling. His last thought before blackness claimed him was that Alex owed him a very *large* boon.

Diana paced Alex's cabin. The ship had set sail some hours ago, just before dawn. With the sun now high in the sky, Alex had yet to venture to his cabin. Where was he?

She plucked at the oversized black shirt and breeches that she had borrowed from Alex's chest. Her own clothing reeked of rum.

Alex's clothes smelled like him, an alluring combination of sandalwood and sea. Wearing his things made her feel very close to him. She hugged the shirt tighter around her and wandered over to look at the maps and charts lying on his desk.

Had she done the right thing in following him? No doubt he would be furious when he discovered her presence aboard, but there was no help for it. She could not let him go after Marcus alone. Not when there was every possibility that he would die in his quest for vengeance.

No, her place was at his side.

The ship rolled suddenly, thrusting her against the desk. She cried out as pain shot up from her knee. Limping and muttering, she made her way to sit on the bed. Her knees and elbows already bore bruises from bouncing around in the barrel. By the time the ship reached its destination, she feared she would be black and blue all over!

Footsteps approached in the passageway. Her head shot up, ears straining to hear more. The footfalls halted outside the door.

She mumbled an unladylike expletive and dove beneath the bed. She had no idea who was about to enter the cabin, and she wanted to reveal her presence only to Alex. Heart pounding, she waited.

Alex stalked into his cabin, his mood foul. Damn Birk! First he was late getting back to the ship, then he started a brawl with Mister James over a bloody cask of rum. What had gotten into the man?

He went to the cabinet and pulled out his bottle of brandy. Not bothering with a goblet, he popped the cork and took a swig straight from the flask. Heat slid down his throat, easing some of the frigid loneliness that plagued him.

Aye, that was what ailed him. Not Birk, not Marcus. Just simple loneliness. How he had hated to leave Diana behind.

He put the bottle aside and stripped off his shirt with short, efficient movements. Tossing the garment heedlessly aside, he perched on the edge of the bed to remove his boots. Then he took up the brandy again and sat back against the headboard.

He sighed, lifting the onion-shaped bottle. Birk was aboard, the supplies stowed safely in the hold. Finally they had set sail. Marcus's days were numbered.

He would go to Port Royal first, he thought as he sipped the brandy. He needed to visit with Morgan and apprise him of recent events. He also intended to call upon Diana's father and assure him of her safety, then acquire the ledger pages that proved Chilton's collusion with Marcus. Then he would hunt the villains themselves.

He expected danger. He knew that death might yet await him at his enemy's hand. Yet he had a new reason to survive his quest. Diana awaited him.

He knew he had made the right decision in leaving her behind. As long as she was safe, he could concentrate on capturing Marcus. Once that was done, he would be free to once more assume his own identity and claim Diana as his bride.

He smiled at the thought. She would make him a fine wife. Though she was a bit headstrong, he had no doubt that marriage would calm her youthful high spirits. As her husband, he would instruct her in her wifely duties with a firm but patient hand. He had no wish to destroy her spirit. Her vitality was one of her most attractive qualities. But she would learn to respect his greater experience in worldly matters.

He could hardly wait to see her again.

The ship listed sharply, jarring him from his thoughts. He grabbed for the headboard to avoid rolling off the mattress, but missed. The brandy bottle went skidding as he hit the floor with a thud. He cursed, opened his eyes, and cursed again.

He was staring straight into Diana's familiar, beloved, and apprehensive gray eyes. She huddled under the bed, her hair a tangled mass around her pale face, her small white teeth biting into her lower lip.

"Hello, Alex," she said softly.

"Bloody hell," he muttered.

Chapter 17

❧

Diana squealed as Alex grabbed her arm and dragged her out from under the bed.

"What in God's name are you doing here?" he thundered.

She flinched at the naked fury on his face, but refused to reveal her misgivings by word or deed. "Obviously, I followed you."

"I told you to stay behind. I even *explained* to you why you should." He seized her upper arms and shook her. "I *needed* you to obey."

The distress in his voice almost made her wish she had complied. "I'm sorry. But I couldn't let you go without me."

"Why? To be sure that I fulfilled my promise to prove your father's innocence? I thought you trusted me."

"I do trust you." She gave him a pleading look. "My father has nothing to do with this."

"I wish I could believe you." He thrust her from him. "But I believed that you would stay behind when I asked it of you. You have betrayed my faith in you."

"Alex, no!" She reached for him, but he crossed the room as if he could not stand to be near her. She stared at his rigid back and pressed her trembling lips together. Dear Lord, what had she wrought by disobeying him? "I only wanted to be with you."

"*You* only wanted!" He turned to confront her, the sneer on his face completely foreign to the tenderness she had often seen there. "It is always what you want, Diana. You are a troublesome child."

"I am *not* a child!"

"You are. Always it is what you want, what you need. What about what I want and need?" He shook his head, his eyes growing dull with disappointment. "I weary of this game you play. You only hear what you want to hear. I am the captain of this ship, and if need be, I will lock you in the hold to keep you safe from Marcus."

She paled. "You would not do such a thing."

He gave a harsh laugh. "Indeed I would, my precious girl. I am a pirate, have you forgotten? A criminal. A seducer of innocents."

"That is not true!"

He raised a brow and flashed a mocking glimpse of white teeth. "Is it not? I seduced you so well that even now you sneak aboard my ship to share my bed."

"Don't you dare talk that way of what is between us," she snapped, her own temper starting to fray. "There is more than lust to our relationship."

"I used to think so."

She locked her hands together. "Alex, don't act like this."

"Like what? Like a pirate?" He advanced on her, his paces slow and measured, like a tiger on the hunt. "Cruel? Insensitive?" He took her chin in his hand. "Dishonorable?"

"You are the most honorable man I have ever known," she shot back. "And I will not stand by while you belittle what is between us."

"And what is between us, sweet lover? Not trust. Not consideration." He caressed her jaw, his dark eyes glittering wickedly. "Just raw passion, my darling. And naught else."

She slapped his hand away. "You are a blind fool."

"Fool, am I?" He raked his gaze over her, his tone dripping with contempt. "Aye, I am a fool for letting my need for you overrule my better judgment."

"You feeble-minded ass." She put her hands on her hips. "I followed you because I was scared that something would happen to you. Did you think I would cheerfully wave goodbye from the safety of Besosa as you sailed to your death?"

"Indeed I did." He folded his arms over his chest. "But instead you followed me in hopes that your presence would somehow protect me."

She stiffened at his patronizing tone. "It is not so far-fetched a notion, Captain. On Marcus's ship, who watched your back when Scroggins tried to put a knife in it?''

He shook his head. "One incident does not make you a warrior, woman! I appreciate your concern, but your fears are unfounded. I have no intention of dying."

"How gratifying." Each syllable dripped with sarcasm. "Then if my presence offends you," she said, "please do return me to Besosa. I assure you I will remain in my luxurious prison like a good little captive until big, strong you comes to fetch me." She pushed a straggling lock of hair behind her ear and added with a sweet smile, "Or until they return your lifeless body for burial. I swear to shed no tears over your grave, dear sir."

"You try my patience, wench," he growled, clenching his hands into fists.

"No more than you try mine, *Alejandro*."

"Don't call me that." The way she sneered his name loosed something in him that he had kept tightly leashed for far too long. With a low sound of need, he reached for her, tangling his fingers in her hair, pressing her into him with a hand on her bottom.

"Since you are already here," he purred, "perhaps I should take advantage of your presence."

"I'm not afraid of you," she breathed, her eyes smoldering with banked desire.

He froze with his mouth only inches from hers. *She wasn't afraid.*

"*Dios*," he whispered. When she had said his

name like that, he had heard Bianca's voice in his mind, had expected her to act like Bianca and flee from him in terror. But instead she looked him in the eye and met his passion with her own. Slowly he released her.

"Alex?" She furrowed her brows, no doubt puzzled by his behavior.

"*Amada*, forgive me." He placed a chaste kiss on her forehead, then closed his eyes and rested his chin atop her hair.

She pressed her face into his shoulder. "I'm sorry I made you angry," she said, her tone growing more agitated now that his anger had abated. "But I had to come with you. I *had* to, Alex."

" 'Tis done." He sighed and held her tighter. "I merely wish that you were safely away from this."

"I couldn't stand staying behind. If something happened to you, if you died and I never knew . . . I love you so much and . . ." Her words trailed off, and she stiffened in his arms. "Oh, dear," she whispered.

"Diana?" He stared stupidly at her as she pulled out of his embrace.

"I'm sorry." She sniffed and swiped a hand across her eyes, damp with unshed tears. "I didn't mean to say that."

"Come here." He drew her back into his arms.

"Please, let me go." She pushed against his chest, her cheeks flaming with chagrin.

"Nay, love." He stroked his hand through her hair. "That I can never do."

"You mock me when you call me that."

"I do not. I mean it." He smiled into her widening gray eyes. "I love you, Diana."

"You love me?" She blinked at him in disbelief. "Since when?"

"Since the night you attempted to prove your independence in your father's garden. I knew as soon as I met you that you are not like other women." His smile faded as he grew serious. "But I am not free to claim you. I am bound by my oath to avenge my brother's death at Marcus's hands. Until that time I must put aside my own needs."

"I will wait for you." She took his hand and kissed it. "Perhaps I can even help you."

"No." Caressing her lips with his thumb, he said, "I will not risk you."

"But—"

"My decision is final."

She tilted her head. "I am not known for my meekness, Alex. You surely do not expect me to stand by and watch you die."

"That is exactly what I expect—though I do not intend to die." He took her hand. "Marcus is dangerous, my love. I will not be responsible for your death at his hands."

"My life is my own responsibility."

"Not when it is *my* quest that would get you killed." He squeezed her fingers. "Please, my sweet. I could not stand to watch you die, too."

She twined her fingers with his and asked

gently, "Who else did you watch die, Alex?"

He let out a long breath. "Bianca," he said. "My wife. I could not bear to lose you as I did her."

"Oh, Alex." She hugged him tightly.

He pulled her closer into his embrace. "For a very long time, I thought that the accident was my fault."

"Tell me what happened, Alex."

He took one look at her determined gaze. "Very well. I was but seventeen when we married, she a mere five and ten. She was from a noble Spanish family and beautiful in a fragile way: fair-haired, blue-eyed, delicate. As the second son, I could marry whom I liked, unlike my older brother. When I met Bianca, I was completely infatuated."

Diana had not realized how difficult it would be to listen to him speak of desire for another woman. "Go on," she whispered.

"She married me to please her family. I did not learn until after we wed that her true vocation was the church, and by then it was too late." He sighed. "I am not proud of my behavior. I was young. Hot-blooded. My bride was shy and innocent. She begged me for time to get used to being married before we shared a bed. I agreed. I thought it would take but a few days. After three months, I reached the limit of my patience."

Diana sank down on the edge of the bed. Thus far everything he'd said gave credence to the rumor that El Moreno was of noble blood.

She wondered if what he was about to confide had been the impetus that had driven him from his privileged lifestyle. "Go on."

His face took on a faraway look, as if he relived events as he spoke. "I came home one night, drunk as a lord. In my arrogance, I decided that I had given Bianca enough time. I stormed into her chamber, demanding my rights as her husband." His voice thickened with self-disgust. "She was terrified. She begged me not to touch her. Cried. Prayed. Called upon God to strike me down before I defiled her."

"Did you . . . ?" She couldn't finish the sentence.

"Nay, she ran from the room." He curled his lip, mocking the youth he had been. "But I was determined to see the issue settled once and for all, so I followed her."

He paused. Diana twisted her fingers together. "Did you catch her?"

"I did." He swiped a hand over his face. "I can still see her, beautiful and ethereal, poised at the top of the stairs. The moonlight coming through the window cast an angelic glow over her."

He stared ahead as he spoke, and Diana knew that he didn't see the cabin around him— only Bianca and that terrible night so long ago.

"I called her name," he continued. "She turned. I could tell she had not expected me to follow her. I came nearer and she put out her hands as if to ward me off . . . whispered, 'No.'

I reached for her, but she took a step back. I can still see her eyes, the terror in them, as she flailed in midair . . . I swear I stopped breathing in that instant. I tried to grab her—I felt her hair brush my knuckles . . . so close . . . but my hands closed on empty air." He paused, his breathing harsh. "She . . . died instantly of a broken neck."

He fell silent. Diana rose and came to him.

"A terrible tragedy," she said softly, taking his face in her hands. "You fell in love. You offered your name to this woman. She accepted. She did not tell you that her heart belonged to the church, so of course you thought she would share your bed. It is what any man would expect."

He enfolded her in his arms. "Only recently did it occur to me that Bianca should never have married. She should have been permitted to follow her heart's desire and join the holy order."

"Indeed she should have. I am sure if you had realized her vocation, you would not have married her."

"No, I wouldn't have." He kissed the top of her head. The tension that had gripped him while retelling the tale faded away, and he changed the subject. "Why is it that your hair smells like rum?"

"Perhaps because I sneaked aboard inside a cask of rum?" She traced her finger over the front of his shirt and refused to meet his eyes.

"You did what?" He gripped her arms and

gave her a hard shake. "Don't you realize how dangerous that is?"

"Of course I do, but 'twas the only thing I could think of at the time."

He closed his eyes for a moment, then opened them again. "You will be the death of me, woman. Perhaps this would explain why you are wearing my clothes? Not that they don't look fetching, you understand."

She stepped out of his arms and gave him a smile of pure seduction. "Would you like them back?" She toyed with the hem of the shirt.

He arched a brow. "Aye, I would."

"Very well." His love gave her a confidence she had never felt before. Inching out of the shirt, she drew out the task until he was all but salivating. She tossed the garment aside triumphantly and smiled at him, bare to the waist.

He took her into his arms, pressing her soft breasts against his naked chest. "You're a wanton bit of goods."

She gave him a cheeky grin. "Aren't you lucky?"

"I am at that." He nuzzled her neck. "So when do I get my breeches back?"

The door crashed open. Birk charged inside, then halted as he took in the scene before him. "Well, now," was all he said.

"Damn it, Birk!" Alex had stepped in front of Diana to protect her modesty. "What the devil do you want now? Haven't you caused enough trouble for one day?"

"Ha!" Birk grinned as much as he was able with his split lip "You should be thankin' me for makin' sure she didna end up buried in the hold."

"*You knew!*" Diana's temper snapped as she recalled every word and deed since Birk had first approached Mister James and young Carver. She all but climbed over Alex to get to the grinning Scot, but her lover held her firmly and would not loose her.

"Easy, my love." Alex laughed. "You are not exactly dressed for battle at the moment."

Her cheeks flushed as she recalled her state of undress. Peering around Alex's muscular torso, she narrowed her eyes at the physician. "You will pay, Birk Fraser. Beware."

"Indeed, lassie." Still chuckling, Birk left the cabin, closing the door behind him.

"What was that about?"

"Your friend has an odd sense of humor," she muttered. "I will tell you the whole of it later. In the meantime, where were we?"

"Right here." He lowered his mouth to hers.

"Ah, Port Royal. A golden treasury of information."

Dressed like a lord in a blue satin coat and breeches with a snow-white shirt, Marcus looked down on the busy street from the window of his room above the Hart & Hound Tavern. Much as he preferred the comfort of his own cabin on the *Marauder*, Morgan had made it virtually impossible for him to drop anchor in the harbor anywhere near Port Royal. So Marcus had been forced to send his ship into hiding farther down the coast while he and a few of his men took rooms in the city. Yet the situation did have its advantages.

"If there is information to be bought about El Moreno, this is the place to purchase it. Anything in this city can be had for a price." He smiled and glanced at the bed. "Wouldn't you agree, my dear?"

The girl tied spread-eagled to the bed gave a frightened whimper from behind her gag and turned her face away.

"Now, none of that." Marcus approached the bed. He stopped about a foot away, admiring the contrast of her pale, naked body against the dark coverlet of the bed. He sipped from the goblet of wine he held, his gaze missing no detail, allowing her no secrets. "For instance, it was quite simple to find a man so fond of drink that he was willing to sell his virgin daughter for the price of a cask of ale."

The girl whimpered again, hiding her face in her long, dark hair.

Marcus chuckled. "Given that, my dear, it should be a simple matter to acquire information about my enemy."

He said no more, merely stood there enjoying his wine and watching her body tremble beneath the weight of his stare. He enjoyed this game, making her so aware of him, so frightened of him, before he even touched her. It made the triumph of bedding her that much more exciting.

A knock sounded at the door. He scowled. "Enter."

Scroggins shuffled into the room. "He's comin', Cap'n."

"Is he?" Marcus turned away from the girl. "Are you certain?"

"Aye. Ship's been sighted. He's comin', all right."

"Excellent." Marcus rolled the pewter goblet between his hands. "Send a man to the docks. I want to know everything he does from the moment he drops anchor. And if that red-haired bitch is with him."

"Aye, Cap'n." With a bob of his head, Scroggins retreated from the room.

Marcus turned back to the bed. "What marvelous news!" He dipped his finger into the wine and slowly traced a line of crimson over her naked thigh. Then he set the goblet down. "We must celebrate. And, my dear, I insist that you share in my joy."

Smiling, he began to take off his clothes.

The return voyage to Jamaica had seemed to pass much more swiftly than the journey to Besosa. Diana stood at the rail and watched the familiar buildings of Thames Street become clearer as the ship approached King's Wharf. Though she knew Port Royal as well as she knew her own estate, the city looked different to her now. More colorful. More alive. More exciting. She knew that Port Royal could not have changed that much in the time she had been gone, which meant the transformation had to be in her.

Alex came up behind her and slid his arms around her waist. She loved him so much, she thought she would explode with it. "Happy to be home?"

"Yes." She let her head fall back against his shoulder and closed her hands over his where they clasped around her waist. "But at the same time I wish we had not returned. What are we to do now? I worry about you walking so freely through the city with so many soldiers about."

"Do not concern yourself," he reassured her. "I have never once been detained by the military."

"There is always a first time."

He laughed and turned her to face him, dropping a kiss on her lips. "There is no need to fear, my sweet. You are the only one who can identify El Moreno."

"I wish we didn't have to return at all," she sighed.

"We must, if we are to help your father. Besides, Port Royal is where Chilton is, and therefore the best place to begin searching for Marcus." He arched a brow. "I don't suppose I can convince you to confine yourself to the cabin while we are in port?"

"No." She tilted her chin, anticipating an argument.

"I didn't think so. But you will obey my every order to the letter, do you understand?"

"I will. I just want to be with you."

"I cannot object to that." He pulled her closer, but she held back from his embrace with her hands on his chest.

"Alex, I would ask something of you."

"Name it."

"Allow me to visit with my father while we are here. I know he must be worried about me."

"No."

"*Please*, Alex!"

" 'Tis too dangerous. You may send your father a message, but you will not leave the ship."

"He will not believe a piece of paper. I know my father, Alex. He will want to see for himself that I am unharmed. Let me go to him."

"No."

"You can send men with me, armed men—"

"No."

"Please, Alex." She stroked the hollow of his throat with her finger. "What if it were your daughter that had been taken? Would you not wish to assure yourself of her safety?"

"I have no daughter."

"Are you certain?" She gave him a mysterious smile. "Perhaps I carry your child even now."

Alex stared at her, images exploding in his mind. Diana, round with child. A dark-haired infant suckling at her fair breast. Himself swinging a dark-eyed little girl in his arms, her giggles filling the air with joy.

His mouth suddenly dry, he placed a trembling hand on her abdomen. "Nothing would please me more."

"Think how you would feel," she said, covering his hand with hers, "if someone like Marcus snatched your daughter away without a word. You have no idea what happened to her. Horrible possibilities haunt your dreams. Frustration eats at you."

Her words struck home. He was a man who was dedicated to his family. Hadn't this whole farce begun because he was determined to avenge his brother's murder? His conscience nagged at him. He did not want to leave Diana's father in torment.

"I will think about it," he sighed. "But that is all."

"Thank you, Alex!" She kissed him.

"I'm going to regret this," he muttered.

"No, you won't." She kissed him again and made him forget his misgivings.

It was time. Frederick removed the ledger pages from behind the portrait of his late wife. The time limit he had given Chilton was up, and there was still no sign of Diana. A man of his word, he would bring the evidence to Morgan and set events in motion to recover his daughter.

He knew the pages could incriminate him as

well as Chilton, but the sacrifice was worth it. His own fate meant nothing. It was Diana who mattered . . . if she still lived.

Tucking the papers safely in the deep pocket of his coat, Frederick left for Morgan's office in Port Royal.

"I cannot fathom it." Diana bit her lip as she contemplated the disturbing news. The sailor who had borne the ill tidings shifted his feet as he awaited her decision.

They had dropped anchor in Port Royal early that morning, and Alex had left but a half hour past on an errand he had declined to discuss. He had refused to depart, however, until she gave him her word that she would remain on the ship until his return. At that time, he said, he would consider allowing her to visit her father. Truly, she had had every intention of obeying him.

But this changed everything.

She closed her hands over the rail and stared unseeingly at the buildings of Port Royal. She needed to determine what she would do next. She longed to keep her word to Alex. But Rico Fernandez, one of Alex's gunners, had heard in the marketplace that her father had become desperately ill shortly after her disappearance. Now, more than ever, she needed to go to him and assure him of her safety.

But she had promised Alex.

She bit her lip and tried to control the rising panic in her breast. Her mother had died of a fever four years past. She did not think she could stand to lose someone else she loved.

There was no choice. She had to go.

Alex would understand. As things stood, she could appreciate his reluctance to let her visit her father. Not only was there danger in doing so, but there was no guarantee that once she returned home, she would be able to come back to him. Knowing Frederick Covington, Diana had every reason to expect her father to keep her under lock and key until she was safely wed to some suitable gentleman. But this was different. Her father was ill, and he needed her. If Alex only knew, Diana was certain he would allow her to go back to Covington Hall. She had to assure her father that she was alive and unharmed.

"Would you arrange some sort of transportation, Mister Fernandez?" she asked, her decision made. "I would like to go visit my father."

Fernandez scratched his head. "The captain no like this," he said in his thick Spanish accent.

"The captain will understand. Now, will you do as I ask, or must I do it myself?"

"No, no. . . . I help you." He slapped his chest and grinned, displaying rotted teeth. "I come, too. Protect the woman of El Moreno."

"Very well." An armed escort would certainly placate Alex. "The captain will appreciate that, I am sure."

Fernandez nodded eagerly. "I go now . . . get carriage."

"A carriage would be perfect." She watched as he nodded again, then scurried away to see to his task. Alex would have no objections, she thought as she turned away from the rail. She knew he would understand that she had to go to her father when he was ill, since one of his own men would be accompanying her. She only wished Mister Fraser had not gone into Port Royal. Though she was acquainted with Fernandez, the only man from the skeleton crew aboard the *Marauder* who had survived Marcus's escape, she would have felt safer with someone she trusted at her side. Also, Birk was a physician.

Alex would have been her first choice, of course. She wanted her father to meet him, so that he could see for himself what a fine man Alex was. She thought they might like each other: both self-made men, both men of the sea.

She would tell her father about him. She would tell him how El Moreno had saved her life. How he had protected her. And how she loved him. Frederick Covington would come to know El Moreno for the man he was, not the legend. Just as she had.

With a contented smile, she went below to ready herself for her journey.

Chapter 18

Diana leaned forward and addressed the driver of the open carriage. "What seems to be amiss?"

"We're stuck, milady," the driver answered. He turned his scarred face toward her. "The mud is deep here, and the weight of the carriage is making it worse."

"I told you to go the other way," she reminded him, still annoyed that he had disregarded her instructions. "This is the long route to Covington Hall."

"My apologies, milady."

She sighed. "There is nothing to be done about it now. Mayhap if we all get out, the horses will be able to pull the carriage free."

The driver smiled, the long scar pulling grotesquely at the side of his mouth. "A fine idea, milady."

Her armed escort consisted of Rico Fernandez and Jean Latierre, two of Alex's crewmen. Each hopped from the carriage, and Latierre extended a hand to help Diana down. She wrinkled her nose as her slippers sank into the muck, but having grown up on the island, she was used to such inconveniences. Hitching up the skirts of Lady Rothstone's borrowed gown, she accepted Latierre's help as she made her way across the muddy road to a grassy slope. Fernandez got in position to push the carriage.

"I hope this will not take long," she called to the driver.

"Not long at all, my dear."

A chill went through her as she recognized the melodious masculine voice. She turned her head to see Marcus step out of the copse of trees behind her.

Latierre turned to face the threat, his hand on his sword hilt. Marcus drew a pistol and fired. The sharp crack echoed off the mountains in the distance; Latierre fell forward, blood soaking his shirt in the middle of his chest.

Diana gaped at the fallen man, then remembered her other bodyguard. She whirled around and found him leaning on the carriage, a bored look on his face. "Aren't you going to do something?" she cried.

"No." He smiled that stump-toothed grin again.

"Fernandez works for me," Marcus said. "He was most useful the night we first met, my dear . . . when your bastard lover clapped me in irons and held me prisoner in my own hold. He obligingly let me out so that I might retake my ship."

"Traitor," Diana hissed at the Spaniard.

"But I believe he has outlived his usefulness." Marcus nodded, and a second pistol shot exploded. Fernandez fell into the muck with a splat, a stupid grin still on his face. "Excellent shot," the pirate commented.

"Thank ye, Cap'n." The driver blew on his smoking pistol.

Diana stared wide-eyed from Latierre to Fernandez and finally to Marcus. "How could you? Fernandez was one of your own men."

"My dear." Marcus took her arm and smiled. "Never trust a traitor."

"Do not touch me," she hissed, yanking her arm away.

"Really, my dear. Your manners are atrocious." He grabbed her arm again and held it firmly. "Scroggins!"

The ugly seaman appeared from among the trees. "Aye, Cap'n?"

"Help Jack get the carriage out. It will be more comfortable riding to Chilton's estate in that rig than on horseback." He gave an evil laugh. "Besides, I've another use for our mounts."

"Aye, Cap'n."

Marcus turned his attention back to her as Scroggins scurried to obey. "My apologies, my dear. Did I not introduce you to your driver? Meet Jack Scabb, first mate aboard the *Marauder*. And, of course, you know Scroggins."

She tried once more to pull her arm from his grasp. Unsuccessful, she glared up into his glittering green eyes. "You will regret this. He will come for me, you know."

To her dismay, he laughed. "My dear, I am counting on it."

"As always, I am pleased to see you, Rothstone." Henry Morgan toyed with a jeweled snuffbox that had been a gift from the king several years before. He traced his finger over the miniature portrait of His Majesty that graced the lid, then pinned Alex with a shrewd stare. "But why are you here if you have not captured Marcus?"

"There was a complication." Sitting on the other side of the desk in Morgan's Port Royal office, Alex smiled as he imagined Diana's reaction were she to hear herself called that. "Marcus abducted Diana Covington."

"So I have heard." Morgan pushed away the snuffbox. "The gossips have been chattering about the incident for the past week. The girl's reputation is ruined."

"Bloody hell." Alex clenched his jaw. "It had to be Chilton. No doubt the blackguard still means to have her as his wife."

"At this moment, he is the only man in Port Royal who would wed the girl, heiress or no," Morgan agreed. "Though I do find it strange that Frederick did not come to me about it."

"Mayhap he feared for his daughter's life."

Morgan sat back in his chair and tapped his fingers on the arm, raising his brows at Alex. "Am I mistaken in believing that you know more of this situation than I do, Rothstone?''

"No, sir, you are not mistaken." He summarized events, explaining about Chilton's partnership with Marcus and how Frederick had discovered it. He told of the plan to blackmail Frederick into producing the ledger pages by threatening Diana's life. He gave the details of the conversation Diana had overheard between her father and Chilton, but avoided all mention of his personal relationship with the lady. Still, Morgan gave him a knowing smile when he finished the story.

"So, you are taken with the girl, Rothstone."

Alex nodded. He should have known Morgan would put the pieces together. "I intend to wed her, sir, as soon as my life is my own again."

"You have my best wishes, of course." Morgan sat back and toyed with his mustache. "But what of Covington? Is he involved in this or not? Is he an honest man trying to stop a crime, or is he one of the jackals himself, seeking to gain from his associate's error?"

"I lean toward honesty," Alex said. "But that is only my opinion."

"Humph." Morgan pursed his lips. "I value your opinion, Rothstone. But I would prefer proof."

"As would I. I hope the ledger pages will exonerate him."

"Perhaps. To my knowledge, Covington has always been an honest man. I shall reserve judgment for now."

Alex nodded, knowing this was the only concession he would get from Morgan. He had spoken for Diana's father and in so doing, had fulfilled his promise. The decision rested in Morgan's hands, as it always had.

A disturbance erupted outside the office. Morgan waved his hand, and Alex slipped from his chair and ducked through the open first-floor window, pulling the shutters nearly closed. He peered through the slats just as the door flew open. Frederick Covington burst into the room.

"Sir Henry, I must speak with you!"

A harried clerk followed Frederick. "I tried to stop him, sir, but he just pushed me aside!"

Morgan stood, his brows raised with interest. " 'Tis quite all right, Milton. Go about your duties."

With a resentful glance at Frederick, the clerk left the room, slamming the door behind him.

"Brandy, Frederick?" Morgan stepped toward the crystal decanter. "It will calm your nerves."

"I fear nothing will calm my nerves," Frederick responded, clenching his hands around the packet of papers he held. "I have much to tell you, Sir Henry, and when I am through, it would not surprise me if you clapped me in irons and hanged me at dawn. But you must be informed."

Morgan poured two measures of brandy and turned back to Diana's father. "You intrigue me, Covington. Sit down, and tell me your tale." He held out one of the snifters.

Covington looked from the offering to the papers in his hands. Indecision swept his blunt features, then his mouth tightened. He thrust the pages at Morgan.

"Take these, Sir Henry. Then if you still want to offer me refreshment, I will accept it. These are—"

"Pages from Chilton's ledger. Aye, I know." Morgan took the documents with one hand and offered the brandy with the other. "I said sit down, Covington. We have much to discuss."

Obviously confused, Frederick took the drink and sank into the chair.

"I understand that Marcus abducted Diana because of these." Morgan sat and leafed through the pages, scanning each one rapidly but thoroughly. "I can see why." He looked up, his shrewd gaze pinning Frederick where he sat. "I even suspected that *you* might have something to do with this."

Covington swallowed hard. "I understand how incriminating it must look . . ."

"Indeed it does." Morgan sat back, scrutinizing Frederick as he tapped his fingers on the arm of his chair. "Still, I am inclined to believe you, Frederick. First of all, you have a reputation as an honest fellow. Secondly, your daughter's life is in danger now that you have brought these pages to me. Only a man of integrity would make such a choice. And thirdly . . ." He gestured, and Alex pushed

open the window and reentered the room.
"Someone else told me the very same tale moments before you arrived."

Frederick jumped to his feet as he spotted
Alex. "Who the devil is this?"

"Frederick, may I present El Moreno?" With
a nod of his head, the lieutenant-governor indicated that Alex take a seat.

Alex grinned and bowed at Frederick, then
settled into the other chair in front of the massive desk.

Frederick remained standing, his mouth
agape. "El Moreno? What madness is this, Sir
Henry?"

"No madness, Frederick. El Moreno has been
looking into Chilton's illegal activities with an
eye toward capturing Marcus." Morgan
grinned. "In short, he works for me."

Frederick's puzzled expression changed to
one of comprehension. "Who better to catch a
pirate than another pirate?"

"Indeed." Impressed with the man's quick
deduction, Alex wondered how much to tell
him. He looked to Morgan.

"As I said," the lieutenant-governor continued, correctly interpreting Alex's glance, "this
man has been working for the Crown. Several
days ago, he engaged Marcus in battle. The
blackguard escaped, but El Moreno was able to
rescue your daughter."

"Diana?" Frederick straightened in his chair
and turned beseeching eyes to Alex. "Was
she . . . is she . . . ?"

"She is very much alive, sir," Alex reassured him. "Diana is a very resourceful woman. She escaped Marcus on her own before he could hurt her."

"Thank God." Frederick sagged back in his chair. "Where is she now?"

"Aboard my ship. I wanted to be certain it was safe before I brought her home." Alex looked Frederick straight in the eye. "Rest assured that your daughter is unharmed."

Some of the worry lines in Frederick's forehead eased. "My thanks, good sir. I feared the worst."

"You had cause." Alex turned to Morgan. "What now?"

Morgan heaved himself from his chair and took a moment to lock the papers in a box on his desk. "It is obvious to me by his own actions that Frederick is an innocent pawn in this dastardly scheme." He tucked the key to the box in his pocket. "Therefore, I propose that we reunite father and daughter and then go after that buffoon Chilton."

"Agreed." Frederick stood as well. "Shall we go now? I am eager to see my daughter again."

Alex remained seated, his mind awhirl as the two men discussed giving Diana into her father's care. He had gotten used to having her with him and was loath to give her up. Still, it was only a temporary measure. Reluctantly, he got to his feet.

"My ship is anchored near King's Wharf."

"Let us away, then," Frederick said eagerly.

Alex turned toward the door just as it was flung open. The pasty-faced clerk stumbled inside, a pistol at his back. Two rough-looking seamen followed him, one holding the weapon that so quailed the dutiful Milton. The other, a huge fellow with matted hair and an even dirtier beard, carried a blanket-wrapped bundle draped over his shoulder.

Alex stared at the bundle, realizing that it was just the right size to be a person. A woman, perhaps . . .

His blood froze. Diana. Was she safe aboard his ship, cursing him for not indulging her desire to see her father? Or had she somehow been lured away? . . .

He could not finish the thought.

The brawny fellow shrugged, letting his burden fall to the floor at the men's feet. The thing landed with a sickening thud that Alex had heard all too often in battle. The thud of lifeless human flesh hitting hard wood.

"A gift for ye," the shorter man sneered, revealing black holes where he had once had teeth. His ragged clothing hung from his scrawny frame, but his skeletal fingers looked strong and sure on the hammer of the pistol. "From Marcus."

"You will dangle for this outrage—both of you!" Morgan roared. "And that devil you call master along with you!"

The two laughed. The smaller one pointed his pistol at the lieutenant-governor and fired. Morgan dived for the floor. Alex took a step forward and found the pistol pointed at his chest.

"I wouldn't do that," the smaller man cackled. "Ye have to open your present. Marcus sends his regards." He fired wildly at Alex, causing him to duck, then the two men turned and fled the room.

"Aren't you going after them?" Frederick demanded. "They might lead you to Marcus."

"No." Alex knelt down. Slowly, carefully, he set about untying the rope that secured the blanket. He heard Morgan come up behind him just as the last knot gave way. The edges of the covering fell open.

"Sweet Jesus," Frederick whispered, his voice thick with horror.

"The bastard is an animal," Morgan growled.

Alex only stared. Black hair, he realized with mind-numbing relief. *Not red.*

The girl had been pretty once, Alex thought. Before Marcus had sliced her into something barely recognizable as human. He reached out and gently closed her blank, staring eyes.

A choking sound drew his attention to the clerk. The young man turned away from the body and promptly emptied the contents of his stomach behind Morgan's desk.

"Blast it all, Milton!" Morgan muttered.

Alex turned back to the body and wrapped the blanket around the girl once more.

"What kind of monster *is* Marcus?" Frederick whispered, his face still chalky from shock.

"To think, he had my Diana at his mercy . . ."
He looked at Alex. "I thank you, sir, for saving
my daughter's life. If she had stayed with
him . . ."

"I know." Alex tightened his lips. "I have
seen Marcus's handiwork before."

"Thank God Diana is safe aboard your
ship," Frederick continued. "I thought for a
moment—"

"So did I." Alex stood and looked down at
the blanket-wrapped corpse.

Frederick let out a relieved breath. "And
now, gentlemen, if you do not mind, I have a
most urgent need to see my daughter."

"I completely understand," Morgan agreed.
He waved a hand at the blanketed body. "Milton, clean up this mess, eh?"

The clerk blanched at the order and rushed
behind Morgan's desk again.

The ex-buccaneer snorted with disgust. "He
wouldn't have lasted ten minutes under my
command. Back to your post, Milton!"

The clerk scurried from the room, still shaking from the horrors he had observed. In the
doorway, he nearly ran right over the dark-
haired man entering the room.

"Alex!" Birk swiped a hand over his sweaty
brow, panting with exertion.

Morgan glared at Alex. "Blast it all, man!"
he thundered. "Did you tell your whereabouts
to every fool on the streets?"

"Calm yourself, Sir Henry," Alex reassured
him. "This is Birk Fraser, my ship's surgeon."

"Hmph." Morgan scowled as Birk came forward.

"Alex." Birk stopped before him, his eyes solemn. "She's gone."

"What!"

The Scot held up a folded piece of paper. "And this just arrived, pinned to the bodies o' Fernandez and Latierre."

Alex took the paper. His fingers trembled. "What happened?"

"From what I ken," Birk explained, "the lassie heard that her father was ill and near to dyin'. She went to see him before he breathed his last. Latierre and Fernandez went with her."

"*I* am her father," Frederick spoke up. "And as you can see, I am in perfect health."

" 'Twas no doubt a ruse devised by Marcus," Morgan said. "That spawn of Satan will dangle for this, I swear it."

Alex stared at the note, his mind numb as he realized what Birk had just told them. *Marcus had Diana.*

"Are you goin' to open that, Alex?"

"Aye, man," Morgan urged. "Let's hear what the bastard has to say."

Slowly Alex unfolded the note. Something fell from within the creases of the paper. He glanced down. A lock of curling red hair drifted gently down to coil over the blanket-clad body.

Alex forgot about the note. He could only stare at the coppery strands as they rested upon the blanket shroud of the murdered girl. *Diana,* he thought with growing anguish. *Dear Lord. Diana!*

Dimly he heard Morgan demanding something, Frederick chiming in. But their words disappeared in the terror that rose like a storm within him. *Marcus had Diana!*

"I'll read the blasted thing," Morgan announced. He snatched the note away. Alex barely noticed. Bending, he carefully took the lock of hair in his hand. He stroked it with one finger, remembering how he had loved the feel of Diana's fiery mane spread over his chest.

Morgan cleared his throat and read, "*Chilton's estate. Your lady awaits. And this time, to the death.*"

To the death. Alex watched how the hair curled over his finger. Aye. This time Marcus would die. Even if he had to sacrifice his own life to ensure it.

"What's this?" he heard Birk say.

"A woman who had the misfortune to encounter Marcus," Morgan replied. "Have a care, man. 'Tis not a pretty sight."

"I'm a physician, sir, and quite used to . . . Sweet Jesu!"

"Warned you," Morgan said.

Birk briefly examined the woman, then covered her again and looked up to meet Alex's gaze. "Good God, he's findin' ways to keep them alive longer."

Alex closed his eyes, anguish and fear blocking coherent thought. No longer was this a game of cat and mouse. This was about life.

And death.

"I'm thinkin' on how he lured the lassie away," Birk said, standing. He gripped Alex's arm, forcing him to open his eyes. "You might remember that Fernandez was the only survivor the day Marcus escaped from you."

"Treachery," Morgan growled. "The poxy wretch must have been in league with Marcus the whole time."

"Aye, that's my thinkin'." Birk studied Alex with concern.

Alex turned from his friend's gaze and came face-to-face with Diana's father.

"Do you mean to tell me," Frederick said with agitation, "that one of your men betrayed you, and now that foul creature has my daughter?"

"Yes." Alex met the accusation in the man's eyes without flinching. The emotions he saw in Frederick's expression echoed his own fear and shock.

"Then as captain, you are responsible for the actions of your men," Frederick charged. "And Diana's fate as well."

"Now, just a bloody minute—" Birk began.

"No, Birk. He is right. I should have foreseen this." Alex took a deep breath, trying to quell the unfamiliar feelings that restrained him from action. He was more used to charging forward, but the burden of guilt proved too heavy to bear into battle.

Frederick pointed a finger at Alex. "If anything happens to my daughter—"

"Stop this at once!" Morgan thundered. "While we stand here casting blame, the blackguard yet escapes us. We must ride for Chilton's estate immediately!"

"Chilton!" Frederick snarled. "I'll throttle that primping popinjay for this! If Diana is harmed, neither he nor Marcus will live to see the sun rise."

"I will summon a patrol of my best men," Morgan stated, clapping a hand on his sword hilt. "This time the scurvy knave will not escape!"

"*I demand that you let me pass!*" The feminine voice carried clearly from outside Morgan's office.

"Bloody hell." Frederick shook his head and sent Morgan an apologetic glance. "Sir Henry, that shrieking harpy is Maude Dunstan, my wife's cousin. She is also Diana's companion, and somewhat outspoken on the subject of piracy."

"You tell that brigand to admit me, young man!" Maude shouted. "I have very powerful friends within the Jamaica Assembly!"

Morgan scowled. "I have no time to argue politics, Frederick, much less with a loud-mouthed shrew."

"I am well aware that Diana's life is in danger, Sir Henry! I will deal with Maude."

"And I will muster the patrol."

Alex heard their voices from what seemed a

long distance away. *Diana's companion . . . life in jeopardy . . . Diana's life is in danger . . . no time to argue politics . . . no time . . .*

There was no time.

Alex shook off the strange paralysis that gripped him. There was no time to wait for the patrol or for Frederick to deal with his argumentative relative. Every second that passed brought Diana closer to death at Marcus's hands.

"Out of my way!" A series of thuds sounded from outside the office.

Alex tucked the lock of hair away in his coin purse. Without a word to anyone, he started for the window.

Birk grabbed his sleeve as he swung one leg over the sill. "Alex, what's the matter with you? I've never seen you so rattled."

"Tell McBride to bring the *Vengeance* to that stretch of beach near Chilton's estate. I have a feeling the *Marauder* will be waiting there."

Birk gaped at him. "You dinna think to confront that madman alone, in this condition?"

"This is between Marcus and me and no one else." Alex heard the door to the office crash open. "Follow with Morgan's troops if you wish, but pass on my orders to McBride first."

"But—"

"Farewell, Birk." Alex slipped out the window just as Diana's companion burst into the room. Her voice carried to him as he ran for Frederick's mount.

"Look at the lot o' you, standin' about while

my bairn is nowhere to be found! Is there no man who means to save my poor Diana's life?"

She continued to harangue them, Morgan's vehement disclaimers going virtually unnoticed. Alex wheeled the bay stallion around and set off for Chilton's estate.

It was a good day to die.

Chapter 19

Chilton looked up from the papers on his desk as Marcus dragged Diana into the library, Scroggins bringing up the rear. The nobleman gaped and sprang to his feet, his chair skidding backward. "What the devil are you doing here?"

"I have brought your bride, Peter." Marcus shoved Diana between her shoulder blades. "Summon the priest. I am eager to claim my reward."

Diana caught her balance by grabbing the edge of the desk. She glared at Chilton. "What is he talking about?"

Chilton came out from behind the desk. "I offered him payment if he recovered you from El Moreno." He caressed her cheek. "That vermin did not harm you, did he?"

She slapped his hand away. "Which vermin would that be, my lord? El Moreno or the one you hired?"

"Now, Diana . . ."

"I gave you no permission to address me so

personally, *my lord*. I demand that you return me to my father at once!"

"You are in no position to make demands." Marcus's voice rang with leisurely menace as he seated himself. "Give me use of a room, Peter, and I shall work some of that arrogance out of her."

Diana eyed him with revulsion. "You can try."

Marcus threw back his head and laughed. "Still she spits at me! I shall enjoy breaking you, my love."

Chilton stepped between them before Diana could retort. He took her hand. "You are overset, my dear. I shall have one of the servants escort you to a room to rest."

"Scroggins can do it." Marcus glanced at the seaman and jerked his head toward Diana.

Chilton frowned. "I do not trust him."

"Nonsense, Peter." Marcus steepled his fingers. "Scroggins will not harm the wench. He knows better than to disobey my direct orders."

"I heard no orders." Chilton held Marcus's stare until perspiration dripped down the fop's face. After a long, tense moment during which Diana held her breath, Marcus broke the eye contact and turned to his henchman.

"You will not touch her, not so much as a finger, Scroggins, or you will answer to me."

"Aye, Cap'n."

Scroggins reached to take Diana's arm, then

pulled back at the last moment. Instead he gestured for her to precede him.

"The second door at the top of the staircase," Chilton directed.

Diana did not move. "What if I refuse?"

The seaman laid a hand on the butt of his pistol. "I don't have to touch ye to shoot ye."

She swallowed and glanced at Chilton. Of all of them, he seemed the most sympathetic to her plight.

He took her hand. "Marcus means to have you," he murmured in a voice too low for the other men to overhear. "But if you consent to marry me, I will protect you."

Never, her mind screamed. She bit back her revulsion and forced herself to smile at him. "I will consider it." She pulled her hand from his. With one last wary look at Marcus, she followed Scroggins from the room.

As soon as she was gone, Chilton whirled on Marcus. "You fool! You almost ruined everything!"

Marcus folded his hands over his stomach and rested one foot on the knee of the opposite leg. "I merely want what is mine, Peter."

"Damn it all, Simon! We have a bargain. Before you can have her, she must be my wife. Otherwise you will not see one gold piece from her dowry."

Marcus grew very still. "How many times have I warned you not to call me that?"

Chilton stared with wide eyes and open mouth. "I'm s-s-sorry. It just . . . slipped out."

Marcus unsheathed his knife and began to scrape the mud from his boots. "You grow bold, Peter."

Chilton watched the clumps of partially dried mud drop on his expensive carpet. Sunlight glinted off the blade, as if flashing a warning. "I—I merely wish for things to progress as they should."

Marcus held up his dagger and blew flecks of dried mud from the blade. "As do I."

"We are in agreement, then." Chilton smoothed the chocolate brown velvet of his coat, surreptitiously wiping the dampness from his palms. "I will instruct the servants to bring refreshments for you, Si—I mean, Marcus. I will also send for the priest."

"Excellent. You are learning, Peter." Marcus tossed the knife and caught it, then slid it into its sheath. "Let us hope you survive the lesson."

Diana Markham, Marchioness of Chilton. Wife to Peter Markham. Mistress of a vast estate. Mother of the future marquis.

Not bloody likely.

Diana snorted and turned away from the window. She stalked through the garishly decorated bedroom in which she was imprisoned. The mere thought of wedding Chilton struck her as only slightly less pleasurable than having a thousand ants crawling over her bare skin. Never—not if he were the last man on earth. Not even to save herself from Marcus.

She could never imagine marrying any man except Alex.

Alex hadn't said anything about marriage, but Diana would accept nothing less. Once a mistress, never a wife: that was the saying. But Alex had said he loved her, and she knew that she loved him; therefore, nothing less than a lifetime commitment would do.

She would be his wife, old sayings be damned.

Where was he? she wondered impatiently. She worried the edge of the crimson and gold bed curtain with her fingers. There was no doubt in her mind that he would come. But as long as Marcus held her prisoner, Alex would be at a disadvantage.

She abruptly let the drapery go. She would not stand about waiting to be rescued. Alex would be safer going up against Marcus if the pirate could no longer use her as leverage against her beloved. Besides, there was no telling what Marcus and Chilton planned for her. As of yet, they did not know that she was aware of their conspiracy to blackmail her father. It would be best to slip away now, before they learned of her knowledge.

She evaluated her circumstances. She had heard Chilton dismiss the servants, so she knew that only the four of them remained in the house. Scroggins guarded her door, which meant Marcus and Chilton were probably downstairs.

The first order of business was to escape

from the room. She thought for a moment, then smiled as a plan formed in her mind. After making certain that all the items she needed were at hand, she called out for Scroggins.

The repulsive little man opened the door. "What the devil are ye squawkin' about?"

"I have need of the chamber pot," she announced in imperious tones.

He squinted at her, one hand on his pistol. " 'Tis likely under the bed, ye haughty bitch. I'm not yer servant to be fetchin' it for ye."

"You blithering fool," she replied in her most arrogant voice. "I know where to find the chamber pot. But 'tis full. I need you to empty it out."

Scroggins hitched up his breeches. "Just dump it out the window."

She looked down her nose at him. "I am certain that is what's done at the flea-infested inns that you frequent, you ignorant little toad. But we of the gentry conduct ourselves with more decorum. I wish to have this emptied properly at once!"

Scroggins stepped forward, pulling the pistol from his belt. "Don't be takin' that tone with me, wench. It wouldn't take much to convince me to put a ball in that pretty head o' yers."

"All I ask is that the chamber pot be emptied," she insisted. "If you do not believe it is full, then come see for yourself."

Scroggins hesitated. "You bring it to me."

She gave an exaggerated shudder. "I will

not. Suppose I spilled something on my gown?''

The seaman muttered an unfavorable remark about females and waved the pistol. "Pick it up."

Diana made a face and picked up the chamber pot, holding it out for his inspection. The contents sloshed loud enough for him to hear. "See? 'Tis almost full to the brim."

Scroggins snorted and came forward, shoving his pistol in his belt. He grunted something about playing lady's maid and reached for the pot.

An instant before he would have taken it from her, Diana tossed the contents right in his face. His angry bellow of surprise died a sudden death as she then shoved the chamber pot itself in his face. He pushed it aside, wiping one hand across his eyes and clawing for his pistol with the other. Diana grabbed the small stool used for climbing into the huge bed and swung it at his head. The stool connected with a sickening thunk, and Scroggins dropped to the floor, unmoving.

Diana stood panting for a moment, checking to be sure that he was indeed unconscious. She put down the stool and yanked the pistol from his belt. The wretched man did not even flinch. She stepped over his inert form and fled the room.

She started running down the hallway, then forced herself to slow to a walk. No need to alert Marcus or Chilton that something was wrong by running! Keeping close to the wall, she crept down the elaborate staircase. She reached the bottom with no incident and darted to the front door. Raised voices made her freeze with her hand inches from the door-knob.

"What do you mean, you will have her now? Damn it, Simon! You said after the wedding!"

Diana cautiously followed the sounds of the argument to the library. One majestic oak door stood open, and the other was closed. She pressed herself against the one that was shut and listened. The first voice had been Chilton's. But who was Simon?

"I told you not to call me that." She shivered as the bell-like tones of the familiar voice carried clearly. "I am Marcus now."

"You can call yourself whatever you like," came Chilton's agitated response. "But you are still Simon Chandler. You will be Simon Chandler until the day you die, and nothing will change that!"

There was a chilling pause before Marcus spoke again. "You dare much, Peter. Does the wench mean that much to you, then?"

"I have worked to have Diana Covington and her fortune since the first day I saw her. I will not let you ruin this for me."

"That is the second time you have called me by that name," Marcus drawled. "Should you utter it a third time, I shall have to kill you."

Diana could hear the promise in Marcus's words, but Chilton seemed deaf to it.

"More threats? You have tormented me since we were children, Simon. And why? Because I am the legitimate heir to the estate, and you are nothing but one of Father's by-blows!"

Dimly Diana registered the sound of a sword being drawn from its sheath, but she was too amazed to pay it much attention. Chilton and Marcus were brothers! Now she knew how the two had come into partnership in the first place.

Chilton's voice drew her attention back to the conversation.

"Now, now, put the sword away. You wish me to call you Marcus? Fine, I shall call you that." The hiss of the blade being replaced in its sheath told her that Marcus had been placated.

"Very wise of you, Peter."

Diana silently agreed.

"If you wish to be called Marcus, then I shall address you as such. But do not think I don't know where you got the name, brother. Marcus. Markham. A play on words, eh? But you shall never be a true Markham."

"I should have drowned you as an infant," Marcus sneered. "I would be more of a credit to the Markham name than a cowardly weakling like you."

"Killing me would do you no good," Chilton reminded him. "You were born on the wrong side of the blanket. You can never inherit."

"One never knows. Stranger things have happened."

"Can you not be satisfied with what you have?" Chilton whined. "You are rich beyond your wildest hopes. You stand to gain half of Diana's dowry once she becomes my wife. You even get the pleasure of bedding her first on our wedding night! What more do you want?"

Diana felt a jolt of alarm as the words rang in her head. Chilton planned to give her to Marcus on their wedding night? What kind of man was he?

She had to escape. Now.

As she whirled away from the library doors, her hip struck a table. The Chinese vase that stood upon it wobbled. She reached for it, but it brushed past her fingers and crashed to the floor. She streaked for the door.

"What was that?" Chilton cried. The two men ran out into the hallway.

"Stop the bitch!" Marcus shouted.

Their booted feet thundered behind her as she raced through the foyer. Just as she jerked open the door, a large male hand reached over her shoulder and slammed it shut again. She spun around and raised the pistol. The weapon was yanked from her hand.

"Going somewhere?" Marcus asked.

To the death. Alex leaned over the horse's neck, urging it on. No more games. Gone was the adventure, the thrill of besting one's enemy in a battle of wits. This time Marcus would die.

A false calm settled over him, masking the roiling emotions that devastated his control.

Once this had been about avenging William's death. But William was gone, and nothing would bring him back. All that mattered was Diana.

From the very first, Alex had been attracted to Diana's vitality. He, who had so long been obsessed with death, was drawn to her warmth and vivacity. And now Marcus threatened to snuff out her life's flame. The world would be so very dark without Diana.

Whatever the cost, Diana must live.

He smiled sardonically as Chilton's estate came into view. Perhaps this was the way it had been fated all along. How many battles had he fought with Marcus, how many men had they sent to their deaths . . . all to bring them to this moment.

Marcus would die this day. Of that Alex was sure. And Diana would live. As he approached the confrontation, Alex knew without a doubt that he would gladly take a killing blow to land a killing blow. Though he wanted to live and spend the rest of his days with Diana, he knew it might not be possible. If his death proved to be the sacrifice that ensured Diana's survival of this peril, then so be it.

But if he did die, he would take Marcus with him to hell.

Marcus laughed and shoved the pistol in his belt. Grabbing Diana's arm, he roughly dragged her down the hallway. "Come, my dove."

Chilton stood near the library doors, worry etched on his thin face. Marcus shoved Diana into the room. Snarling, she whirled around with her fist raised. Marcus caught her hand before it struck his face. In a lightning-quick move, he seized both her wrists and pinned them behind her back.

"I love a woman with spirit," he declared, amusement heavy in his voice.

"What shall we do now?" Chilton followed them into the room, twisting his fingers together. He looked to Marcus for guidance.

"Commence with the wedding, of course."

"You are mad if you believe I would consent to marry *him*!" Diana snapped.

"Do you hear that? She refuses! Now what?"

Marcus applied more pressure to his grip, twisting her arms even more. "She will agree. Or she will die."

"Then I will die," she vowed, wincing at the pain.

Marcus chuckled at her response. "I believe she finds you unattractive, brother! Perhaps she prefers a real man in her bed." He squeezed one of her buttocks, laughing as she squirmed away from his touch.

"Are you mad?" Chilton yelped.

Marcus turned his predatory gaze on Chilton. "Cease your squawking, Peter. You remember our agreement: I get first turn on the wench. You can have what is left." He chuckled. "I doubt you could handle much more than that."

Chilton flushed and clenched his hands together so tightly that his knuckles showed white. "But it was supposed to be after the wedding! You are going back on your word, Simon!"

Releasing Diana's wrists, Marcus shot out a hand and grabbed Chilton by the throat. "I warned you about calling me that, Peter."

"S-sorry," Chilton rasped. "I am overset."

"I can see that." Marcus shoved him away.

Chilton fingered his throat. "Ever since we were children, I have called you Simon. You cannot expect the habits of a lifetime—"

"Enough." Marcus turned his back in dismissal. "And as for you, my dear ..." He grabbed Diana as she tried to slip toward the terrace doors. "You cannot mean to leave so soon."

Diana looked down at the fingers locked around her wrist, then raised her eyes. "Apparently not."

He chuckled and stroked his palm over her cheek. "I have a mind to sample your charms ... immediately." Marcus pulled her against his body. Clamping his arm around her waist, he insinuated one thigh between her legs and slowly wound her hair around his hand. "Do you really want such a one as she for your wife, Peter? Is your greed for her gold so great that you would accept a soiled bride?"

"What do you mean, soiled bride? She is the granddaughter of a duke!"

"And the whore of my enemy." Marcus

yanked her head back so that she looked directly into his piercing green eyes. "Tell me, bitch, how does that hellspawn El Moreno perform in bed? Does he plow you well as a man should? Or can he do the deed at all?"

"He is more of a man than you can ever hope to be," she said with biting certainty.

"Do you think so?" He gave her a cold, savage smile. "Allow me to change your opinion." He crushed his mouth to hers in a brutal kiss, scraping his teeth over her tender lips and drawing blood. Then he released her.

Her mouth throbbing, she glared at him. "If I had a sword, I would run it through your black heart," she declared passionately.

"Fight me," he dared her, staring into her eyes. "Do it."

Chilton tugged on Marcus's shoulder. "Stop this, do you understand? You get her *after* the wedding!"

Marcus shrugged him off and glared. "What difference does it make if I take her before or after the vows are said?"

Chilton spluttered and could not look the pirate in the face.

Marcus narrowed his eyes. "Or is it that you want her all for yourself? Perhaps you intend to renege on our bargain, brother?" He shoved Diana aside.

She stumbled and grabbed a chair to stop herself from falling. As she watched the two men circle each other, she inched toward the terrace. Clearly, Marcus was mad.

"Of course I mean to keep our bargain!" Chilton backed away as Marcus stalked him. "I never said otherwise!"

Marcus grabbed his brother by the front of his coat. "You mean to betray me, don't you, Peter? After all, everyone betrays me eventually. Perhaps your whore means more to you than your brother."

"N-no! Of course not! Never!" Chilton's voice trembled, and he glanced at Diana as she edged closer to the terrace doors. His eyes held a plea, whether for aid or forgiveness she did not know.

"You lie!" Marcus roared. "Your lust for the wench has made you foolish. That you would turn on me . . ." The pirate released him, raking his contemptuous gaze over his brother as Chilton stumbled to regain his footing.

"N-no, Simon! I swear, I would never betray you!"

Marcus whirled Chilton around, hooked an arm around his neck, and jerked the nobleman back against him.

"I warned you not to call me that, brother." Drawing his blade, he slit Chilton's throat with one efficient stroke.

Her hand on the door latch, Diana watched with horror as blood spurted from the wound, raining on the carpet and splattering the papers on the desk. Wet, gurgling sounds came from Chilton as he thrashed in Marcus's arms. With a horrible choking sound, his struggle ceased.

Marcus let Chilton's limp body crumple to

the floor. Bending, he wiped his dagger clean on his brother's expensive silk coat. When he straightened, he pinned her with his merciless stare.

"You are next."

His visible pleasure at the prospect sent her whirling to unlatch the doors. Her trembling fingers refused to obey her. A sob caught in her throat as she rattled the door handle frantically.

A hand clamped down on her shoulder. She shrieked as Marcus spun her to face him.

"Too late," he smirked.

"No, Marcus," came another voice. " 'Tis too late for you!"

Diana's heart soared. Alex! She met his gaze over Marcus's shoulder, smiling tremulously to show him she was all right.

Marcus turned to face his nemesis, keeping Diana behind him.

"El Moreno," he hissed. "At last."

Alex allowed himself one glance at Diana. Once assured of her safety, he kept his gaze fixed on his enemy. Marcus was a master at escaping tight situations.

"You are finished, Marcus," he said. He aimed his pistol at the other man's heart. "If you step away from Diana right now, you may yet live to walk from this room."

"So concerned for your whore?" Marcus sneered. "How touching."

"Move away from her, Marcus."

"As you will." Marcus stepped to the side,

then yanked Diana in front of him as a shield. He drew his dagger and held it to her throat. "Go ahead," he taunted. "Fire." He rested his chin atop Diana's head and smirked. "But you might miss and hit your lady love."

Alex tightened his fingers around the pistol to stop the uncharacteristic trembling. He longed to put a ball in Marcus's black heart. Then all of them would be free. But he could not risk Diana.

He glanced at her. She looked back, wide-eyed with fear, but said nothing. She didn't cry, didn't beg. She simply watched him with complete trust and total love. Her faith in him almost cracked the fragile restraint that held back his uncontrolled emotions.

"Put the pistol on the floor and step back from it," Marcus instructed. "The sword as well."

Alex complied. He never took his eyes from his enemy.

"Very good. I had not credited you with such intelligence."

Anger flared, but Alex tamped it down. If he let loose his rage, then none of them would survive this. "Let her go, Marcus, and I will let you live."

"Brave words from an unarmed man!" Marcus laughed and tightened his arm about Diana's waist. "I do not take kindly to threats, as dear Peter discovered to his misfortune."

Alex glanced at Chilton's body. "He is dead, then?"

"Quite."

"One less neck to stretch on the public gibbet. Morgan will not be pleased. Of course there is still you to entertain the crowd, Marcus." Alex tried to inject sarcasm into his voice, but all he could think about was the blade at Diana's throat.

"I have no intention of dancing at the end of a rope, and certainly not for Morgan's amusement," Marcus sneered.

"A pity. I had thought to enjoy the sight myself." Alex took a step forward.

"The only sight you will enjoy is that of your doxy's demise should you move again." Marcus lifted Diana's chin and caressed her bared throat with his blade.

Alex halted. He glanced at Diana. She gave him a tremulous smile. Then her eyes widened in alarm.

A foul stench alerted him to danger. He spun aside just in time to avoid the blade intended for his back. With a sweep of his arm, he sent the dagger flying from his assailant's fingers.

"Ye've the luck of the devil!" Scroggins cursed. He aimed a fist at Alex's midsection.

Alex blocked the punch and countered with a powerful stroke to the jaw. In the blink of an eye the wiry seaman came back with a series of vicious blows. Behind him, Alex heard the terrace doors crash open. He kicked Scroggins in the kidneys and whirled to see Marcus drag Diana out of the house.

"Diana!" he roared. Madness shattered his

brittle control, and rage flared like a flame.

Scroggins leaped on Alex's back and locked his arms tightly around his throat. Alex slammed his elbow backward into the man's midsection. The henchman lost his grip and fell, but leaped to his feet. Alex turned, raining blow upon blow on the seaman, aware that every second brought Marcus closer to a successful escape—with Diana.

A clatter of footsteps echoed in the hall. Morgan burst into the library, followed by Frederick and a patrol of soldiers.

"Morgan!" With a mighty strike, Alex sent Scroggins stumbling backward. The henchman landed in the arms of Sir Henry Morgan.

"Where is my daughter?" Frederick demanded.

Alex scooped up his sword and pistol. He ran for the doors to the terrace. "With Marcus. But they will not get far."

Morgan shoved Scroggins into the arms of one of his soldiers. "Wait! We—"

"No time." Alex slipped through the doors and picked up Marcus's trail. He would rescue Diana. And then Marcus would die . . . whatever the cost.

Chapter 20

"**B**last those scurvy bastards!" Marcus stood on the beach and studied the horizon. "Where the devil are they? I told them to meet me here."

Diana turned her gaze from the empty sea and looked up the rocky incline they had just descended. At any moment she expected to see a familiar figure in black appear atop the craggy cliff. She wished she could summon him with sheer force of will, but wishes were as plentiful as the sand that surrounded them. Reality was Marcus's bruising hold on her arm.

"It seems we must wait. Whatever shall we do with the time?" Marcus turned his attention from the horizon to smirk at her. "What say we begin the festivities while we await my ship?"

"I say no."

"Ah, such fire in you, my dear." Marcus forced her chin up and smiled into her eyes. "You add spice to the feast."

"Add this to your feast." She kicked him hard in the shin.

Savagery twisted his expression. "So. You wish to play, do you? So be it." With his clenched hands, he ripped open her gown to the waist, breaking the laces and tearing the fragile chemise to leer at her bare breasts.

She fought him, cursing him, using every dirty trick her father had taught her. He laughed and jerked her hard against him.

"Resist," he grated in her ear, his voice gritty with lust. "Scratch me. Bite me. 'Twill make the conquest so much sweeter."

Tears streamed down her face as she struggled against him. He squeezed her sensitive breasts. The rough skin of his hands chafed the tender flesh, and he twisted her nipples roughly, sending pain splintering along her nerve endings. His open mouth crushed hers, his teeth digging into the lips she tried to close against him, his tongue finally taking victory and thrusting into her mouth until she could barely breathe. The threat of his hardened sex rubbing against her hip sent new terror streaking through her. Then suddenly she was free.

"I shall enjoy breaking you," he said with a smile. He backhanded her across the face, sending her sprawling into the sand. "I shall make you forget that puling spawn you spread your legs for."

Diana sat up. She touched her throbbing mouth, and her fingers came away stained with blood. "You are not half the man he is!"

"Whore!" he snarled. He dropped to his knees beside her. "There are many ways to cause pain, my dear. And I look forward to showing you all of them." He shoved her skirts upward.

"Marcus!"

The pirate's head jerked up at the shout. He cursed and rose to his feet. Diana looked past him to see Alex scrabbling down the last few feet of the rocky incline. Her heart soared.

"I should have known better than to trust Scroggins. I shall have to take care of the matter myself." Marcus drew his sword.

"Alex!" Diana scrambled to her feet away from Marcus, holding the torn edges of her garments together.

"Diana." He came to her. Cupping her cheek, he slid his dark gaze over her, touching her ruined clothing and bleeding lip. His jaw tightened. "I love you," he said softly. "And my one regret is that I didn't have the chance to wed you."

"Oh, Alex." Tears stung her eyes. She laid her hand over his, but he pulled away.

She watched in confusion as he turned to Marcus, every muscle in his body taut. Drawing his sword, he touched the blade to his forehead in mocking salute.

"To the death," he challenged.

"Aye." Marcus copied the gesture. "To your death."

A small, ferocious smile tugged at Alex's lips. "Perhaps."

The battle began.

Clutching her bodice closed, Diana moved

back from the fray. Steel hissed against steel as the two men advanced and retreated. Tension hummed like a live thing between them. Death was in the air. But whose?

Diana worried her lower lip between her teeth as she watched Alex. Something was wrong. She had seen him fight Marcus before, the day he had rescued her from the *Marauder*. He had laughed then, smiled—thoroughly enjoyed the duel as if it were only an amusing exercise. But this time he did not laugh. His smiles were cold. This time, he was serious.

She recalled the murderous look in his eyes when he had seen her ripped clothing and bloody mouth. As she noticed the tension of his body, the emptiness in his eyes, she realized that he was not in control. Emotion drove him—pain and rage. And that could mean his downfall. Without control, he would make mistakes. And that could mean his death.

Fear gripped her heart.

Steel clanged. She watched the two men circle, her eyes fixed on Alex as he countered Marcus's moves. The two men were evenly matched in their skills; today she dreaded the outcome.

Marcus lunged suddenly and slashed. Alex hissed in pain, and blood welled from a slice in his upper arm.

"First blood to me," Marcus sneered. "But not nearly enough to suit me."

Alex pressed his lips together. "First blood," he agreed. Then he went at Marcus like a man possessed, his blade flashing in the sunlight.

Diana bit back a whimper as the blood slowly soaked Alex's sleeve. Already he had lost his edge. He fought recklessly, as if he didn't care whether he lived or died. All he wanted was to destroy Marcus. She wanted to cry, scream, beg him to stop. But she dared not distract him.

The battle swept the two men up and down the beach, the surf licking at their boots. Alex's weapon appeared a flashing blur as he attacked and retreated. Marcus thrust, and Alex whirled and came around to meet steel with steel. They locked together, sword to sword and shoulder to shoulder.

"I shall enjoy your whore," Marcus taunted. "Mayhap I shall take her as you slowly bleed to death, that you might enjoy her screams as you breathe your last."

"You will be dead," Alex snarled. Then he shoved Marcus, breaking them apart.

Marcus landed on his back in the sand, his sword falling from his grasp. Alex stumbled backward but quickly regained his balance. With a howl of triumph, he charged Marcus, his sword arcing down to finish the battle.

"Bastard!" Marcus rolled out of the way and stumbled to his feet. "I swear I will see you in hell this day!" He thrust his hand forward, flinging sand into Alex's face.

Alex cried out, clawing at his eyes.

Marcus grinned and aimed his sword at Alex's heart.

"Look out!" Diana screamed. She leaped on Marcus's back, reaching around to gouge at his face with her nails. He grabbed her by the hair and hauled her off his back, then he flung her to the sand at his feet.

"Bitch!" he snarled, kicking her viciously in the ribs. "Once I dispose of *him*, you'll regret you did that!"

He rounded on his blinded prey. Pain throbbing in her side, Diana pressed her lips together to keep from moaning and stumbled to her feet in time to see Marcus charge his opponent. Alex squinted at Marcus through the tears streaming from his abused eyes. A moment before the villain's sword seemed destined to spear his heart, Alex dropped to his hands and knees. The blade whooshed harmlessly over his head, and Marcus tripped over him. With a muffled curse, the pirate tumbled into the sand. Blinking rapidly, Alex struggled to his feet. He glanced over at Diana, his eyes red and watery from the sand. "Are you hurt?" he barked.

"No." Her breath hissed through her teeth as pain splintered through her side. "I'm all right."

Alex faced Marcus, who gasped to regain his breath. The two staggered as they circled each other, the fury of their fight obviously a physical drain on them. Marcus looked at Alex, his eyes narrowing with pure hate, and lunged. Alex spun out of the way, Marcus's blade missing his chest by inches.

"You are damnably hard to kill," the pirate complained, once more bringing his sword to bear.

"Too much of a challenge?" Tears still streamed down Alex's face from the sand, but Diana could tell as he focused on Marcus that his vision had returned completely.

"Weep not," Marcus crooned with a mocking grin. "I promise to kill you quickly."

Alex gave him a chilly smile. "I promise just to kill you."

Marcus came at him. The combat escalated into a storm of rapid moves and clashing blades. Neither gave quarter. The surf erased the footprints they made in the wet sand as each strove to gain the upper hand.

Then the boom of a cannon thundered over the roar of the sea. The *Marauder* appeared just offshore, the *Vengeance* hard on her tail. A wisp of smoke trailed from the deck of Alex's ship.

"How touching," Marcus taunted. "Your crew shall die with you."

As he spoke, the *Marauder* fired on the *Vengeance*. Only a sharp maneuver prevented her from being hit broadside. Water sprayed upward as the cannonball landed in the ocean.

"Perhaps not," Alex said.

Marcus roared with rage and came at him again.

"Diana!" a familiar voice called.

She was stunned to see her father and Sir Henry Morgan striding across the beach, followed by a dozen soldiers, one of whom pushed a prisoner before him.

"Papa!" Unable to take her gaze from the combatants, she fell into her father's arms with a sob. "Papa, you must stop them!"

"Thank God you are safe." Her father hugged her tightly and stroked her hair. "I thought never to see you again. Sir Henry said—"

"Sir Henry!" Pulling loose of her father's embrace, Diana turned to the lieutenant-governor and grabbed his arm with both hands. "Sir Henry, you must stop them! Please, stop the duel!"

"My dear girl—"

"Please," she begged, cringing as Marcus missed skewering Alex by a hair. "Please, before he gets killed!"

Morgan shrugged off his coat and draped it over Diana's shoulders. "Mistress Covington, no one will be killed this day. Marcus will stand trial for his crimes, as will this pathetic wretch." The ex-buccaneer indicated Scroggins.

The henchman glared. "And what about El Moreno? Is he goin' to hang as well?"

"El Moreno!" the guard captain exclaimed. "Where?"

"Right there, crossin' swords with the cap'n!"

The patrol leader gaped at the two battling pirates, then whirled on Morgan. "Do you want us to arrest them both, sir?"

"Of course we will take El Moreno into custody," Morgan announced.

"No!" Diana cried.

"Then should we break this up, sir?" the patrol leader asked.

"No." Morgan focused on the clashing swordsmen. "I am curious as to who the victor will be."

"You would let them kill each other out of curiosity?" Diana exclaimed, appalled.

"Young lady, I merely give the devil his due."

Frantic, Diana turned back to the battle. Her gaze locked on Alex as he struggled between life and death. Behind the combatants, the two ships mirrored the struggle between good and evil.

The smell of smoke drifted across the water as the guns boomed and cannonballs whistled through the air. Distant cries of alarm sounded from the *Marauder*. Then, sails aflame, Marcus's ship sank slowly into the sea.

"No!" Marcus cried. He moved into a position where he could see his vessel without letting down his guard. Faraway splashes indicated that Marcus's crew was abandoning the sinking craft. "Damn your hide, El Moreno! This is your doing!"

"No, Marcus." Alex nimbly fended off his opponent's wild swings. "This is your *undo-ing*."

"A pox on you! You think to take my life?"

"As you have taken others'. As you tried to

take Diana's." Alex countered Marcus's attempt to slice open his chest.

"So noble," Marcus sneered, slashing at Alex's midsection.

Diana inhaled sharply, then slowly exhaled as Alex jumped back to avoid the blade. He immediately engaged Marcus again.

"Tell me," Marcus taunted, "do you mean to avenge every death attributed to me?"

"You killed my brother," Alex growled. Violent grief twisted his face. "And you meant to harm Diana as well. For that you will die."

"Your brother?" Marcus swiftly eluded Alex's thrust. "I have killed so many Spaniards, I cannot possibly remember them all."

"He wasn't Spanish. He was English, aboard the *Marie Louise* out of France." Alex's breathing grew harsh as Marcus became more aggressive. His voice roughened. "You tied him naked to the mast and made him beg for his life. Then you butchered him, one body part at a time, and threw him to the sharks."

Diana's heart clenched with pain as he recited the horrors done to his brother. With each word that passed his lips, his movements grew more agitated, more frenzied.

"Oh, dear." Marcus smiled. "Was that whining bugger your brother? How pitiful he was, crying for mercy like a woman. 'Twas a relief when he finally died."

"You bastard," Alex snarled.

Marcus began to laugh. The sound grew louder and louder, drowning out the roar of the waves and the clash of the swords. While he gasped and howled as if demented, Marcus's guard dropped.

Alex moved in for the kill.

The laughter ceased. Marcus came around, his face a mask of mad determination. He swung a full circle, his blade arcing for Alex's throat. Alex ducked, and the sword whizzed over his head. He came up on the other side of Marcus's arm and pivoted, bringing his own blade down to slice through muscle and bone. Marcus screamed in pain. His spasming fingers opened; his sword fell into the sand; and he dropped to his knees, holding his half-severed arm.

Alex raised his sword.

Diana held her breath. His face looked hard and fierce, primitive, like a warrior chieftain about to destroy his enemy. He stood there for a long moment, poised to deliver the killing blow to the foe who knelt weaponless at his feet.

"Do it, goddamn you," Marcus spat.

Alex blinked. He frowned slightly, like a man trying to remember an elusive dream. Slowly he lowered the sword.

"It seems we will both live this day," he said.

Diana closed her eyes, beginning to tremble with relief. It was over.

"Arrest them." Glancing at the captain of the patrol, Morgan indicated the two pirates with a nod of his head.

"No!" Diana started toward Alex, but her father pulled her back.

"Let it be, daughter," he said.

"I cannot." Diana pulled free and ran to Alex as he was led up the beach by the patrol. She threw herself into his arms, despite her throbbing ribs. Resting her cheek against his chest, she gloried in the sound of his beating heart. She had never thought to hear it again.

One of the soldiers tried to pry her away, but Alex glared at him so fiercely that the man backed off. "Don't touch her," he growled, enfolding her in his arms.

Diana sent a pleading glance at Morgan as she embraced her beloved. "Sir Henry, not only has this man saved my life, but he captured Marcus as well. He has rid our island of a terrible evil. Does that count for nothing?"

"He will have a fair trial," Morgan answered.

"Fair? Nothing about this situation is fair!"

A soldier came forward and gently pushed Diana aside, then clapped manacles on Alex's wrists. Another claimed his sword belt, pistol, and the knife in his boot. The same was done to Marcus.

"What are you doing?" Diana stared at the chains in horror, then at Morgan. "Please, Sir Henry! Is this really necessary?"

Morgan looked away.

"Diana." Alex's soft tone held a command she could not ignore. She turned back to him, her heart clenching at the depth of emotion shining in his dark eyes. He smiled tenderly. " 'Tis best this way, my love," he said. "Go home with your father. Get married. And forget that you ever knew El Moreno."

"But I love you." She gripped the sleeves of his shirt with desperate fingers. Tears welled in her eyes. "It cannot end like this."

Alex lifted his manacled hands and brushed a teardrop from her cheek. "Do not cry, *amada*. All will be well."

"Come on." One of the soldiers grabbed his arm. " 'Tis the lockup for you."

"No!" Diana tightened her grip, forcing him to either stop or drag her along in the sand. Cupping Alex's cheek, she whispered, "I will find a way to free you."

"There is no way." His expression tender, he gently tugged his arm from her grasp. "*Amada*." Heedless of the people watching, he leaned forward to brush a kiss on her lips. "Just remember that this is not the end, my sweet. I love you."

His loving smile was the last thing she saw as the soldier shoved him forward.

"Easy, now!" Morgan went over and pushed the soldier aside. "This is a valuable prisoner, you know. You would not cheat us of a hanging by injuring him before he can stand at the gallows, would you?"

The soldier protested, but Morgan dismissed him. "See to the other. I will accompany this one myself." He went to Alex and rattled his chains to check their security, then signaled to the patrol and led the way toward the rocky path. Diana watched them go, helplessness weighing on her like the chains her beloved dragged with him.

Frederick frowned after Morgan and the patrol as they passed him, then turned to his daughter and opened his arms. Diana threw herself against him with a sob, clinging to him like she had when she was a little girl.

"He saved me," she sniffed, a tear trickling down her cheek. "I love him. And they are going to kill him!"

"El Moreno? But . . ." Frederick stopped midsentence and stared after at the patrol winding up the cliff with a confused expression.

"I know you probably think him a pirate, but—"

"On the contrary, I owe him a great debt." Frederick pulled forth a handkerchief and dabbed at the wetness on her face. "He brought you back to me."

"Sir Henry says he is to be hanged!"

Her father sighed. "I will talk to Morgan. But for now, let us go home."

She nodded, emotionally drained. Her father would be able to help, she thought. Morgan would see that delivering Marcus far outweighed any crimes Alex may have committed at sea. Her father slipped an arm around her shoulders, and she let him lead her toward the path.

They had just reached the bottom of the cliff when they heard a commotion.

"What the devil?" Shading his eyes, Frederick squinted upward. Diana did the same.

A shot rang out.

Diana's heart leaped into her throat. She saw Alex's dark form teeter for a moment at the edge of the cliff, one hand clutching his chest. Then he fell, plummeting to the sea below.

"No!" Her anguished cry echoed off the cliffs around them.

"By God," her father murmured.

"No, no, no." Diana clenched her hands and lifted them to her trembling lips, her gaze fixed on the water where Alex had disappeared. "Where are you? Alex, where are you?"

"Diana . . ." Her father reached for her.

"No, do not say it!" she cried. "He is alive. I know he is."

The moments ticked by, and still no dark head broke the surface.

"Diana, I think we had best go home."

The sympathy in her father's voice almost undid her. "No, I—"

"He is dead, child," her father said gently. "No one could stay underwater that long. The weight of the chains—"

"No," she said again, her voice little more than a whisper. Tears spilled down her cheeks. He was dead. She knew he was, had seen it with her own eyes. The pain was too much to bear.

"He was wrong," she said in a dull tone,

tearing her gaze from the sea. "This is the end, after all."

Frederick pulled her close and slowly led her up the path. They met the patrol captain halfway. He gave Diana a look of sorrow.

"They sent me to tell you . . ." He cleared his throat, obviously uncomfortable. "El Moreno tried to escape, and Henry Morgan shot and killed him. I'm sorry."

Diana closed her eyes and gave herself up to grief.

Chapter 21

E l Moreno was dead.

It seemed that everywhere she turned, Diana heard the grisly tale repeated over and over. How El Moreno had trapped Marcus, only to be killed by the great Morgan. The story was told with much relish and embellishment in the taverns, the forts, and the marketplace.

Diana had taken to remaining within the walls of Covington Hall so that she could avoid hearing the tale repeated over and again. Yet even in her own home she could not escape the wagging tongues. The servants gossiped while carrying out their duties, never realizing that every time El Moreno's name was mentioned, their mistress's heart broke all over again.

Even witnessing Marcus's hanging had not dulled her pain. The villain had gone mad moments before death, swearing on his mother's grave that he saw El Moreno in the crowd. Of course that was impossible, and so Marcus died with his enemy's name on his lips.

Diana found Marcus's madness to be fitting justice for the wrongs he had done to Alex and his family.

She had taken to wandering the gardens, away from the chattering servants, where she comforted herself with bittersweet reminiscences of the short time she had known Alex.

She stood near the doors to the ballroom. Though the sun shone brightly in the blue sky, in her mind she saw the moon in a velvet night sky, and a black-clad man had just stepped from the shadows and into her heart.

"Diana?"

Maude's familiar burr startled her from her memories, and the sun suddenly seemed overbright. Diana frowned at Maude. She hated to be awakened from her daydreams into a world that did not have Alex.

"What is it, Maude?" she asked without much interest.

"Your father requests your presence in the study," her companion said.

"Now?" Diana plucked a blossom from a nearby bush, wishing Maude would leave her alone so she could return to the meager comfort of her fantasies. "What does he want?"

"I dinna ken. He told me to fetch you, and so I have."

"Very well," she said with a sigh. Dropping the flower, she took up her skirts and wandered toward the house.

Her lethargic pace increased to a normal walk as she made her way down the hall to

Frederick's study. The sooner she answered her father's summons, the sooner she could return to the garden. She gave a short rap on the closed door and entered the room.

"You sent for me, Papa?"

Frederick looked up from the document he was reading. "Yes, I did. Be seated, Diana. I have some wonderful news."

She took the chair across from her father's desk, where she had an excellent view of the gardens. "And what news might that be?" she asked indifferently.

"I have just arranged for your betrothal."

"You did *what*?" She surged from her seat. "Papa, how could you?"

Frederick frowned at her until she sat down again. "I am your father, my dear, and seeing to your future is my responsibility. You did not think to remain unwed forever, did you? Especially given recent circumstances?"

"The thought had occurred to me," she snapped, her heart throbbing with grief. "I have no need of a husband."

"I disagree, daughter. I believe you do need a husband. A strong man who can handle your headstrong ways."

"Headstrong!" She started to rise again, but the expression on her father's face made her sink back into the chair. "I need no man to order me about."

"The agreement has been signed," Frederick said. " 'Tis done."

"I will refuse to wed him."

"You *will* wed him, else you will be turned out of this house to make your own way in the world."

She gaped at him, shocked at his heartlessness. "You wouldn't."

"I would. Daughter, you do not seem to realize that your recent adventures have done considerable damage to your reputation. This offer may very well be the only one you ever receive."

She shrugged. "So be it."

Frederick slammed both palms down on his desk and rose. "You will marry this man, daughter. He is a man of great courage and honorable name."

"Courage? He is so courageous that he cannot face me and claim my hand himself? And honorable?" She choked on the words. "The most honorable man I know died before my eyes but five days past."

Frederick looked down at the betrothal agreement on his desk. "Nevertheless, you are betrothed. I think you will like the man. He is fair of face and well titled—"

"Do you think I care about good looks or titles?" She locked her gaze on her father's. "The man I love is dead. Yet you expect me to marry a stranger within days of his passing?"

"You must get on with your life, Diana. I have been remiss in not seeing to your marriage sooner. But after your mother's death I felt like a ship with no rudder, drifting with no direction."

"Then you understand how I feel," she whispered.

"I do understand, but it changes nothing. The agreement has been signed. You *will* wed this man, even if I have to clap you in irons and drag you to the church."

She felt the blood drain from her face. "Nothing I say will change your mind?"

"I'm afraid not." He reached across the desk and touched her hand. "He is a good man, my dear. Handsome, titled, wealthy. Trust me—I think you will be pleased."

"Pleased?" She stepped away. "How can I be pleased with a man who cannot even ask for my hand himself? When shall I meet this coward? When he creeps into my room under cover of darkness to perform his husbandly duties?"

Frederick flushed at his daughter's reference to the marriage bed. "You may meet him now if you like," he said. "He awaits you in the gardens. I had Maude send him through the other doors."

She turned on her heel and headed for the door. "We shall see how long it takes to flush that craven fool from behind Maude's skirts and out of my life."

She slammed the door behind her.

Minutes later, Diana burst into the gardens like a satin-clad hurricane. Her "betrothed" stood with his back to her, his feet planted in the very spot where she and Alex had first exchanged words. As she stormed up to him, she took in his great height and the broad shoulders that were no doubt due to the excellent cut of his dark blue coat. Ink-black hair flowed over his shoulders from beneath his broad blue hat with its white ostrich plume. He put his hands on his hips as he looked around, and Diana's steps faltered. The gesture was so familiar! An invisible hand squeezed her heart as she recalled the many times she had seen Alex do that very thing. She stopped and took a deep, audible breath.

He turned at the sound, his hands dropping to his sides. The sun behind him cast his face in shadow beneath the wide brim of his hat.

Diana regained control of her rioting emotions and lifted her chin. If she intended to send the man packing, then she needed to project an image of strength. "So, you are the man who would take me to wife?"

He nodded, and she smiled. So, he was too shy to even speak to her, was he? All the better to be frightened off by a shrewish tongue.

"You do realize, do you not, that I am soiled goods? I was the captive of the pirate El Moreno for an entire week. He ravished me and made me his mistress."

He made a noise that sounded suspiciously like a stifled chuckle.

"You think it amusing?" she asked with annoyance. "Or perhaps you think me a liar? I assure you that El Moreno used me shamelessly, like the veriest bawd. He did things to me that people speak of in whispers, subjected me to exotic pleasures that he learned in his voyages to the Far East. I am not fit to be a wife, sir."

He cleared his throat loudly, but though she waited, he said nothing. She rolled her eyes.

"Once a mistress, never a wife, is that not what they say?" she continued. "There is every chance that I contracted some sort of disease from the man, you know. I could very well have the pox or something worse. And there is every chance that I may yet carry the black-guard's babe. You would not wish your heir to be a pirate's get, would you, sir?"

His shoulders shook. He began coughing rather violently.

Diana glanced askance at him and took a step backward. "Given the circumstances, sir, I think it would be best if you withdrew your suit."

He stopped coughing, tossed back his head, and laughed.

Diana blinked. Her blood froze as the familiar laugh echoed throughout the garden and he swept off his hat.

She stared at him, her eyes widening as she took in every feature of his familiar, beloved face. "*Alex?*"

"Aye." He let his hat tumble to the ground as he pulled her to him. His touch was warm, firm, and amazingly real. "Tell me again how you were ravished by a pirate," he teased. "And about those 'exotic pleasures' that El Moreno taught you."

She jerked away from him, her face heating with mortification. "You . . . you . . ."

"I fear not any disease the rogue may have given you," he continued with a grin. "And I would accept any babe of that sordid union as if it were my very own."

"Indeed? Well, I will not accept you as a husband! How could you do such a thing?" She slapped him hard across the face. Then she turned her back on him, fighting tears, confused. Her heart sang because he was alive. But pain flooded her veins because he had tricked her.

He caught her as she took a step toward the house. "What do you mean, you will not accept me? I assure you, my days as a pirate are over. As far as the world is concerned, El Moreno is dead."

"Aye, he is." She faced him, anger and hurt bubbling over. "I saw El Moreno die. I heard the shot; I saw him fall. Do you have any idea how I felt? I died, too, that day."

"I did not mean to hurt you, Diana, but there was no other way."

"No other way," she echoed with derision. "How did you survive? You had been shot, and you had those chains on."

"Morgan passed me the key to the irons. 'Twas he who fired the shot, well over my head. I resurfaced on the other side of the cliff and stayed in the shadows of the rocks until the soldiers left."

"Why would Sir Henry do such a thing?"

"Because 'twas his idea that I become El Moreno. I was working under his orders to track down Marcus and bring him back to face the gallows. El Moreno had to die so that I might assume my rightful identity."

"You might have told me. You might have hinted that . . ." She stopped and took a breath, realizing that she was becoming overset. "Now you have somehow convinced my father that we should be wed."

"We *will* be wed, my sweet." He took her hands in his, tightening his fingers when she would have pulled away. "I never committed half the crimes attributed to me. Most of those rumors were Morgan's doing. It was all a pretense to capture Marcus."

"And our relationship? Was that a pretense, too, Alex?" She shook her head. "Or is Alex even your name?"

"Oh, it is my name. And you were the only real thing amid all the pretending, Diana. I fought my feelings for you, but in the end, they won out."

"Who are you really?" she whispered, staring up into his dark eyes. "Are you the man I fell in love with? Or are you someone I don't even know?"

"I am the same man I always was," he answered, bringing her hands to his lips. "And more."

Her flesh rippled with pleasure at his touch and brought to life all the feelings she thought had died with El Moreno. Confused, she yanked her hands away.

"What of your ship? And your men?"

He sighed and accepted her withdrawal. "Birk and McBride are both good friends of long standing. I hired the rest of the crew as El Moreno."

"And the ship?"

"The *Vengeance* is mine and always has been. Before my brother died she was called the *Miranda*. I changed the name when I became El Moreno."

"Miranda." Diana closed her eyes. "The countess. You do love her."

He cupped her face. "Yes, I do love her. Diana . . ." He waited until she opened her eyes. "She is my mother."

"Your mother!" She gaped at him, then glared and yanked away. "Do you think me so simple a maid that you could not confide in me? You knew what I thought!"

"Never have I accused you of being simple, my love. And as for being a maid . . ." His voice trailed off suggestively.

"You are no gentleman!" she snapped, blushing.

He seized her about the waist, dragging her against him with the tender mastery that made her melt inside. "Never have I pretended to be. No gentleman would be able to handle a spirited wench like you."

"I am no mare to be broken, Alex," she retorted, fighting the urge to beg him to make love to her. "Take me as I am or not at all."

"Oh, I shall take you, *amada*. To wife."

"I have not yet decided to accept your suit." With effort, she turned her face away when he bent to kiss her.

"You decided the day you offered yourself to me," he growled, sensuality heavy in his voice. "I knew the first time I took you that I would have you for my wife."

"Another unimportant detail that you did not tell me? I do not think I shall marry you, sir. You keep too many secrets, for my taste."

"Taste this," he murmured, covering her mouth with his.

Diana closed her eyes and let passion take her. She curled her fingers into his shoulders, kneading the warm muscles she found there. His heart beat against hers as he deepened the kiss, proving in a most pleasurable manner that he was not some ghost come to haunt her, but a flesh-and-blood man.

He finally broke the kiss, and Diana sighed, resting her cheek against his shoulder in contentment. A moment later she lifted her head up and looked at him with a stunned expression.

"Alex, if the Countess of Rothstone is your mother, what does that make you?"

He released her and bowed. "Alexander Rawnsley, Earl of Rothstone, my lady."

"Another secret? How many more must I discover?" she huffed in exasperation.

He grinned. "As many as I can think of to keep you entertained, my sweet."

"Just tell me this," she said, going back into his arms. "You do not have a secret wife lurking about, do you?"

"No, my love." He tightened his embrace. "I have told you about my first wife, and she is dead. There are no others, I promise you."

"And you are a man who keeps his promises." She eluded him when he would have kissed her again. "What about mistresses? I cannot go about waiting to be assaulted by your jilted lovers, sir. Must I always carry my dagger with me?"

"Nay, love. Rosana was the only woman who could come close to being called my mistress, and she has left Besosa. I doubt we shall see her again."

Diana wrapped her arms around his neck. "No children, either?"

"Only the ones I shall have with you. Provided you accept my offer." He pressed her against him.

Diana marveled at how well they fit, as if they had been molded especially for each other. She gave an exaggerated sigh. "I suppose I shall. After all, my father has informed me that my reputation is ruined, thanks to the dreadful pirate who ravished me. You are my last hope for a husband."

"No one will dare utter a word against the future Countess of Rothstone," Alex assured her. "The rumors will stop once it gets about that we are to wed."

"I hope so, for Papa's sake."

"Your father will quell what talk he can. He knew me as El Moreno, but once he understood that I was working for Morgan, he was most pleased to sign the betrothal agreement."

"I do not doubt it."

"We shall be wed immediately," Alex continued. "There is bound to be someone who insists on spreading lurid tales of your abduction, and I do not want it whispered about that my firstborn child is a pirate's get."

"I do not think I am with child," Diana said with a smile. "I only said that to be rid of a tiresome suitor."

"It had the opposite effect," Alex said with a gleam in his eye. "Getting you with child is the one activity certain to keep me in port."

"Does this mean you intend to ravish me again?"

"To be sure. And again and again."

"Oh, good." The rest of her words were lost as she gave herself up to the familiar magic of her beloved's embrace.

Dear Reader,

If you've enjoyed the Avon romance you've just read, then don't miss next month's exciting selections, beginning with Cathy Maxwell's latest historical Regency romp, *Because of You*, an Avon Treasure. When a disowned rake returns home, he never dreams that he'll be forced to marry a vicar's innocent daughter. And he never expected to feel the passion that soon flares between them.

A stolen kiss with a prim and proper debutante proves the undoing of a masterful duke in Sabrina Jeffries' *The Forbidden Lord*, an Avon Romance. This sparkling, powerful Regency-set historical is unforgettable.

Do you love stories set in the wild west? I sure do, and there's nothing like a sexy cowboy to pique my interest. In Maureen McKade's Avon Romance *Untamed Heart*, a local lawman decides to clean up town…and that includes shutting down a sassy saloon owner's establishment. Can this unlikely couple find true love?

And if you're looking for a delightful romance, then don't miss Sue Civil-Brown's utterly delicious *Chasing Rainbow*. Opposites attract when a globetrotting scientist settles down in the town of Paradise Beach, hoping for a little peace and quiet…and along comes a free-spirited heroine who's destined to shake him up…

Avon continues to bring you the very best in romance, so enjoy!

Lucia Macro

Lucia Macro
Senior Editor

AEL 0199

Avon Romantic Treasures

*Unforgettable, enthralling love stories,
sparkling with passion and adventure
from Romance's bestselling authors*

****

PERFECT IN MY SIGHT *by Tanya Anne Crosby*
78572-2/$5.99 US/$7.99 Can

SLEEPING BEAUTY *by Judith Ivory*
78645-1/$5.99 US/$7.99 Can

TO CATCH AN HEIRESS *by Julia Quinn*
78935-3/$5.99 US/$7.99 Can

WHEN DREAMS COME TRUE *by Cathy Maxwell*
79709-7/$5.99 US/$7.99 Can

TO TAME A RENEGADE *by Connie Mason*
79341-5/$5.99 US/$7.99 Can

A RAKE'S VOW *by Stephanie Laurens*
79457-8/$5.99 US/$7.99 Can

SO WILD A KISS *by Nancy Richards-Akers*
78947-7/$5.99 US/$7.99 Can

UPON A WICKED TIME *by Karen Ranney*
79583-3/$5.99 US/$7.99 Can

Avon Romances—
the best in exceptional authors
and unforgettable novels!